"I will never submit to you," Melissande declared boldly.

"And should you force me, then you will prove that you are no more of a nobleman than your sire."

Quinn's knuckles hit the wall on either side of her shoulders with a soft thud; then he was close, too close. She closed her eyes and willed him not to notice the unsteadiness of her breathing.

Had she been born a man, she would never have been in this position! Curse all men for their need to lord their power over women!

Curse Quinn for making her want him to touch her. That one thought resonated with frightening clarity in Melissande's mind, and she squeezed her eyes tighter against the truth.

"No, my lady," Quinn whispered. "I am not my sire. I shall make you shiver," he pledged. "I shall make you moan, and I shall make you beg me to touch you...!"

Dear Reader,

In the nine books since her first was published by Harlequin in our 1993 March Madness promotion of brand-new authors, Claire Delacroix has continued to delight audiences with her stories of romance, passion and magic. *My Lady's Champion* is another captivating medieval tale that will transport you to another time and place. Don't miss this story of a noblewoman forced into marriage to save her ancestral home.

Whether you're a longtime fan of Mary McBride or have just discovered her, we know you'll be delighted by her new book, *Darling Jack*, the touching tale of a handsome Pinkerton detective, driven by revenge, and the steady, unassuming file clerk who poses as his wife for an assignment.

Our other titles for the month are *Dulcie's Gift*, from Ruth Langan, the prequel to the contemporary stories in the Harlequin cross-line continuity series, BRIDE'S BAY, and a Western from newcomer Carolyn Davidson, *Loving Katherine*, about a lonely woman who is struggling to keep the family horse farm, and the ex-soldier who teaches her that there is more to life.

We hope you'll keep a lookout for all four titles.

Sincerely,

Tracy Farrell
Senior Editor

Please address questions and book requests to:
Harlequin Reader Service
U.S.: 3010 Walden Ave., P.O. Box 1325, Buffalo, NY 14269
Canadian: P.O. Box 609, Fort Erie, Ont. L2A 5X3

Claire Delacroix

My Lady's Champion

Harlequin Books

TORONTO • NEW YORK • LONDON
AMSTERDAM • PARIS • SYDNEY • HAMBURG
STOCKHOLM • ATHENS • TOKYO • MILAN
MADRID • WARSAW • BUDAPEST • AUCKLAND

ISBN 0-373-28926-X

MY LADY'S CHAMPION

Copyright © 1996 by Deborah A. Cooke

All rights reserved. Except for use in any review, the reproduction or
utilization of this work in whole or in part in any form by any electronic,
mechanical or other means, now known or hereafter invented, including
xerography, photocopying and recording, or in any information storage
or retrieval system, is forbidden without the written permission of the
publisher, Harlequin Enterprises Limited, 225 Duncan Mill Road,
Don Mills, Ontario, Canada M3B 3K9.

All characters in this book have no existence outside the imagination of
the author and have no relation whatsoever to anyone bearing the same
name or names. They are not even distantly inspired by any individual
known or unknown to the author, and all incidents are pure invention.

This edition published by arrangement with Harlequin Books S.A.

® and TM are trademarks of the publisher. Trademarks indicated with
® are registered in the United States Patent and Trademark Office, the
Canadian Trade Marks Office and in other countries.

Printed in U.S.A.

Books by Claire Delacroix

Harlequin Historicals

*The Rose Trilogy
†Unicorn Series

CLAIRE DELACROIX

An avid traveler and student of history, Claire Delacroix can be found at home when she has a deadline, amid the usual jumble of books, knitting needles and potted herbs.

For Mausi

Chapter One

February 1102

Quinn de Sayerne was home.

He sighed with satisfaction as his gaze raked over the mountains. They were etched permanently in his mind's eye, yet to see them before him again was a gift.

Home. Finally.

Quinn had waited twenty years to return. Now the moment was upon him and his heart pounded in anticipation of seeing Sayerne once more.

Nothing could spoil this moment.

He plunged through the snow, breaking a path for his companions where he recalled the road to be. No column of smoke rose from the château when he crested the last rise and it came into sight.

Quinn saw nothing but home.

"There it is!" he exclaimed to his companions.

When no one responded, he glanced back to find their expressions less enchanted than his own. Bayard looked more doubtful than usual, but even that could not diminish Quinn's pleasure.

He was finally home. He had always feared that somehow his father would contrive to deny him his legacy. It would have suited the old man well, but Dame Fortune had smiled upon Quinn.

After all these years, beloved Sayerne was his.

He spurred his horse forward, refusing to note that the river in the village outside the château walls had frozen over. The mill wheel was lodged in heavy ice. Quinn discarded the evidence of neglect, telling himself that the property must be well managed for all the wheat to be made to flour already.

It was a lie and he knew it, but he could not relinquish his lofty recollections of this place. For so long, Sayerne had been a dream that buoyed his spirits, a touchstone that he might never even see again. He had come too far on that dream to readily discard its allure.

Disrepair was to be expected in a land without an active lord. He had been prepared for that.

But this apparent abandonment was more than Quinn had bargained for, and closer scrutiny made it harder to evade the truth. He gritted his teeth as he urged his steed onward.

A desolate wind whistled through the village. Not a single face peeked out from the darkened doorways. Quinn's disquiet grew as a straw roof tumbled to the ground.

The village remained silent, except for the rush of the wind.

It was too cold to stir, even for a neighbor, Quinn reasoned as he blinked away the snow that blew before him. Another lie, and a less artful one, yet Quinn could admit nothing else.

Still, Quinn did not look back to see Bayard's expression. He forced himself to continue, determined to maintain the euphoria of homecoming until he stood within the château itself. Then and only then would he assess the damage done to the estate.

That simple conviction was difficult to hold as he rounded the last bend of the road. Quinn reined in his steed and stared, feeling Bayard and the four squires falter to a halt behind him as they did the same.

The very gates of Château Sayerne stood open, unmanned.

That was a sign of abandonment that he could not deny. Quinn gazed uncomprehendingly as one gate swung in the wind, its hinges creaking.

Where had everyone gone? And why?

"It seems that the rumor of your boots' foul stench has preceded you," Bayard commented from behind him. The squires laughed, their voices falling silent when Quinn did not join in their sport.

It was the hand of his father that Quinn saw at work. He had the estate, but his bitter sire had ensured that Quinn had nothing else with which to abandon his fighting life.

Betrayed yet again. He had been a fool to expect anything different.

It seemed that Quinn had granted his sire less credit for his vindictiveness than was the old man's due. Quinn's lips thinned in determination. The old man had sorely underestimated his son. Quinn would claim his legacy, in whatever condition it might be.

In the center of the bailey was a magical place that Quinn had loved as a child. The bailey rose there and from the back of a horse, one could see over the walls to the land beyond. He rode directly there and paused, lifting his nose to the wind. His gaze danced over the familiar curves of the land, his heart thundering in his chest.

Far beyond the walls of Sayerne, the land made an undulating path to mountain peaks that rose in turn to meet the crisp blue of the winter sky. All was clothed in thick white that reflected the sunlight with a brightness that hurt the eyes. The walls of the château cast stark shadows across the snow and the wind sang slightly within the confined space. A tear rose to Quinn's eye at the sight of Sayerne's familiar beauty. His father's neglect could not destroy Quinn's own memories or the beauty of the land itself.

He was home, despite the odds.

"Good morning!" Quinn called toward the stables with a boldness he was far from feeling.

He knew that no one would answer and the echo of his unanswered cry confirmed his suspicion. He stared up at the familiar yet silent tower of the château and finally confronted the truth.

Only snow and wind occupied Sayerne.

The snow had blown into deep drifts in the bailey and even the way to the stables was not cleared. No one had been here in a while.

But Quinn would not be so easily daunted. He straightened in his saddle with determination. He would rebuild, he would reclaim. He would prove that he was not like his father.

"This place is abandoned," Bayard commented.

Quinn nodded at the reminder of his companions' presence. "That it is, but no less mine for all of that," he declared. His voice rang out across the bailey. "I am Lord de Sayerne, and I stake my claim on my ancestral holdings!"

Quinn leapt from his saddle purposefully and abruptly found himself hip-deep in snow.

Bayard, curse him, laughed aloud.

Quinn felt the snow slide its icy fingers into his boots and noticed the squires' surprised expressions. It would be easy to laugh along, but instead he forced himself to scowl at his old companion.

"Laugh while you may, for this snow is wicked cold in the boots," he retorted.

"That I can see from here," Bayard said.

"Well, maybe you should confirm how cold it is in one's tunic." He lunged with a fistful of snow before Bayard could guess his intent.

His weight threw the other knight off balance in his saddle and landed the two of them in the deep snow. They tussled playfully, laughing and shoving handfuls of snow into each other's garments by turn. The young squires laughed, well used to the antics of their knights.

"Woho! It is indeed cold in the tunic!" Bayard bellowed. "How does it fare within the chausses?"

Quinn yelped as a healthy handful of snow was shoved into his chausses. He spun and pelted his chuckling companion with snowballs. They chased each other, dodged and feinted, until Quinn leapt and landed solidly atop his friend.

Bayard's dark hair was already dusted with snow but Quinn still pushed him headfirst into a drift. The knight squirmed to escape, then gained the surface again with a roar that sent the horses stepping sideways. The squires yelped in surprise as Bayard made a menacing face in their direction.

Quinn's gaze lifted slowly to the disrupted state of Bayard's hair and he could not help but laugh. "Your hair," he sputtered as he began to guffaw. Once Quinn had begun to laugh at the sight, he could not stop.

"It was you who frightened everyone away," Quinn jested when he caught his breath.

Bayard grinned and cocked a brow eloquently to the watching boys. "*Quiet,* Quinn promised us, but I expected *some* life to greet us here," he commented to the squires. Bayard turned back to Quinn with a grin. "Are you certain that no one sent one of your boots in advance to warn these poor souls?"

"Not by my doing, though I would not put such a feat past you," Quinn said.

"Me?" Bayard shook his head in mock disappointment. "Sadly, the thought did not occur to me in time. I could have dispatched a warning with that messenger from your lord if my wits had been about me."

"As your wits desert you, so my villeins desert me." Quinn shrugged and smiled wryly as he met his friend's gaze. "Mayhap we should both check our boots," he whispered conspiratorially. They chuckled together as Bayard brushed off his garments. Quinn cast a hopeful glance around the bailey, not really expecting to see anyone appear.

"If the villeins were so dismayed at the prospect of a new lord, it is best that they left," he said finally. He beckoned to the squires and indicated the stables. "See whether you can make your way there and tend to our steeds. They have traveled far this day and are in sore need of rest."

"Yes, my lord." The youngest boy, Michel, eight summers old and flushed with excitement at being squired to Quinn, leapt enthusiastically from his palfrey's back.

And disappeared into a drift of snow.

"No!" Quinn shouted in dismay. Bayard choked on a laugh.

Quinn trudged through the deep drift that rose against his own chest and reached into the hole left by Michel's passing. An instant later, he hauled the boy back above the surface of the snow and gave him a shake.

Michel sneezed.

Quinn knew Bayard chuckled silently without even looking at the other man. He barely restrained a smile himself, but little Michel from the sunny south had been granted a surprise he would not soon forget. Quinn tucked Michel protectively under his arm and held one cautioning hand up to the other boys, whose expressions ranged from shock to mirth.

"Make a pathway with your steeds before you dismount," he suggested, somehow managing not to smile. "Use my destrier and Bayard's first, for they will cut a larger path." All three boys nodded in hasty agreement.

"Perhaps Michel could help us in the hall," Bayard suggested.

Quinn nodded as he waded back through the snow to the central rise where the snow was less deep. He set Michel on his feet and determined that the boy was no worse for wear, despite his unfamiliarity with such winter conditions. Michel had been born in the Holy Land and Quinn had kept a watchful eye on the boy as they traveled north.

"That was my thought exactly," he agreed.

Bayard shook the snow out of his hair and turned a doubtful eye on the château. "It might not be any warmer in there."

Quinn waved off his companion's concerns with a blithe hand. "If nothing else, there must be wood and tinder left behind," he said with a confidence he was far from feeling.

Surely his father would have left him enough for a blaze? Quinn was less certain than he would have liked to be. Michel rushed ahead of the knights, undaunted by his experience with the snow, and the pair followed the enthusiastic boy.

The hall was dark and musty. Only a shaft of light drifted into the lower hall from the open portal, but the winter sunlight was bright enough to reveal more than Quinn would have liked to have seen.

His customary optimism faltered before the truth. It would take a lot of hard work to bring Sayerne even close to its former glory. Determined not to be daunted, Quinn strode purposefully into the hall.

The room was barren except for the dust stirred by their arrival. The fire screen Quinn remembered was gone, as were the poker and pail, the spit from the great fireplace had disappeared, as had his mother's beautiful tapestries. Even the trestle tables and benches had been removed. Tufts of abandoned herbs had blown into the corners but there was not so much as a candle stub else remaining.

"Betrayed again," Bayard muttered. Quinn did not even look up.

"No," he said. "You cannot be betrayed by one you do not trust."

This was more than a departure. Someone—and Quinn knew who—had made certain that there would be nothing to aid him here. From his death bed, his father had probably ordered the villeins to clear out Sayerne. Quinn should have expected no less.

It was as cold as a tomb within the hall and Quinn shivered despite himself. And there was not a stick of wood to be seen.

Curse his father! Quinn kicked at the few stale rushes in frustration. A squeal made him jump, followed by the sound of little feet scratching against the flagstones.

"Fetch that, boy!" Bayard bade Michel with a terseness that commanded obedience. Michel leapt to do the knight's bidding, then halted uncertainly at his next words. "We shall need something for our supper!"

The boy turned, his horrified expression enough to make Quinn laugh aloud. Bayard maintained a serious expression by some strength of will and Quinn did not dare chuckle.

"My lord?" Michel asked tentatively.

"Do not worry," Quinn counseled him. "We haven't even checked the kitchens yet."

"And they will be bountifully stocked?" Bayard responded with rare impatience. "It is time you faced the fact, Quinn, that we cannot remain here. It is good that you have inherited an estate, but you must admit that you have been granted an ill turn. Man cannot sustain himself on snow and the occasional rat alone. We cannot afford to remain here."

Quinn was immediately insulted by his companion's lack of faith.

"I have not gained my inheritance only to walk away from it!" he argued. "The château is solid and well built, the property extensive enough to support many more than we six. It will take work, I admit, but the power to return Sayerne to its former glory lies within our own hands.''

"Quinn, I see the advantages and I do not suggest that you walk away.'' Bayard's voice had dropped and Quinn was reassured by his words. "I only suggest that we return in the spring, when something can be made of the place. Coin will not solve this alone, my friend, unless there is someone selling what you need.''

As much as Quinn hated to admit it, there was sense in Bayard's conclusion.

"I will stay with you, my lord Quinn, even should the others decide to go,'' Michel said steadfastly and came to stand beside the knight.

Quinn smiled for the boy and ruffled his fair hair. Was Bayard right? Should they leave? But what would happen to Sayerne if it was abandoned?

Before he could respond to Bayard, someone cleared his throat in the portal. Bayard glanced over his shoulder, then moved abruptly out of the doorway to reveal a short, spare man. The new arrival was carefully attired in a livery that made Quinn's heart leap in recognition.

He was a messenger from the liege lord and the news could only be good. Maybe the Lord de Tulley had a plan to help Quinn to remain here.

"Quinn de Sayerne?'' the man asked in the precise manner of a well-trained servant.

Quinn smiled and nodded. "Yes, that is my name.''

"Yes.'' The man looked Quinn up and down as a frown lodged between his brows. Quinn realized belatedly the state of his appearance and brushed some of the snow from his hair. The man didn't appear to notice Quinn's gesture but he cleared his throat.

"I have a message for you from the Lord de Tulley.'' He snapped his wrist and Quinn saw the silhouette of a roll of parchment. Quinn took the presented scroll and stepped back outside into the bright sunlight.

A quiver of excitement danced through Quinn when he held the roll of parchment within his hands. His name was written across the curve in a spidery hand. This fine missive to a lord was for him! Quinn de Sayerne was now a man of property.

For the sake of his audience, Quinn endeavored to appear nonchalant. It would not do for this messenger to guess that his heart was pounding in anticipation and pride.

"How did you know I had arrived?" Quinn asked absently, running his fingers across the bright red wax seal and delaying the moment of breaking it. The touch of the wax beneath his finger sent a thrill through him.

"We had watchmen posted to inform us of your arrival. The lord knew that you would return once our missive regarding your father's demise had found its way to you."

"I appreciated the lord taking the time and trouble to inform me," Quinn responded in an echo of the man's formal tone. "It cannot have been easy to seek me out in the Holy Land."

"The Lord de Tulley is most fastidious about ensuring the line of succession is maintained appropriately," the messenger sniffed.

"Still I appreciate his efforts," Quinn said with a smile.

The servant nodded brusquely. "I shall inform him, sir."

The moment already delayed as long as possible, Quinn reluctantly broke the seal and unfurled the parchment, feeling a smile spread over his features as he scanned its contents. He glanced up and, finding Bayard's questioning gaze upon him, could not restrain his pleasure.

"I am summoned to the lord's home," Quinn informed his companion proudly. His investiture awaited him, he was certain.

"That's a fine invitation, indeed." Bayard turned and clapped Michel on the back good-naturedly, his expression so sober that any other than Quinn would not have doubted his sincerity. "Do not worry about the rat tonight, boy," he solemnly advised the squire. "We will leave him for our return. The Lord de Tulley will probably offer finer fare."

"Rat?" the messenger repeated with evident distaste. He peered into the shadows of the hall once more and his complexion paled. "There are rats here in the hall?"

He swallowed carefully and his gaze flicked between the two knights. "And you planned to dine upon them?" he asked in a thin voice.

"Well," Bayard hedged in the manner that warned those who knew him that he meant to make a joke. "Actually," he confided, "it would have been difficult, as there is no fuel to be found here for the fire."

He leaned closer to the messenger and his voice dropped. "They are not so good raw, for they tend to *writhe* on the way down." He made a gesture with one hand meant to clarify his meaning.

The messenger stepped hastily away from Bayard and regarded him warily.

"Maybe you would like to try one?" Bayard suggested amiably. He snapped his fingers at Michel and the boy obediently ducked back into the hall.

The messenger gulped, then turned and fled, calling the remainder of his message over his shoulder as he ran. "The lord will expect you at the board as soon as you might see fit to present yourself," he said. "A long ride it is from here, so the lord suggested you might stay with one of his villeins this night. Take the westbound road. I shall tell the miller at the river fork to expect your presence this night."

"I thank you!" Quinn cried, his spirits restored by both the missive and the promise of a warm meal.

The messenger however did not respond. He was in the saddle with a speed better suited to fleeing the dogs of hell than the bailey of Sayerne.

"Do you imagine he could run any faster?" Bayard demanded scornfully. "And over the rumor of a rat." He snorted in disdain. "We could tell him tales that would keep him sleepless for a fortnight."

"But it is better that those tales are left untold, my friend," Quinn said quietly, his mood tempered by the reminder. There was a moment of silence as both men remembered what they had endured in the East. Bayard's lips thinned, then he turned away.

"My lord, I could not find the rat," Michel admitted, his expression crestfallen when he emerged back into the sunlight.

Bayard shook his head with amusement. Quinn followed his gaze to the gate, but the messenger was long gone. "It seems that the lord's messenger lost his appetite anyhow."

"Or maybe he knows more about the lord's board than we do," Quinn commented.

"Woho! Now there is a thought!" Bayard's brows rose at the promise of food. "Let's hasten to this miller's board before we miss the evening meal. And then—" he wiggled his brows and Michel giggled "—on to the bounty of the lord's own table."

"If I didn't know better, I might think you had only accompanied me to have food in your belly," Quinn accused genially. Bayard laughed.

"I anticipate more than *that* pleasure now that we are home. Do you think this miller has a pretty daughter?" He winked, then sobered as he glanced over the ailing château. "But trust you to find a haven for us that will actually require solid labor from our hands."

"It will be good for you," Quinn counseled, seeing that Bayard was unconvinced. "You are getting too old to earn your way with a blade," he added teasingly.

"Too old to fight? But not too old to work like a peasant?"

"You do not have to stay," Quinn responded, knowing that his companion was happiest when he had something to complain about.

"Leave?" Bayard demanded in mock outrage. "First I am old, now I am not even good enough to move millstones. This *is* a sorry day for my pride."

He leaned closer and poked Quinn companionably on the shoulder. "Do not imagine that you will shake me from your side in this adventure," he growled. "I owe you a great deal already, but to have a home would be the greatest gift a man might give to another. Should anyone be able to rebuild this place, it will be you, Quinn. I have never raised a blade with a man of such will."

Quinn smiled, knowing the words came from the heart. "Then consider yourself at home, my friend. We have battled alongside each other for too long to part company now."

The two knights paused in the middle of the snow-filled bailey and smiled as they shook hands under the bright winter sun. Then they let out a simultaneous whoop and dashed through the snow to their waiting steeds.

"A husband?" Melissande kept her voice under control with difficulty.

She glared back at her liege lord and noticed that the lord was looking older than when last she had seen him. Though his blue eyes still sparkled bright with intent, the lines were etched more deeply in his brow. He looked smaller, but no less determined.

Melissande braced herself for the rest of his idea. It was Tulley's right to choose her spouse since her father was gone. She supposed she had been foolish to hope that he had forgotten his obligation since he had not insisted on her marrying before this point.

"Yes, Melissande." He stroked his chin and leaned back in his chair as he regarded her, his bright gaze appraising. "You are still young but it is time we saw you wed."

Melissande had a feeling that Tulley did not intend to see the match made that she desired. But nothing was gained by silence, as her sire had often said. Melissande cleared her throat before voicing her concern.

"Dare I assume," she said carefully, "that you have found Arnaud de Privas?"

Her lord snorted in a manner that provided a more than adequate answer. "I have already told you to put that childish whimsy behind you," he maintained.

Melissande schooled herself not to show her disappointment. "A pledge is not whimsy," she stated quietly.

Tulley leaned forward and braced his elbows on his desk as he resolutely held Melissande's gaze. When he spoke, his voice was low and compelling.

"If your sire were alive, he would have seen that childhood pledge dismissed long before now. There is more at stake here than you might guess."

The implication that she could not understand the import of her choice rankled Melissande as nothing else could. Her chin shot up and she knew that her own gaze sharpened.

"My word is at stake and that, sir, is of immeasurable value to me."

A slight frown appeared between the lord's brows. "My lands are being challenged by your insistence upon this nonsense," he countered hotly. "Annossy is a point of weakness for me, as long as you administer the estate alone. It is hard enough to be troubled on the borders, but even you must admit that Annossy has been attacked more than my other periphery properties."

"My lord, might I remind you that you promised me the opportunity to administer Annossy alone and prove my abilities," Melissande retorted. "I had hoped that you might have invested me with the seal of my father's estate by now."

"And I am glad that I have not taken that step, given these recent attacks on Annossy!" Tulley snapped back.

Melissande held her tongue as Tulley warmed to his theme. She could not argue that there were no attacks and so far, she had not been able to stop them.

"The marauders know Annossy is governed by a woman alone and have probably guessed that you have not been invested with your family's estates officially," the lord continued, his tone savage. "You know that their actions reflect their perception of weakness."

"Weakness?" That charge did not sit well with Melissande. "I am not weak! My father saw me well trained, sir! The villeins are satisfied, the tithes have been beyond expectation. Annossy is well ruled and you have had *no* complaints since my taking the reins! You should invest me formally, for there is no reason to not do so!"

"Annossy is governed—by my grace only—by a woman alone and that is reason enough. I hold these lands for the king by grant of the Count of Burgundy and should any of them be lost, my own position would be compromised. You know that I cannot risk that." The lord met Melissande's regard and held it as she reluctantly acknowledged the truth in his remarks.

Melissande could make no argument, for her estates had borne the brunt of the attacks, precisely as Tulley maintained. Not for the first time, she cursed the fact that she had not been born a man.

The lord seemed to sense her reconciliation to his opinion, for he continued in a more measured, yet still resolute, tone. "Whatever you or I or even your villeins might think, these bandits perceive the weak link in my holdings to be Annossy. I will not risk any loss for the sake of your pride. I might let you temporarily administer your family holdings, but I will not invest you and break openly with tradition."

In that instant, Melissande saw the warrior the Lord de Tulley had once been, and appreciated anew his reputation as a man who would see his will done against all odds. She regarded him silently, knowing she would be forced to bow to his bidding in this.

If she had been a man, she would have openly defied him. If she had been a man, there would have been no criticism of her administration. If she had been a man, she would have chosen her own mate freely. Or taken no spouse at all.

But Melissande was not a man, so she bit down on her rising defiance. Still, she could not simply agree without attempting to change the lord's mind.

"Do not imagine that I will permit this to continue," Tulley stated. "I intend to lose no land in this fight, especially if the only price is seeing you married suitably."

"But..."

"But nothing, Melissande," the lord said testily. "This situation has continued for too long now and the time for action has come. You will wed and, as befits my right as your liege lord, I will decide to whom."

Melissande caught her breath and straightened slowly, knowing that she had to ask the question in her mind.

"I understand that you regard my childhood vow to Arnaud childish whimsy," she stated cautiously, well aware of the sharp glance the lord shot her way, "but might he not be considered? It would please me to keep my pledge."

That was an understatement in the greatest extreme. Her word was her bond and that was a source of pride for Melissande. Tulley's brow darkened threateningly, though, and Melissande knew to dread his next words.

"Do you think, child, that after all these years I would ignore what I know to be important to you?" he demanded in exasperation. "I did seek out that rogue Arnaud whom you inexplicably hold so dear."

Tulley had sought out Arnaud? Melissande regarded the older man in surprise. Her heart skipped a beat at the possibility that Arnaud would be her spouse, though the lord's tone was surprisingly disparaging.

His next words surprised her even more.

"It seems he has taken a wife himself."

"A wife?" Melissande choked out the words.

The lord glanced up and deliberately met her shocked gaze. His eyes narrowed. "It would appear that your loyalty has been misplaced," he concluded tightly.

No! This could not be!

There could be only one explanation. Tulley was trying to deceive her so that she would agree to his plan.

"Liar!" she raged before she could check her words. The way Tulley straightened told Melissande that she had made a mistake in blurting out her suspicions.

The lord's features set coldly at her audacity. "The source was reliable beyond doubt," he said stiffly. "Apparently, Arnaud is now your neighbor. He wed Marie de Perricault a year past."

"Marie!" Although Melissande had not seen the older woman in years, she remembered her testy manner. "Arnaud would never marry Marie and break his word to me!"

The lord's lips tightened. "But he did exactly that. I would suggest you come to terms with the truth."

Melissande did not believe him.

"Your source is deceived in this," she charged hotly. The lord's eyes flashed angrily. Knowing her temper would gain her nothing, Melissande fought to rein in her response. She took a deep, steadying breath and forced her hands to unclench.

"All these years," she began calmly, though indeed, she felt her voice rise with each word. "All these years, you have treated me with respect and honesty. Please do not abandon that path now, my lord."

Her heart began to pound as Tulley said nothing, his regard coldly impassive.

"Tell me that you did not find Arnaud," she demanded. "Tell me that you refuse to seek him out for whatever reason, but do not lie to me about his fate. Do you think that lies will reconcile me to your will?"

The lord's lips tightened dangerously. "You will be reconciled to my desire, whether you wish it or not." He pushed to his feet and pounded his fist on the desk to enunciate his pronouncement. "*You will be wed,* by my command, or you will forfeit your holdings to me."

"This you cannot do!" Melissande protested. The lord's eyes narrowed and, in that moment, she knew he could. "Annossy is my family's ancestral holding."

Melissande knew she pushed the bounds but was too infuriated to stop. "Should you wrongfully take Annossy from me, I shall see your word tested. I shall appeal to the king himself!"

"Whose authority is thin this far from Paris," the lord responded. "Do you think that he will test his relations here over the pleas of a landless noblewoman, however fetching she might be? Remember that you are not even invested with the estate. Annossy is mine to grant as I see fit and it was only by my grace that you have administered it these five years. I could easily make a case that your determination not to wed threatens the security of my estates."

The lord settled back in his chair again and regarded Melissande with satisfaction. "Do you truly imagine that he would take your side?"

Melissande stared at her leather-clad toes, took a deep breath and reluctantly faced the truth of her situation.

Tulley—curse him!—was right.

"Put aside your childishness, Melissande," the lord counseled in a calmer tone. "You cannot avoid marriage, and it would be easier to make your peace with the fact soon."

"I took a vow," Melissande insisted.

Tulley arched a brow. "And now you will take another."

Anger rolled within Melissande, but the lord's gaze was resolute. She would be wed, she realized, regardless of her own will. At Tulley's command. And likely to a man whom she did not know.

A man who would seize her holdings and consign her to the bedchamber, as the law fully granted him the right to do. Melissande could imagine no worse fate than this.

"At least, you have seen the wisdom of holding your tongue," Tulley muttered.

Everything her father had built would be stolen away from her and there was nothing she could do! Melissande forced herself to remain calm, so that she might learn the worst. She took three deep breaths before she trusted herself to speak.

"Who would you have me wed?" she asked in a flat voice that did not resemble her own.

A rap at the door to the lord's office interrupted whatever Tulley might have said. The lord looked up and smiled, his welcoming expression prompting Melissande to glance to the portal.

A knight filled its frame. No, not a knight but a renegade. A shadow of foreboding crossed over Melissande's heart and the room, which had seemed too warm just a moment past, suddenly chilled.

No, her first impulse had to be wrong. This had to be some man-at-arms in Tulley's employ, no one else. His arrival at this moment was nothing but a coincidence.

But still Melissande looked.

The arrival was tall and broad of shoulder, though his travel-stained garb said little of repute about him. His mail glinted in the candlelight, half-hidden beneath a tabard with a torn hem. A well-worn cloak was tossed over his shoulders, his thick leather gloves scuffed from years of heavy wear.

He removed his helmet with a grunt of satisfaction and ran one hand through the length of his untrimmed chestnut hair. It was wavy but clearly unclean. There was stubble on his chin and a streak of mud across his cheek.

Melissande was certain he must be plagued with lice, and retreated a hasty step. He must have sought out the lord to pledge his blade.

Melissande's mouth went dry with the sudden certainty that the chatelain would never have shown him here while she remained, if that had been the case. The vagabond would have been left to wait in the hall.

In that moment, she knew who this man was. But surely Tulley would not wed her to such a barbarian?

"My lord," intoned Tulley's chatelain. "Quinn de Sayerne, son of Jerome de Sayerne, as you requested."

Son of Jerome de Sayerne! That news dismissed any possibility of her greeting this man with the slightest favor. Melissande regarded the new arrival with shock. Trust that lecherous serpent to have spawned a son of no greater repute than himself!

And she had thought her troubles over when Jerome died, resting peacefully in his own bed. Melissande had never suspected that Jerome had sired a mercenary for a son. She recalled only too well the way that Jerome had pledged to join Annossy and Sayerne under his hand. Her stomach churned as she stared at the new arrival and recalled the thievery Jerome had initiated against her family's holdings.

If sire and son were cut from the same cloth, it was not unlikely that this man was behind the raids on Annossy!

Chapter Two

It was unfortunate that a woman so fair of face insisted on scowling.

Quinn immediately noticed that the noblewoman in Tulley's office had the long fair hair of northern women that he found so alluring, although it was twisted and braided so that its golden glory was difficult to see. He could easily imagine that this lady enjoyed being contrary.

But even her foul mood did not deter from the simple beauty of her heart-shaped face, or dismiss Quinn's admiration of her slender form. Her green eyes were intriguingly tipped upward at their corners and heavily lashed, despite her fair coloring. They snapped as she glanced to him, as if he were guilty of some crime. Her full, ruddy lips were set with decided disapproval as her gaze swept over him.

Her low opinion of him made Quinn even more aware that he had had no chance to bathe before meeting his lord. He had been troubled enough about that fact, but the chatelain had insisted he bend his knee first, and so Quinn had complied.

In all honesty, Quinn recalled few of the niceties of polite society and had relied upon the chatelain's understanding of such matters. Now he feared he had made a mistake. The company of noble ladies was also a distant recollection for him and this moment would do nothing to boost his confidence.

With luck, he would be able to refine his image before he needed to find a bride.

"My lord de Tulley?" he said, knowing his voice dropped lower in his effort to appear composed. The lord's smile seemed genuine and Quinn dared to hope that all was not lost.

"Yes, Quinn. I suspect that you barely recall our last meeting." The lord rose from his chair and rounded the desk in a most amiable manner to shake Quinn's hand. "You were only a boy, then."

Quinn regarded the older man with surprise at his unexpected familiarity. He studied the bright blue eyes, the aquiline nose and relentless set to the older man's lips, the sight nudging a vague recollection. Although the thick mane of white hair was new, there was a vigor in the lord's grasp that recalled a long-ago summer afternoon to Quinn's mind.

"It was you who told me to leave Sayerne and seek my fortune," he said slowly.

The lord nodded as he released his hand. "Yes. I always knew that you would grow up straight and true, despite the challenges laid at your door." He looked Quinn in the eye again. "How are matters at Sayerne?"

Quinn flicked a glance to the lady's silent condemnation, disliking that he had to answer before her.

Although, it seemed unlikely that she could think less of him.

"Neglected," Quinn admitted. The lady sniffed indignantly at his admission and averted her lovely face. Obviously she thought the fault for that lay at his door and Quinn immediately longed to defend himself.

It was not because of him that Sayerne was neglected! How dare she make such presumption about a complete stranger?

Quinn was tempted to take issue with her attitude. Although Sayerne was less than it could be, it still was a fine estate. It bothered Quinn that this woman thought so little of something he prized.

That she evidently thought less of him was not something he would admit to finding troubling. Bayard had warned him often enough of the fickleness of courtly women for Quinn to let such a frosty stranger's judgment bother him.

And it would be inappropriate to argue with her here before the lord, he reminded himself irritably.

He fired a hostile glance in her direction when the lord turned away, and found himself wishing unexpectedly that she might smile.

Decidedly uncomfortable with the thought, Quinn resolutely turned back to watch Tulley pace behind his desk. That man folded his hands carefully before himself and pursed his lips before he glanced up with assessment gleaming in his eye.

"You appear undaunted by Sayerne's state," the lord mused thoughtfully. His manner was much that of a cat toying with a mouse and Quinn eyed him for a long moment before he responded.

Surely the lord did not intend to grant Sayerne to another? Quinn realized suddenly that the missive had only summoned him here. It had not mentioned his investiture, although he had assumed . . . Quinn swallowed his fear and resolved to learn the truth in short order.

"Sayerne is my inheritance," he said carefully. "And there is nothing wrong there that hard work will not put right."

The lady snorted. Quinn watched her fold her arms across her chest and noted how the move complemented the full curve of her breasts. He hauled his gaze to her face, only to find contempt shining in those glorious green eyes.

"And who will do this work, now that your abused villeins have fled?" she asked acidly.

"It is only natural that villeins would leave an estate without a lord," Quinn commented. Though his confidence was faltering in this strange interview, still he plunged onward. "I am convinced that they will return when they hear that I have arrived and intend to rebuild."

"You?" The lady scoffed openly. "Surely the return of the son of Jerome de Sayerne will have no appeal for his hard-pressed tenants! Any fool would guess that you two are cut from the same cloth!"

That he should be accused by a stranger of being like his father prompted Quinn's anger as nothing else could. He had never abused another! He had never cruelly taken whatever he desired and thought nothing of the repercussions!

"If the villeins cannot be troubled to see the manner of man I truly am, then I shall rebuild without such cowards on my estates!" he growled. "And should I be obliged to do so, my lady, you may well rest assured that *I* will rebuild Sayerne, stone by very stone, with the labor of my own hands!"

Her eyes narrowed as she regarded him, but clearly her opinion did not change. "How touching that the new Lord de Sayerne has such a pretty manner with words."

Tulley cleared his throat delicately at that point. Quinn spun to face the older man, heat rising on his neck that he had forgotten that man's presence. Out of the corner of his eye, he saw that the lady's cheeks tinged pink and he savored the sight of her embarrassment.

Maybe she was not made of stone, as she might have him believe.

Quinn realized suddenly that he did not know who she was. He scolded himself silently for neglecting his manners in such a fundamental way.

It was no consolation to know that the lady had certainly noted his error and would remind him of it, if she were ever given the chance.

"An assumption is being made here," Tulley commented. His bright gaze flicked between Quinn and the lady standing beside him.

An assumption? Panic took up residence in Quinn's stomach with a fluttering sensation. Surely it was not outrageous to assume that his inheritance would be granted to him?

"Sayerne has not yet been invested upon anyone," Tulley continued.

With those words, the bottom dropped out of Quinn's universe.

"My lord?" Quinn asked, though his voice was no more than a croak.

Could the lord intend to grant Sayerne to this forthright lady? Why else would Quinn have been admitted to the lord's offices in her presence? He slanted a glance in her direction, mildly reassured that she looked as surprised as he felt.

Tulley smiled. "Do not worry, Quinn, my intention is still that you will hold Sayerne. However, times demand that I place a condition upon your investiture."

He paused and Quinn regarded him in confusion. A condition?

"I would see you married, Quinn," Tulley concluded.

"Married?" The word burst from Quinn's lips before he could halt it.

"Yes, the line of Sayerne must be assured and I cannot let you take the reins of the estate without some succession—if it is not secured, then it should be in the process of being assured."

"Married?" Quinn could not reconcile himself to this curious demand.

Tulley eyed him carefully. "Surely, Quinn, a man such as yourself is not a man who dislikes women?" The lord's precise manner of speech made his implication clear and Quinn hastened to set the matter straight.

"No, no, my lord," Quinn clarified hastily. "It is only the timing that troubles me. I had assumed that one day I would take a wife, but not at this moment. Sayerne is in need of repair and I would not condemn any lady to endure such circumstances."

Quinn's voice gained assurance as he made his argument. "Grant me but a year, my lord, that my home might be fitting for a bride and then the matter may be discussed more leisurely."

To his disappointment, Tulley frowned.

"No, Quinn, a year will not do. The matter must be resolved immediately or I cannot invest you with the estates."

Quinn's mouth dropped open in shock to have his fear so calmly uttered, but Tulley merely seated himself at his desk with a preoccupied frown. "Other, greater troubles are there to be addressed and your marriage will solve more than you know."

The lord darted a coy glance to the lady beside Quinn. "Will it not, Melissande?" he asked softly.

To Quinn's astonishment, the lady stamped her foot in outrage. He noted now that she was more affronted by the suggestion than he, but had little time to consider that before she spoke.

"Spare me your pretty words about this vagabond!" she snapped. "It is bad enough that some spawn of Jerome has come to claim that cursed family's holdings, without your greeting this mercenary as a saint!"

Quinn felt obligated to argue. "I may be no saint, but do not call my family cursed." The lady turned upon him with furious eyes.

"No?" she demanded archly, and her voice rose in challenge. "Tell me then why villeins fled your father's land at every opportunity. Tell me why no less than two dozen of his bastards born of serving wenches populate the countryside, each and every one denied the bounty of his hall. The women themselves were cast to the winds when their state became evident. Explain to me, if you will, why every year until this one I have been obliged to argue with that foul man over the precise location of boundaries between Sayerne and Annossy. Maybe you can tell me where the grain has gone that was stolen out of my warehouses every winter."

Her lips tightened and her frosty gaze swept over him, her unflattering judgment of Quinn reflected in her green eyes. "Jerome de Sayerne was a dreadful neighbor and it is difficult to expect any better from the likes of you!"

She lifted her chin and glared directly into Quinn's eyes. He could smell the sweetness of her skin and cursed silently that his body responded to such a woman. She was nearly as tall as he, but the finger she poked solidly into his chest stole his thoughts away.

"Maybe you, mercenary that you are, might explain to me who raids my estates even now," she accused, and poked her finger into him once more. "I would not put such a deed past the leavings of Jerome de Sayerne. One way or the other, he pledged to merge my Annossy with Sayerne, but I tell you, *this will not be done.*"

Annossy. She was the Lady of Annossy. Quinn remembered that estate bordered upon Sayerne, then decided to set matters straight with his new neighbor.

When she made to enunciate her last point with another jab of her finger, Quinn snatched her hand in one deft move. The hand suddenly enfolded within his own was surprisingly soft, but he ignored the impression.

She was so startled that her eyes widened slightly. She made to move back, but Quinn did not release her hand.

"And I tell you, my lady, that my sire and I parted ways twenty years past because of our differences," he growled. "Do not again make the mistake of confusing our tempersaments."

"Sayerne has need of a strong administrative hand, not simply a marshal," she retorted. "What skills could *you* have with any tool other than a blade?"

Quinn leaned closer to her as his voice dropped. "And surely a clever lady like yourself has learned to not take matters at first appearances," he said.

Her green eyes narrowed with suspicion. "Mercenaries plague my borders," she hissed, her meaning clear when she flicked a glance over Quinn's attire. "And you appear to be a mercenary." She tilted her chin and held his gaze boldly. "How much do you know about the raids on Annossy?"

"Nothing," Quinn responded flatly. He shook his head when she appeared unconvinced. "I have returned from the Holy Land this very week, my lady. You see not a mercenary before you, but a knight in sore need of a bath."

Quinn smiled slowly, but the lady stared at him in disbelief. She seemed slightly disarmed by his jest and Quinn savored the minute victory. Her gaze flicked from his smile to his eyes, then to his hand grasping hers as though she knew not what to conclude.

"He speaks the truth, Melissande," Tulley interjected. "I sent for him and set sentinels to mark his arrival. Quinn speaks the truth, as he always did."

At the unexpected endorsement, Quinn's tension eased. His smile broadened and he was surprised to note a flush staining the lady's cheeks. She flicked a significant glance to her hand trapped within his.

Quinn realized that he enjoyed her discomfiture too much. It emboldened him. Carefully he unfurled her slender, graceful hand and brushed his lips across its back.

The lady caught her breath and for an instant, her bold facade slipped. Quinn found himself intrigued by the soft-eyed woman he glimpsed.

"I beg your pardon for my appearance, my lady, but it is my pleasure to make the acquaintance of a neighbor."

The lady's cheeks flamed and she hastily withdrew her hand. She wiped it upon her kirtle surreptitiously as she backed away, as though she would remove all evidence of Quinn's touch. Her lips tightened and the maiden braced for battle returned with vigor.

Quinn felt the weight of Tulley's gaze upon him and reluctantly met the lord's vividly blue eyes.

"Melissande d'Annossy will be far more than your neighbor, Quinn," Tulley mused. "It is she that I would have you take to wife."

"To wife?"

Too late, Quinn put the pieces together and realized where this conversation had been directed all along. He felt like a fool for not seeing the truth sooner, but this Melissande had confused him with her hasty accusations.

"My lord, no!" the lady gasped.

Quinn turned upon her with annoyance. "You would protest wedding me?" he demanded. Those green eyes were cold once more as they swept over Quinn in a manner that left no doubt of her opinion.

"I would protest wedding anyone claiming blood with your sire," she snapped.

"And I would protest wedding any woman with ice coursing through her veins!"

"And neither of your protests have any meaning at all," Tulley interjected. "For I have decided."

"It is unfair!" Melissande protested.

"It is unreasonable!" Quinn added.

Tulley arched one silver brow high and that coy smile played on his lips again. "And it is how it will be. Might I remind you, Quinn, that you are not invested yet with your estates. Should you not do my bidding, as any obedient vassal should, I will be obliged to find another to whom I might trust with Sayerne.''

Quinn's heart stopped at the threat, but Tulley was not done. He turned his piercing gaze upon the lady and Quinn heard her catch her breath. ''And you, Melissande, are nothing but a woman, whatever you might desire to the contrary. No obligation have I to leave you to continue to administer Annossy. Indeed, those estates could well be offered to another and you will be obliged to live here until I find you a suitable spouse.''

''But Annossy is my ancestral home!'' the lady protested angrily, her words stopping when Tulley held up a hand for silence.

''Instead of these options which you both find unacceptable, I have arrived at a solution that will serve the needs of you both. Both of you will keep your estates, should you do my bidding. Additionally, this match may eliminate the raids on my periphery holdings, most particularly Annossy.'' He fixed Quinn with a bright eye. ''I believe these mercenaries perceive weakness in Melissande's unmarried state.''

The lord folded his hands together and calmly regarded the pair before him. Quinn was irked at being manipulated—as apparently was the lady—but he would not sacrifice everything he had gained on a whim.

''I would have Sayerne,'' he said reluctantly. ''Should this be your condition, I will make this marriage in good faith.''

The lady sniffed with clear displeasure. ''It is clear that you leave us no choice,'' she said begrudgingly.

Tulley's gaze flicked between the two of them. ''It seems that there is a decided lack of enthusiasm for this match. Maybe even now one or both of you harbor plans of annulment.''

No one denied the accusation.

Tulley leaned forward, his voice intent. "There will be no annulment. Do not expect otherwise, for I will demand proof of consummation on the morning after the ceremony."

Quinn could not look to the lady after such a deliberate mention of intimate matters. He readily recalled his first impression of how splendidly he had thought her made.

Somehow Quinn doubted that the lady shared any of his dawning sense of anticipation.

"Maybe I named the wrong man barbarian," she muttered through her teeth, as though she could not restrain herself from comment.

Quinn's gaze flew to the lord's, certain she would be chastised for her rudeness, but Tulley merely smiled.

"Since I have known you so long, Melissande, and understand the strain of this situation, I will let your audacity pass." He stood and brushed an invisible speck of dust from his tabard.

"Shall I consider the matter settled?" he asked brightly.

Quinn nodded. He looked up in time to see the lady reluctantly do the same.

Tulley smiled jovially. "Such a matter as this should be sealed with a kiss, don't you think?" he suggested.

The lady's cheeks flamed scarlet. Quinn found a lump suddenly in his throat and his pulse hammered in his ears. It had been so long since he had touched a woman, and Melissande's manner was decidedly less than encouraging.

But Tulley watched expectantly. Quinn had little choice.

The lady remained stubbornly motionless and Quinn knew that he would have to make the gesture. He stepped closer and the softness of her scent caught at his nostrils again. Something tightened within him, but she did not so much as look up to acknowledge his presence.

Curse her! She intended to leave him fully responsible! Quinn gritted his teeth, knowing that riding into battle was easier than this. He hoped that she mustered some enthusiasm for his touch by the wedding night.

But regardless of the lady's mood, Quinn de Sayerne did not intend to lose his inheritance.

Quinn lifted his hand and gently touched two fingers beneath the lady's chin. She did not move. He coaxed her chin upward, but she resolutely closed her eyes. No doubt she wanted to leave him ignorant of her thoughts.

Quinn deliberately quelled his rising annoyance as he bent and brushed his lips across hers. He felt the lady shiver beneath his touch, though her frozen expression revealed nothing.

It was after his hand had fallen away that he saw the shimmer of her single tear. Immediately Quinn felt like a knave, although he knew that he was not responsible for this situation. Surely one fleeting kiss could not cost her so dearly?

Tulley cleared his throat. By the time Quinn glanced to him and back to the lady, it was as though that tear had never been. Had he imagined the shimmer of light? The lady exhaled shakily and Quinn saw that she opened her eyes, although she did not look at him.

He knew that was deliberate. What manner of woman had he agreed to marry? A woman of ice, no doubt, with a tongue as sharp as a viper's. Quinn could only hope that she reconciled herself to the matter by the day of the ceremony.

"Well," Tulley said. "It seems that the match is met with much less enthusiasm than I might have hoped. This matter is important to me and I do not intend to give either of you the opportunity to conjure some excuse." He stepped out from behind the desk and spared them each a significant look.

"I shall tell the chatelain to prepare for a wedding this evening," he concluded, and stepped out of the office.

"This evening?" Quinn repeated in shock.

"My lord, you cannot do this!" Melissande protested.

But Tulley merely waved one hand and disappeared down the corridor.

Leaving Quinn to confront his betrothed alone for the first time.

Melissande was in no mood to exchange sweet words with this boor of a mercenary. It was bad enough that she would be forced to marry Jerome's son without the humiliation of Tulley checking the linens in the morning for evidence that the match had been consummated. Now she was left with no time to even come to terms with the situation.

It was clear enough to Melissande who lay at root of her troubles.

"You!" she said, turning her frustration upon the rough-clad and dirty knight. "It is your fault that this situation is forced upon us! Could you not have simply remained abroad?"

"Me?" Quinn responded with a leisure that was decidedly uncalled-for under the circumstance. How could he be so calm, when Melissande was ready to throw something? "What crime is there in returning to claim one's inheritance? I see that you did not leave yours to fall into fallow."

There was an accusation that made sense!

"Well, you are too late to save Sayerne from that fate," Melissande commented dryly. "Sayerne is neglected beyond hope of repair and you are a fool to even think it can be restored." She folded her arms across her chest again and eyed Quinn skeptically.

He had a charm about him, that much she had read correctly. He was the perfect picture of a rogue misunderstood now, but Melissande was not fooled. Although there was certainly an attraction about the man. She imagined that lesser women might have granted him favors for that thoughtful manner of his, but Melissande was not so readily swayed.

And having that warm amber gaze fixed upon her might have disturbed Melissande under other circumstances than this. Her gaze dropped to the firm outline of his lips, but she tore it away before she could even imagine anything at all.

Quinn de Sayerne had accepted her hand only to obtain his inheritance.

It was no consolation that he didn't appear to have the skills to run his holdings. What did a crusading knight know of such matters? And what would happen if he should fail? Would he destroy her Annossy, as well?

The very thought was unbearable. Both Melissande and her father before her had labored too hard to lose everything.

"How do you imagine that you will make Sayerne prosper again?" she demanded sharply. "The estate has been mismanaged for as long as I can recall. You would be better off to pledge your blade elsewhere and move on. You don't even have a villein to call your own."

Color rose ruddily on Quinn's neck. Melissande wondered whether she had pushed him too far, although she had done no more than state the unvarnished truth.

"Undoubtedly because they have all moved to the finer pastures," he retorted more harshly than he had thus far. His gaze bored into hers with a determination hidden until this point and Melissande took a cautious step backward. "Might I guess that some of them graze no farther than at your exalted Annossy?" he asked silkily.

That was too close to the mark for Melissande's taste. She flushed but refused to abandon the fight.

"Yes, even a villein will seek out a place where he might fill his belly once in a while," she answered. "And your sire saw that most on his lands spent their nights in hunger."

"Yet, is it not an offense to harbor the villeins of another estate?" Quinn asked. His bright eyes belied his casual manner. He guessed the truth, and Melissande hated him for his perceptiveness.

"You were so quick to charge those of Sayerne with theft, yet it seems the opposite is true," he mused. "Maybe we should tell Tulley of your theft of labor from Sayerne!"

Melissande gasped at the accusation, then set her lips firmly together. There had been extenuating circumstances, although she knew that Tulley might not see matters her way.

It was no consolation that this rough knight knew at least some increment of the law.

"They were being abused," she admitted tightly. "How could I turn them away or compel them to return to that abuse?"

"And the word of the thief herself is to be adequate proof of that, I suppose," Quinn countered skeptically. "Somehow it is difficult to imagine you as a compassionate judge." He folded his arms across his chest as he confronted her, and his manner did nothing to settle Melissande's nerves.

All the same, Melissande's indignation rose that he should call her both liar and thief.

"Truly," he continued conversationally, and took a step toward her, "it must be an interesting court you hold at Annossy."

Melissande could smell his skin. He was too close and she caught her breath, even as her gaze was snared by his.

Her court? He would question *her* court? His audacity was unbounded! This accusation from a man who had never administered an estate? He had never even troubled himself to learn his father's lackluster administration skills and he presumed to criticize her?

He took another step closer, his gaze glittering purposefully, and before Melissande could guess her own response, she had raised her hand to slap him for his boldness.

Quinn caught at her wrist with lightning speed and pulled her close. Melissande was stretched to her toes, her breasts tantalizingly close to his chest. His proximity fanned the flames of whatever his chaste kiss had awakened within her, but Melissande would have died rather than admit it.

His lips were against her hair, his breath in her ear, but Melissande refused to shiver. She averted her face and stared resolutely at the opposite wall, as though she were supremely unmoved by his touch.

She could not afford to show him that he had any effect upon her.

"Do not imagine, my lady, that I will permit you to strike me," Quinn murmured.

Melissande twisted away from his warm whisper only to find herself trapped by the tawny gold of his eyes. She swallowed but could not look away. Despite herself, she noted the firm outline of his lips and recalled the butterfly-light brush of his lips over hers.

Suddenly it seemed that there was not enough air in the room.

Quinn was a mercenary, Melissande reminded herself forcefully.

"Scoundrel," she muttered. "You care for nothing but your own ends. I can see clearly that you are your father's son."

Quinn's eyes flashed like lightning for the first time, but he kept his voice low. "My sire and I had nothing in common, and you, my lady, will soon enough learn the truth of that." Their gazes locked for a long moment and Melissande knew she had engaged an opponent who would not back readily away.

His gaze dropped lazily to her lips before he looked to her again and smiled.

"Maybe we should seal our pledge anew," he whispered. The mischievous glint dancing in his eyes caught Melissande so by surprise that she did not move away in time.

Then Quinn's lips were on hers.

His kiss was firm, his lips coaxing, the strength of his hand on the back of her waist before she guessed what he was about. Never had Melissande tasted a man so thoroughly as this. It was shockingly intimate, yet tempting, all the same. Quinn smelled of sun and leather and horses, but beneath it all was the heady scent of his skin. Her breasts were crushed against his chest and she was lifted to her toes.

Melissande was overwhelmed by his touch. She guessed that this was not the first time for him to kiss like this, but that awareness still did not check her response.

He angled his mouth deliberately across hers and a curiously soothing warmth spread within her. Melissande could not fool herself any longer that it was the room that grew warm, for she felt the heat swell from deep inside herself.

She was aware of every fiber of her being as she never had been before and found herself shamelessly leaning closer to him. Melissande's eyes fluttered closed in pleasure despite herself and she felt his fingers fan out against the back of her waist.

He was trying to disarm her.

The thought came like a bolt from the blue. Melissande tore her lips from Quinn's and laid her hands flat on his chest to push him away.

She shoved and he obediently stepped back.

Quinn eyed her warily, but made no sign that he intended to pursue her. He stood completely motionless. He still watched her with that warm gaze.

Melissande backed up hastily. Her lips burned. She felt rumpled and flustered as she never had before. Her skin was heated and she knew that her cheeks were stained crimson. She wagged one finger warningly in his direction, hating how breathless her voice sounded when she spoke.

"You will beat me, as your father beat his women," she asserted.

Quinn shook his head resolutely and propped his hands on his hips. "I told you that we two were different," he said flatly. "Never will I lay a hand upon you."

His manner was so reassuring that Melissande was tempted to trust his word. Quinn appeared much like a solid, firmly rooted oak, or as resolute as a large stone that has stood in one place for aeons.

Melissande had the sudden, inexplicable sense that she could rely upon him.

But no! The man only toyed with her! Despite his claim, he was his father's son. Surely she could not so readily abandon her suspicions that he was behind the raids on Annossy? She would not have put it past Jerome to have arranged such attacks in order to see his will done.

Was Quinn as different from his sire as he would have her believe? He was more charming, to be sure, but beyond that, Melissande did not know.

She would believe the worst, she resolved, until proven otherwise. And considerable proof would she require to ease her mind.

It was evident that this was a man from whom Melissande should keep her distance if she wished to think clearly.

"Yes, you are right in that, for you will *never* lay a hand upon me in any manner," Melissande said. She deliberately challenged him, but it seemed she could not stop herself.

The heat he had sparked within her with only one kiss was terrifying. Melissande had never imagined that she might yield so readily to a man's touch.

And she could never permit herself to yield her independence to this man. There was too much at stake.

Quinn's eyes narrowed. "What precisely do you mean?" he asked carefully.

Melissande swallowed, knowing she could not back away now.

"I shall not couple with you," she declared wildly. Quinn's eyes flashed, but she plunged on regardless. "I may be compelled to marry you, but I will not be under your hand in any way. You will keep your distance from me, at all times!"

Quinn's voice dropped and already Melissande knew him well enough to be warned that his temper was thinning. "Understand that I do not intend to lose my estate over your whimsy," he said with deliberation. "And I do not intend to battle you this night to secure my inheritance. Remember that Annossy also hangs in the balance."

Melissande held up one quivering finger. "I have already agreed to this one night, but you will not find me a willing participant even tonight," she warned.

"And ever after you would deny me?"

"Yes."

Quinn watched her for a moment, then deliberately stepped closer. Melissande scurried backward, but Quinn did not halt. He closed the distance until Melissande abruptly found herself backed into the wall of Tulley's office.

"Rest assured, my lady, that marital vows will not be meaningless from me," he growled as he stalked her with measured steps.

Melissande caught her breath at the threat. She glanced wildly from side to side, but Quinn was too close to permit her to escape. She could not dash past him and make the door without being caught.

She waited because she had no choice.

But she was not defenseless as long as she could talk.

"I will never submit to you," she declared boldly. "And should you force me, then you will prove that you are no more of a nobleman than your sire."

His knuckles hit the wall on either side of her shoulders with a soft thud, then he was close, too close. Melissande closed her eyes against the bright amber of his gaze and willed him not to notice the unsteadiness of her breathing.

Curse Tulley! Had she been born a man, she would never have been in this position! Curse all men for their need to lord their power over women!

Curse Quinn for making her want him to touch her.

The thought resonated with frightening clarity in Melissande's mind and she squeezed her eyes tighter against the truth.

"No, my lady," Quinn whispered. Melissande swallowed at the warm fan of his breath against her cheek. "I shall make you shiver," he pledged. "I shall make you moan and I shall make you beg me to touch you."

Foul man! How dare he imagine that she was a wanton who would enjoy his caresses! How dare he imagine that she would grant him such power over her! Melissande's eyes flew open and she glared up at her betrothed, knowing that her eyes snapped in anger.

"Never!" she repeated with newfound vehemence. "I will never yield willingly to your embrace, on this night or any other!"

Quinn, to her surprise, smiled wolfishly.

The evidence that his roguish charm could make her pulse skitter was not reassuring.

"I shall take that as a challenge, my lady," he murmured in a manner that did, in fact, make her shiver.

He leaned closer and Melissande readily guessed his intent. Desperate to escape another of his intoxicating kisses, she twisted and kicked her knee vehemently upward.

Quinn blanched as her knee landed solidly in his crotch.

"Barbarian," she muttered.

Quinn grunted in pain, but Melissande had ducked beneath his arm already. She ran for the doorway with all the speed she could muster, certain that Quinn would catch her and take his vengeance.

To her relief, she gained the portal. She desperately grasped its edge to haul herself hastily out into the corridor. She ran down its length, Quinn's bellow echoing in her ears.

"My lady! You would test the patience of a saint—and I have already told you, *I am no saint!*"

It was only once she had retreated up the stairs to her room, and spent several moments catching her breath under the curious gaze of her maid, that Melissande realized something quite astonishing.

She had not thought once of Arnaud after Quinn had walked into Tulley's office.

The air left her lungs in one breath at that realization. She sank down onto the floor and covered her face in her hands at her own fickleness.

What curious power did this barbarian have over her? And how could fate be so cruel as to cast her into a marriage with Jerome's son?

And was it victory or failure that she had induced the resolutely calm Quinn to raise his voice?

Chapter Three

Quinn stormed into the bathing room, kicking open the heavy wooden door and slamming it behind him. Three unfamiliar servants, as well as Michel, jumped and turned to regard him in surprise.

Ye gods, but the woman set his blood to boiling as nothing else could! He had never been so infuriated—let alone by a woman's caustic words. And as yet, Quinn had barely made Melissande d'Annossy's acquaintance.

To what manner of hell had he consigned himself?

Bayard was the last left bathing, characteristically taking his leisure in the hot water. The room was filled with steam and the smell of wet cloth. A fire blazing on the hearth was the only source of light, but none of this tranquillity soothed Quinn's mood in the least.

Michel approached Quinn cautiously, his deferential manner telling Quinn that his unusual bout of temper showed.

"Would you bathe, my lord?" he asked.

"Yes." Quinn bit out the word.

"Then we will need more hot water." Michel flicked a glance to one of Tulley's servants, who hesitated. When Quinn glared at him, the man bowed hastily and immediately fled the chamber, bucket in hand.

Quinn shed his cloak and unbuckled his belt, acutely aware of the filth layering his skin. She had called him a "barbarian." The very word made his blood seethe. Michel silently folded Quinn's hastily discarded garments.

"I don't think I have ever seen you in such a foul mood," Bayard commented.

Quinn knew the look he tossed his comrade was a dark one.

"If you wish to see a foul mood, then come to my wedding banquet this night," he countered savagely. "Just one glance at the bride will teach you all a man needs to know about foul moods."

Michel froze in mid-gesture to look to his lord and blinked.

"Wedding banquet?" Bayard laughed in disbelief. "You are to be married? On this very night?"

Quinn shot an eloquent glance to his old companion. "Yes, or else Sayerne will not be mine," he admitted. "There is little to find amusing in that." His tone became ironic as he continued. "The lord has even been so courteous as to choose the bride."

"Married!" Bayard repeated, as though he were having trouble with the idea itself. "And so quick as that! Now there is a marvel I had not thought to see soon."

"And if you continue to comment, then it will be a marvel you will not see," Quinn said sourly.

When had he last felt so out of sorts? He could not recall. The lady Melissande certainly showed a gift for irking a man as thoroughly as nettles against the skin.

And now Bayard needled him on top of all but showed no inclination to abandon the tub. Quinn felt the chill against his bare skin, although the room was warmer than most.

Bayard eyed him and smiled as he settled deeper into the steaming bath.

"Have you not soaked the flesh from your bones by now?" Quinn demanded with impatience. "I would not catch my death on the eve of my wedding."

Bayard, the selfish cur, still showed no sign of budging from the tub.

"Then the woman cannot be so unpleasant," he jested amiably. "Although, one must wonder at her looks for the Lord de Tulley to be so anxious to see her match made. And in such a rush." He took a brush to his nails with unconcern. "It is almost as though he wanted to give you no opportunity to reconsider."

That charge struck too close to the mark for Quinn's taste, although the lady was finely made indeed. He expected that the full extent of her liability was her sharp tongue.

He was spared from response, though, by Tulley's servants. From the shadowed corner, they retrieved a second wooden tub that he had not noted and rolled it out to the middle of the room as the servant fetching water returned.

Two tubs? Quinn's eyes widened slightly in surprise as Tulley's boys set to the work of filling it with steaming water. It been a long time since he had visited anywhere blessed with such luxury. In fact, Quinn and Bayard had shared bathwater on so many occasions in their travels, that who would indulge first was an ongoing jest.

"This is a well-equipped keep, Quinn," Bayard commented amiably, evidently seeing the direction of his gaze. "And your reward for leading us here is no small one, for you will not have to be second after me into the bath on this night."

Bayard grinned and leaned back in his tub, beckoning the servant to add hot water to his bath. "By the saints above, it will take me a week to soak this filth from my hide." He sighed and closed his eyes with satisfaction as his water was warmed.

"If you are as dirty as you admit, then that is a blessing," Quinn commented, feeling a vestige of his usual manner return.

Bayard, though, eyed him assessingly from deeper in the steaming tub. Feeling the weight of the perceptive gaze and knowing any such perusal did not bode well for his privacy, Quinn struggled not to show his discomfiture.

"It cannot be a bad sign for this lady to have you so troubled after only one short interview," Bayard commented. Quinn tried not to wince visibly. He might be troubled, but it was not a good sign at all! "You will make the best of this match in the end, Quinn."

There was a thought Quinn did not want to consider. The very idea restored every scrap of his impatience. The lady's assault had been painful enough that he would not soon forget the impact of her knee. To even *think* of the future in her company was beyond him at this moment.

"This match can have no best!" Quinn declared vehemently. "The woman is a termagant of the worst order. There could be no peace for a man wherever she dwelt!"

Too late, he realized that his voice had shown more agitation than he had intended and he hunkered closer to his friend. His tone, though lower, was no less troubled. "The woman is as frosty as the winter wind, and there is no reasoning with her."

Bayard said nothing for a long moment. Surely he did not doubt Quinn's word? Why, anyone would agree with him about the lady—it was probably her manner that had left her unattached for so long.

And it grated upon Quinn that Tulley had found the perfect bait for his trap. Sayerne. The older man had guessed only too well that Quinn would be unable to turn his back on that prize, regardless of the cost.

Although he might grind his teeth at the price for the remainder of his days.

"It is unlike you to be so troubled about any matter," Bayard finally observed.

Quinn flung out his hands in frustration. "It is unlike me to be accused of being a mercenary, a brigand, a liar and the image of my sire in one short interview! The lady tests my patience with her insults."

With that, Quinn deliberately shut his mouth although he could have said more. He imagined that fumes rose from his ears, for everything within him raged at the way Melissande had spoken with him.

The lady exceeded her place.

Bayard propped his elbows on the side of the wooden tub and sat up, an inquisitive glint in his eye. The water in his tub sloshed at his move. "Is she foul to look upon?" he asked with apparent idleness.

Quinn was not fooled. The question concerned his comrade mightily, and curiously, that troubled Quinn. Clearly his riled temper affected his thoughts.

All the same, he did not even turn to Bayard as he responded. "No," he growled when he knew he could evade answering no longer.

Bayard's knowing chuckle did nothing to ease his mood. Quinn was grateful for the relative darkness of this place, for he felt self-conscious color was rising on the back of his neck.

"Dare I suggest that this is nothing but a matter of pride, Quinn?" Bayard asked playfully. "And, what manner of lady would she have been, if had she swooned before you? No woman you would welcome to wife, of that I can be certain."

"I had thought of taking no woman to wife at this time," Quinn declared vehemently. "The timing is inopportune. No woman—let alone a contrary one—would enjoy living at Sayerne before all is right once more. Her character is of little importance beyond that."

With that assertion, he climbed into the tub.

It was blessedly hot. Quinn closed his eyes and leaned his head back against the rim, willing himself to relax.

"Maybe *I* could coax a response from your bride of steel," Bayard mused.

Quinn sat bolt upright and regarded his friend in outrage, but Bayard remained—no doubt deliberately—blissfully oblivious of Quinn's response. "As we both know, my skill on the field of love far exceeds your own," Bayard added with feigned modesty.

Quinn's blood boiled and he bounded to his feet. He pointed at his comrade with a dripping finger. "You will not touch my wife!" he bellowed, water running off his flesh in rivulets. "If nothing else, my sire showed me the results of faithlessness in marriage and I will tolerate none of it in mine, regardless of my circumstance!"

Suddenly aware of the servants' eyes upon him, Quinn deliberately took a deep, steadying breath. When he continued, his voice was closer to his usual modulated tone. "Make no mistake in this, Bayard," he warned. "Should you test me in this matter, it will be you who pays the price."

With that, Quinn sat heavily into the bathwater again, his mood not alleviated in the least. He scowled at the steam unfurling from the swirling water and tried to slow the pounding of his heart. With one blow, the lady had addled his wits.

Could there be something to what Bayard said?

"Well." Bayard splashed playfully in the water, apparently unoffended by Quinn's outbreak. "It does seem that this is a matter that concerns you greatly," he commented. "But you are certain that you have no interest in this lady for her own charms? You did say that she was fair."

"I never said..." Quinn fell sullenly silent when he saw his friend's teasing grin. He turned back to his bath, knowing Bayard would not miss his heightened color this time. The man was cursedly observant.

"Although she is fair." Quinn found himself forced to admit this, albeit begrudgingly. The recollection of Melissande's lovely green eyes swam into his mind's eye and did nothing to improve his mood.

Yes, she was beyond lovely. And blessed with the tongue of a viper. Quinn frowned at his own admission as he took the soap from Michel and worked up a lather in a most purposeful manner.

"But I am making this alliance purely to ensure my inheritance," he added firmly.

"Ah." Bayard snapped his fingers as he rose from the bath, and a pair of boys brought him heavy linens to dry himself. He fixed Quinn with a skeptical eye as he did so. "So, it is completely meaningless that in all the years we have traveled together, despite all the foes and trials we have faced, I have never seen you agitated about anything but this."

Quinn fidgeted and could not hold his friend's gaze. "It is the unexpectedness of the condition," he said. Curiously his voice was less resolute in stating the truth than he might have expected.

Bayard, curse him, smiled. "Quinn, you and I have faced many an unexpected situation in the past, but you have never turned a hair."

"It is Sayerne at root," Quinn insisted, knowing that nothing else could stir his passion so. "That place is too close to my heart. It is nothing but the possibility of losing my inheritance after waiting so long that unsettles me."

Bayard chuckled but mercifully let the matter go. "Ah, good sense does that make," he conceded in a tone that belied his words.

Quinn fired a glance to his comrade, distrusting his manner. Bayard wrapped a length of linen about his waist with a flourish and propped his hands on his hips to regard Quinn quizzically.

"So, might I safely assume that you don't care what you wear to make this match?" He picked up Quinn's tunic, which Quinn realized in that instant was looking sorely used. Bayard granted it an assessing eye. "Your travel garments will do well enough, despite their wear and stains, if this wedding is only a formality to be endured. Won't they?"

Bayard met Quinn's gaze with all the innocence of a new babe.

Curse the man, he was right again! Quinn fought the impulse to growl in frustration. He could not attend his own wedding in such garb, with his hair untended and his jowls unshaved! The lady already thought him a barbarian of the crudest sort and, perversely, Quinn wanted nothing else than to prove her wrong.

"No," Quinn said hastily, disliking the gleam that lit Bayard's eye but plunging on regardless. "The institution of marriage must be respected, if nothing else, regardless of the reason for the match."

He turned to Tulley's servants, who yet lingered in the shadows, and deliberately ignored Bayard's smug grin. "Maybe one of you could discover whether the Lord de Tulley might consider lending me some fitting garments for this occasion." One of the boys bobbed a bow and ducked obediently out the door.

Quinn turned to his own squire. "Michel, sharpen a razor if you would, for I am in need of a shave. Maybe you could see whether you might lay hands on some shears, as well, for my hair is in dire need of a trim."

Michel grinned as he produced precisely those two items from behind his back. "Bayard said you would be needing these."

Quinn glanced to his companion, who grinned unabashedly. Bayard waved vaguely into the air and narrowed his eyes, as though he spied something elusive from afar. "My dame often said I should have been a seer," he said with an affected air.

Quinn threw the soap at him. The resounding splat of the soap landing on Bayard's chest made that knowing man jump so satisfactorily that Quinn laughed aloud.

Melissande was still shaking long moments after she gained her quarters. Her maid, Berthe, met her gaze for only an instant before she began her characteristic monologue.

"My lady, you look to have had a shock of the worst order. And you are too cold." Berthe pressed Melissande's hands between hers for a moment, then tutted under her breath. "Now, come over here and sit yourself down by the fire. I have a nice blaze going and it will warm you through to your toes."

Melissande did as she was bidden, her stomach still churning. She was to be wed to Jerome de Sayerne's son. It was beyond belief.

Her independence would be sacrificed this very night.

She spared a glance to the light filtering through the wooden shutters and knew by its orange cast that the sun was sinking. It would all be done soon enough. By the dawn, she would be wedded to and bedded by that rough barbarian.

Her heart took an unruly skip at the thought.

The ever-bustling Berthe urged a stoneware mug into Melissande's hands. It was warm. Melissande glanced down to its ruddy contents, the smell of cinnamon teasing her nostrils.

"A cup of spiced wine is what you need, my lady, for that will warm you through and through. It encourages the blood to race and heats you from the very core." Melissande sipped the soothing brew and, satisfied temporarily, the clucking maid frowned at the shuttered window. She tossed her dark curls and fixed her bright gaze on her mistress.

"It is cursed cold this winter. It doesn't even matter what a body dons in this weather, for the chill goes straight to the bones. I do not know what was in Tulley's mind to summon us so far in such a season. Surely anything of import he had to tell you could have waited until finer weather had come.''

Melissande knew she did not imagine the speculative gleam in the girl's gaze, but she was not ready to talk about her fate.

''Well.'' Berthe shrugged. ''If nothing else, the lord's keep is well equipped and we can eat at his expense for the inconvenience.'' She glanced pointedly to Melissande's cup and nodded brightly. ''Drink it up, then.''

Melissande sipped. The wine did warm her, just as Berthe had promised. The girl babbled on about this household occupant and another, but Melissande ceased to listen.

She was to wed. She took a deep draft of the wine.

By the time the wine was half-gone, Melissande was markedly less troubled by the entire situation. She looked to her expectant maid.

''I am being married tonight,'' she confessed.

Berthe smiled genuinely, Melissande's confession loosing another torrent of words. ''Yes, my lady, I heard the news in the kitchens and I could scarcely believe your good fortune!'' She clasped her hands together and gazed down in delight at an astonished Melissande. ''All of the women are declaring how handsome this Quinn de Sayerne is and saying how they would like to be in your place this night.'' Berthe smiled coyly and Melissande blinked.

Handsome? *Quinn?* She admitted the man had an appeal, in a rough sort of way, but she had never imagined that any would be envious of her being wed to a stranger on such short notice.

''Yes, Dame Fortune has smiled upon you, my lady, for that rogue Tulley—pardon any disrespect, my lady, but that man is one who sees to his own interests first—could have seen you wed to the first that came along, and not waited for a fine specimen such as Quinn.''

To have her maid address her betrothed in such a familiar manner was shocking to Melissande, but the wine lulled her into refraining from comment.

It was difficult to be riled about much of anything with this unaccustomed warmth coursing through her veins. She indulged in more than a sip of wine so seldom that this heady brew of Berthe's was having a strong effect upon her.

Though it was indeed delicious. Melissande drained the cup and leaned back against the wall, feeling much more tranquil about the entire prospect of marriage to Quinn.

She *had* thought him an attractive rogue, she mused. And he had the most wonderfully warm eyes...when he wasn't angry, of course.

Maybe she should have another cup of wine.

"You must tell me, my lady, are his eyes the shade of honey or of a deeper hue, like that of amber?"

A jolt tripped through Melissande that Berthe's question should so closely echo her own thoughts, but the girl continued unaware.

"There is great dissent in the kitchens over this and I—for the sake of accuracy, of course—would like to be the one to set the matter straight."

Berthe paused, her eyes gleaming, and regarded Melissande in anticipation once more.

Melissande cleared her throat delicately. Only too easily could she recall the precise shade of Quinn's eyes, and the way they changed when his temper flared.

The room was suddenly too warm and Melissande wondered how she could have imagined it cold. She glanced down to the empty cup in her hands. Although she was not one to encourage talk among servants, it seemed that the gossip mill was well at work already on this matter.

"It depends upon his mood," she admitted, hoping against hope that her cheeks were warm because of Berthe's brew.

"His mood," Berthe breathed. She clasped her hands together, rolled her eyes heavenward, then spun across the room in a flurry of wool skirts.

"I was thinking, my lady, that you might be wanting to wear something special on this eve, seeing as it is your wedding night and all, and also I was thinking that you would want to be looking your best for your groom."

With that, Berthe cast a sly wink over her shoulder. "So, I have laid out that kirtle you just had made with the samite we purchased from that trader from the East. I do like that emerald shade upon you, for it makes your eyes even more green and highlights the fairness of your hair."

Berthe glanced back to her choice and sighed with satisfaction. "With the gold embroidery upon it and your red chemise beneath, it seems fitting enough for a bride. And I have borrowed some red ribbons and pearls from one of the other women, that I might appropriately dress your hair."

Berthe ran one appreciative hand carefully over the kirtle laid out on the bed. "My lady, you will look beautiful."

Beautiful. For a barbarian.

Melissande frowned with the effort of collecting her thoughts. She hoped that her finery was not destroyed by the brute in his consummation of their match. He had threatened her that the deed would be done, and although Melissande did not intend to lose any hope of holding Annossy over this matter, still she dreaded the inevitable.

Too late, she wished she knew more of these delicate matters.

She eyed Berthe but knew she could not possibly ask her maid. The girl was charming, but everything passed from her lips to another's ears. Melissande would not deliberately make herself the laughingstock of the servants.

She held out her cup to Berthe, knowing that boldness would come from wine. The first draft had settled her fears better than anything else.

"I am still chilled," she lied, and Berthe's expression immediately turned sympathetic. "Would it be possible for you to prepare another cup for me?"

By the time Melissande descended the stairs to the hall in all her finery, she was warm through and through. Three cups of Berthe's spiced wine brew was almost enough to dismiss every vestige of her trepidation.

In fact, she felt curiously like giggling.

Melissande tripped on the bottom stair and a strong hand caught her elbow. She gasped as she righted herself and glanced up.

Whatever words she might have uttered in thanks died on her lips when she met Quinn's amber gaze.

At least, she thought it was Quinn. His eyes alone remained the same. He had shaved and she saw the strong outline of his features for the first time. His hair was trimmed, his garments fine. Melissande swallowed as her gaze danced back to his and she could not look away.

How could she have questioned whether the man was handsome? In this moment, he looked every bit the noble knight.

A lazy smile crept across his firm lips—lips that only recently had been kissing hers, she recalled—and Melissande knew she had had too much wine. Why else would it suddenly be so difficult to catch her breath?

"My lady, you are a vision," he said simply. His voice was pitched low, for her ears alone, Melissande realized. That they exchanged a confidence, even over such an inconsequential matter, seemed intimate beyond belief.

It reminded Melissande of precisely how intimate matters would be between them before the night was through. At that thought, her knees, oddly enough, seemed uncertain as to whether they would continue to support her.

"I thank you," she said as breezily as she could. "You, also, have managed to look reasonably reputable."

There was an understatement. Quinn's chestnut locks were thick and curly, combed to some measure of order despite their unruly nature. The torchlight in the hall picked out coppery tones within their waves in a most intriguing manner. His shaved jaw was squared and determined. Melissande realized now how cleanly shaped his features were, his nose straight and aquiline.

And still there were the attributes she had noted before. The green brocade tabard, though simple in pattern and cut, emphasized the breadth of his shoulders to her eyes. The wool chausses of darker hue merely accentuated the lean strength of his legs.

Melissande caught her breath as he leaned closer and her gaze dropped to his hand. He had the hands of a man who wielded a broadsword with ease, yet his touch was surprisingly gentle. She could feel its warm weight on her arm and she stared at his strong fingers, noting the few calluses.

Quinn was no mincing courtier, but a man who swung a blade to earn his way. The thought made Melissande tingle in sudden awareness of his masculinity.

"My lady," he whispered against her hair. His breath made Melissande shiver unwillingly and she kept her gaze resolutely locked on his hand. "Surely we might call a truce for the duration of our wedding night, at least."

The way he murmured "our" with such ease made Melissande's heart skip a beat.

But she would show him nothing of her weakness for his form. She summoned a bright smile, took a deep breath and looked him directly in the eye.

"It would only be civilized," she said with a crispness she was far from feeling. "Shall we see the dastardly deed done?"

Quinn's eyes narrowed and Melissande's smile faded at the awareness that she had said the wrong thing.

"That comment is hardly in the spirit I intended," he said brusquely. Melissande felt bereft when he turned abruptly away, his lips set firmly. "But it shall be your way," he added. "The worst may as well be done sooner rather than later."

The very idea that he might not be any more enamored of this forced match than she was not music to Melissande's ears. Quinn offered her his elbow with deliberate politeness and she slipped her hand into it in poor temper.

How dare he? *She* was a fine catch for a wife. Melissande understood that she was not hard on the eyes of men *and* her Annossy was a prosperous estate.

Unlike a certain Sayerne administered by an inexperienced ruffian who simply happened to clean up rather well.

She jabbed her chin into the air, determined not to show Quinn how he had pricked her pride, and sailed into the chapel on his elbow.

Melissande might be forced to wed this barbarian, but she would grant him no more of herself than was absolutely necessary.

On this night or any other.

The Lord de Tulley looked smugly pleased at their arrival.

Quinn was not surprised.

Neither was he surprised that his bride was as frosty as ever. He should not have been surprised by his own heated response to her manner and comments.

Presumably time would diminish her ability to so readily irk him. He gritted his teeth and led his bride to the front of the chapel, wondering if he made as dreadful a mistake as he feared in doing this.

As they stood side by side before the altar and the priest's blessing rolled over him, Quinn carefully considered whether he was making the greatest error of all his days. It was his last chance to change his mind, for once the priest's words were spoken, he would be bound to this woman forever. Quinn flicked a glance to Tulley's intent features and his heart sank.

Take this virago to wife or lose everything. That was the offer and it was only too easy to believe that Tulley would see his threat through.

To lose Sayerne was unthinkable.

And that left Quinn little choice. It was no solace to know that Tulley had guessed the truth.

After this night though, Quinn resolved, he would avoid the lady and her barbed tongue. Between their two estates and the work required to rebuild Sayerne, it should be easy enough to do.

Even if the prospect of a loveless marriage tugged at his heartstrings. He had always hoped for better for himself, but his determination to keep his inheritance had decreed that that would not be the way.

"You may seal your pledge with a kiss of peace," the priest murmured. Quinn started, then glanced to Melissande in time to see her gaze flit nervously to his.

Then she lifted her chin proudly, the ice queen once more.

Quinn was intrigued. Certainly the lady had responded earlier to his embrace. Was it possible that she was not unaffected by his touch, either?

Was it possible that there *was* promise in this match?

A man could only try.

"Yes," he said firmly. "One must adhere to tradition."

There it was again! Quinn heard her catch her breath and knew he could not turn away. Clearly the lady was not as cold as she would have him believe.

Maybe this night would not be such an ordeal after all.

Quinn leisurely fitted his hand beneath Melissande's chin, drawing her closer and turning her to face him in the same moment. Her eyelids fluttered closed when he cupped her face between his hands, but Quinn did not intend to let her escape him so easily.

"Open your eyes, my lady," he whispered. "I would have no doubt in your mind to whom you are wed."

She did as she was bidden and Quinn felt her tremble as he leaned closer. That she was fearful only launched a protective urge within him and made him yet more gentle. He smiled at her, his heart skipping a beat when she tentatively smiled back.

"To the future," he murmured just before his lips brushed across hers.

Melissande quivered, then her slender fingers were on his own face. She tasted like wine and cinnamon and the same sweet warmth he recalled from earlier that day.

Quinn wondered whether all of her flesh tasted as sweet, and found the chapel suddenly lost its chill.

It was only with the greatest effort that he recalled their place and put her aside. To his surprise, the lady's eyes were dancing with mischief.

"And to the boredom of peace," she added unexpectedly. Quinn smiled and she giggled outright, clapping one hand over her mouth at the sound as she looked guiltily to the priest.

Quinn realized he had never seen her smile and his heart swelled that she had done so at this moment.

That was a good sign for the future. Maybe he had been too hasty in his conclusions. Maybe Bayard, with his irritating comments, had been close to the truth.

Regardless, Quinn could not resist the impulse to tease his new bride.

"Maybe you will not find peace so boring as you think," he whispered loudly enough that the others might hear. Quinn heard Bayard's chuckle at the same moment as Melissande gasped at his audacity. Her eyes still twinkled, though, and he grinned slowly as he watched her flush.

Quinn was tempted to toss her over his shoulder and make for privacy immediately, before this fleeting moment passed, but the priest cleared his throat disapprovingly.

"The cook has endeavored to assemble a wedding feast on short notice," Tulley interjected. "Maybe it is time we sample the results of his efforts."

That comment, Quinn noted with disappointment, effectively banished the intriguing imp Melissande had been just a moment past. She sobered, regal again, and coolly slipped her hand into his elbow.

Disappointment welled up within him until he recalled that she had not been playful at all earlier. Quinn had made the lady relax once already. Should he make an effort, especially now that the ceremony was past, he could undoubtedly glimpse that smile again.

And Quinn knew he would have to ensure that Melissande's composure slipped this night if their mating was to be enjoyable.

Clearly what the lady needed was a goodly quantity of wine to dismiss her reservations. And Quinn intended to personally see that she had it.

Melissande was certain that she had never quite finished her cup of wine, but still it seemed that there was always another sip within it. It was most curious and a puzzle well beyond her reasoning capabilities by the end of the meal.

But nothing troubled her this night. She was warm and without a care.

She could not even trouble herself to recall the names of all present or to follow any of their conversations. It was unlike her to be so oblivious to all about her, but Melissande dismissed that with a mental wave. This was her nuptial feast. She could do or not do as she willed.

The meat was good, the wine was better and the soft brush of Quinn's elbow periodically against hers was enough to keep her tingling from head to toe.

She knew she was all too aware of his presence but could not stop herself. As the evening continued, Melissande found a buzz of awareness taking up residence within her.

She covertly watched Quinn's deft handling of his knife, enjoyed the grace of his purposeful hands. She smelled the heat of his skin so close beside her and was aware of the precise moment he pressed the length of his thigh to hers.

Melissande was half-certain that the move had been deliberate, but Quinn's expression was unconcerned.

She did not move away, though the muscled imprint of his leg against hers made it more difficult to concentrate on all around her. Tulley sat on her left and periodically tried to converse with her. Melissande nodded, smiled and sipped, relieved each time that the lord abandoned his efforts.

She wanted to touch Quinn. The wanton urge shocked her to her core, yet Melissande could not dismiss it. He laughed amiably at something his comrade Bayard said and she decided she liked the hearty sound of his laughter.

Quinn smiled at Melissande when she rose at Berthe's urging to retire. Melissande nearly lost her footing when her heart turned a somersault in response, but he caught her elbow within his strong grip once more.

"I shall be along shortly, my lady wife," he murmured in that bone-melting low tone to which Melissande was already falling victim.

"Yes," she managed to whisper in response. She turned hastily and the room cavorted around her in a most peculiar way. Melissande giggled under her breath in an unladylike manner at its antics.

"Do you need my aid?" Quinn asked politely. Melissande panicked at the thought, her sluggardly mind suddenly recalling what would happen when they were alone together upstairs.

She was still unprepared for that moment! To enjoy the press of a man's leg against her own was one thing, but whatever mystery awaited her this night was sure to be quite another. Let him remain down here as long as he desired!

"No, no, no," Melissande said as hurriedly as she could. She backed away with a smile and nearly stepped back off the edge of the dais.

"Whoa!" Bayard declared as he caught her elbow.

"I thank you." Melissande was surprised to find that this knight's touch launched no tingles along her skin.

There was another puzzle, for Bayard was not hard upon the eyes, either. He had an engaging smile to which Melissande was certain many maids had succumbed. She lifted her gaze to Quinn, who winked in a most alluring manner.

"But a moment and I will be with you," he vowed.

And Melissande knew what he meant by that. Well, not *precisely* did she know, but she understood it would be intimate. And likely painful. She turned hastily and made for the stairs, hoping her dawning consternation did not show.

"My lady, do take my elbow for the stairs," Berthe bade her.

Melissande felt Quinn's gaze upon her but did not dare to look back. These stairs required every scrap of her attention. It was curious how they shifted and moved. Melissande knew that they had not acted in such a manner before, but this was yet another puzzle best left for later.

But she conquered them, as well as the hall above, which seemed to have developed a markedly uneven floor. Finally they reached the room and Melissande breathed a sigh of relief. A fire burned brightly in the grate and the mood was that of a welcoming haven.

Until she noticed that the bed linens had been changed and turned down. The import of that could not be mistaken.

This was a room prepared for an assignation. Melissande caught her breath, but Berthe was behind her.

"Come along, my lady. My lord Quinn said he would be along immediately and we will not be wanting to keep such a fine gentleman waiting."

Melissande might have fought to remain dressed, so certain was she that it might not be so terrible to keep him waiting, but she was helpless in her state against Berthe's too-quick hands. All too soon, she was as nude as the day she was born and being hustled toward the bed.

There was nothing for it. At least she might be covered in the bed, for it was clear she was not to gain so much as a chemise this night. Melissande climbed in and pulled the linens up to her chin while Berthe unbraided her hair. Her heart rose to lodge in her throat as the sounds of men's voices drew nearer.

"Do not trouble yourself, my lady," Berthe cooed confidently. "Your Quinn is a kind man, any woman could see that, and I am certain that you have nothing to fear on this night."

Melissande's pulse pounded in her ears. The men fell into an unruly, shuffling silence outside the door, then a knock resonated through the quiet room.

"Good evening?" Berthe called when Melissande said nothing.

"Good evening, my lady," roared one who might have been Bayard. "A gift have we found for you in the hall!"

An instant later, the door burst open and Quinn was bodily shoved through. His tabard he clutched in one hand and his shirt was torn open. Laughter erupted from the half-dozen men outside and rude jests were made.

Melissande found she could not look away from the russet patch of hair on Quinn's chest. His skin was bronzed, no doubt from the sun in the East, and the torn shirt revealed the most fascinating glimpses of his chest.

But a lady should have no interest in such matters. Melissande burrowed beneath the covers, suddenly feeling the weight of every curious male eye upon her. She could easily guess that they all sought to glimpse *her* nudity.

"Come, Quinn," Bayard cajoled. "It is time we put you naked to bed with your bride!" The other men laughed, but Melissande scurried deeper beneath the covers in shame.

Surely they would not!

"I believe that I can manage from this point," Quinn countered amiably. An undertone of determination was there in his tone and Melissande wondered if he had noted her response.

"It is time that we all should be leaving," Berthe said briskly when Bayard might have pursued the matter.

"But..." Bayard protested. He yelped when Berthe crossed the floor and firmly grasped him by the ear. The other men erupted into gales of laughter.

"But nothing," she said firmly. "No business have any of us here, for it is clear to even the most dim-witted fool that a man and a woman need their privacy at this moment." Berthe hauled a cursing Bayard back into the corridor by his ear, much to the delight of the other men.

"I might have expected finer behavior from a knight, especially one who has taken up the Cross and gone to the Holy Land, but it is painfully clear that I have overestimated you...." she continued, despite Bayard's inarticulate protests.

Then the door was closed and there was nothing in the room but the glow of Quinn's eyes. The fire crackled and the silence flooded Melissande's ears. Her heart beat fit to burst as she stared back at her husband.

Husband. Melissande swallowed. She could not avoid the truth any longer. The moment was upon her and the wine, mercilessly, had abandoned her to her fate.

Chapter Four

His wife resembled a cornered and terrified rabbit. Quinn stepped into the room and deliberately laid his tabard aside, moving slowly that he might not frighten her further.

Only her eyes showed above the linens and they were fixed resolutely upon him. They were wide and of a darker emerald in her uncertainty. Quinn took a deep breath at the realization that this night would not pass as easily as he had hoped.

Sayerne hung in the balance. That was both a sobering and a fortifying thought. The certainty that Tulley would rap on the door with the very dawn in search of his evidence did little to help.

The deed must be done, though. Maybe it was that certainty that fueled Melissande's fear.

The thought gave Quinn a new perspective and dismissed his own fears. It was his task to gain her trust in this. He must prove himself different than she feared he would be.

He must prove himself different from his sire. With difficulty, Quinn looked away and made his tone deliberately conversational.

"Ah, that Bayard is such a rogue!" he mused. He deliberately eyed the remnants of his shirt and shook his head sagely. "He never misses an opportunity for some jest or

another. Mercifully, your maid showed no hesitation in
dealing with him precisely as he deserved."

The lady said nothing but Quinn fancied her grip loosened slightly on the linens.

"Was that not a fine meal?" he asked in the same bright
manner. "I could hardly believe Tulley's cook concocted
such a feast in just a half day's notice. Tell me, are all cooks
hereabout so talented, or is Tulley particularly fortunate in
his staff?"

Melissande cleared her throat delicately and Quinn dared
to be encouraged. He did not look to her, but unbuckled his
belt with a leisure he was far from feeling and laid it aside.

"Tulley's cook is particularly gifted even among those
talented cooks in the region. He has been here long," she
offered. She spoke carefully and Quinn imagined that she
was still feeling some effect of the wine.

"Ah, well, I shall have to be careful of becoming plump,
then, now that I am home," he said amiably. Quinn heard
a soft rush of his wife's breath that might almost have
passed for a laugh and was reassured that she might be re-
laxing a bit.

He pulled off his shirt, unable to keep from glancing over
his shoulder to his waiting bride. Melissande hastily averted
her gaze, but twin spots of color burning in her cheeks revealed that she was not immune to the sight of his nudity.

The evening showed more promise than just moments
past.

On impulse, Quinn strode over to the bed and sat on its
edge. Deliberately he left on his chausses. Melissande scurried toward the other side and lay down on her back, eyeing him warily all the while. She clutched the linens before
herself like a shield.

She did not flee, though, and Quinn took encouragement from that. He took his time removing his boots before he turned to her anew.

He was doomed to savor only one night of lovemaking, and that consummation had been gained solely upon threat from the lord. It might have been tragic enough to make Quinn laugh, if only to keep himself from weeping.

He had always wanted more and, ever the optimist, he still dared to hope that somehow he might find it here.

"Do you think that I am too plump now?" he asked teasingly. Melissande's cheeks flamed, but he noted that she did not seem able to keep her glance from darting over his bare chest anew.

"I think you are vain," she retorted, but her voice was more breathless than he might have expected.

Quinn grinned as he leaned closer and propped his hands on the coverlet beside her.

"Are you plump?" he asked in a devious whisper.

Melissande's lips clamped shut and her fingers perceptibly tightened their grip on the linens. "I will not show myself to you like some tavern whore!" she hissed.

Quinn quirked a brow. "What needs to be done *cannot* be done with the linens between us," he commented.

Melissande glanced away and then back, fire in her gaze. "Then close your eyes," she challenged.

Quinn chuckled at the very suggestion. Close his eyes? Never!

"If I am to be condemned to only one night of lovemaking for the rest of my days, then be assured, my lady, that I shall not keep my eyes closed."

His bride breathed an exasperated sigh. "Must you make such a show of it?" she snapped. "I know well enough that you will hardly sleep in a cold bed, even should mine be forbidden to you."

Quinn met her gaze in surprise. "Surely you do not imagine that I would be unfaithful to you?" he asked. Her gaze faltered for only a moment before her eyes narrowed coldly.

"Like sire, like son. Your sire seldom slept alone, should the number of his bastards be any indication."

Her certainty of his lowly character was sobering indeed.

"I have already told you," Quinn said with measured calm, "that my sire and I have nothing in common. I left Sayerne because that man and I did not see eye to eye. On that day I vowed that I would not return while he drew breath and so it has been."

"You mock me!" his bride charged hotly. "You offer only sweet words so that I won't resist you! Once you have had your way, your tune will change."

Quinn abruptly rolled until he lay on his side, looking down at her. "No, Melissande," he whispered urgently, willing her to believe him. "This is our wedding night. You cannot in fairness ask me to close my eyes for this moment."

He leaned toward her and she deliberately closed her eyes. Quinn heard the lady's breath catch in her throat although she did not move farther away. Disappointment filled him and Quinn knew that somehow he had to reassure her.

"If this is to be the only time we couple," he murmured, "I would make the mating sweet. And I would look upon your beauty, if only this once."

Melissande did not respond.

"I do not mean to hurt you," Quinn murmured reassuringly.

Her eyes flew open and she stared at him for a long moment, then nodded tentatively. "I understand it cannot be helped," she whispered, and Quinn saw the source of her fear.

He could not argue with that, though he wished he might have been able to tell some sweet lie to reassure her. "So I have heard, but I will be careful," he vowed.

Quinn extracted her fingers from the linens and took her hand within his. Her fingers were cold. "But you know that this task cannot be avoided on this night."

Melissande closed her eyes again and took a deep breath as though she gathered her strength. Then her eyes flicked open and she nodded purposefully.

"You speak the truth," she said with a firmness that sounded more like the lady Quinn had met in Tulley's offices. "Come to bed, husband, and do your deed."

With that, Melissande hauled back the linens to expose her nudity and lay back stiffly against the sheets. She closed her eyes and placed her hands at her sides.

She looked like a corpse. Quinn regarded his bride in horror.

Although his astonishment was not quite enough to keep him from noting either her slender perfection or the ripe curve of her breasts.

But no! Not like this! Quinn was insulted that she thought he would couple with her like some animal. A man did not merely inflict his desire upon his wife.

In fact, Quinn rapidly felt his desire deserting him with her demand. He shoved irritably to his feet and paced away from the bed as he pushed one hand through his hair. Confound the woman, but she tested him!

"You do this on purpose," he accused irritably.

"On purpose?" she demanded. Quinn turned and saw that she had sat up, her eyes bright with indignation.

"Of course, I submit on purpose!" she declared with a vehemence that Quinn found curiously reassuring. The spark was back in her eyes and although she irritated him like this, he felt he better knew the terms of battle when she was annoyed. "Is that not what Tulley and now you want of me? I simply do your bidding, like any dutiful wife." This last was spat with a vigor that Quinn might have noted under other circumstances.

"A *dutiful* wife!" he roared instead. "Ha! Now *there* is something I clearly am not destined to enjoy!"

"Oh! You push me too far!" Melissande bounded from the bed to shake a finger beneath his nose with outrage. "If

obedience is what you desire of me, then you should forgo
Tulley's test and let the match be annulled!''

Quinn barely heard her words, so transfixed was he by the
cloud of gold that followed her leap from the bed.

"Your hair," he whispered admiringly.

It was beautiful. Melissande's hair hung loose to her hips,
spun gold with the sheen of the finest silk. It shimmered as
she moved as though it possessed a life of its own, and in
that moment, Quinn could think of nothing but touching it.

He had never seen the like. Since he had left the Conti-
nent fifteen years past, Quinn had not glimpsed any sight so
fine.

Melissande forced a laugh in a most uncharacteristic
manner. "It is simply hair," she said with a shrug, but
Quinn knew with curious certainty that she was flattered.

"May I touch it?" he asked in wonderment.

Something of his awe must have shown in his eyes, for
Melissande nodded hastily in agreement. She turned slightly
and Quinn took in the majesty of these golden tresses cascading down her back. Her hair gleamed in the firelight and
bounced slightly as she moved.

He took a step closer and was surprised to find a tight-
ness lodged in his chest. Quinn reached out, noting how
rough and heavy his hand looked in contrast to her hair.

He hesitated, but he could not deny himself the temptation.

Her hair ran over his hand like a golden waterfall and
writhed about his fingers as though it possessed a will of its
own. It was soft beyond soft, silky and smooth. Quinn lifted
a gleaming handful to his gaze and the sweet scent of Melissande rose to tease his nostrils.

His body responded with a healthy vigor that caught him
by surprise. He looked to his bride, but she kept her face
studiously averted, her hands folded before her like a Ma-
donna. Quinn glanced down and saw the rosy curve of

Melissande's buttocks revealed by his lifting the handful of golden locks.

Then he could not help but look. He lifted her hair deliberately away, loving the feel of it as it spilled over his fingers.

She was beautifully wrought, from head to toe, he realized with rising anticipation. Her skin was fair and smooth, her curves delicate and feminine. Every facet of her body was so different from his own. The gently flared hips led his eye upward to the neat indent of her waist and thence to the sweet curve of her breasts, her nipples ruddy and beaded in the cool air of the room. Her neck was long, her chin held high.

Never had Quinn imagined he would find such a bride, let alone be cast such a prize by fortune's lot alone. Their argument was chased from his mind with such speed that he could not imagine why he might have even been irritated with a woman of such sweet beauty.

"Melissande," he murmured, hearing the reverence echoed in his low tone. She turned slightly and the emerald of her eyes glowed in the firelight. "You are beyond beautiful," he confessed, feeling again the rough warrior ungraced with the words of a courtier.

Her full lips quirked in amusement and the expression in her eyes was warily indulgent. "You say that only to gain my willingness this night," she accused, though her voice had lost its earlier sting.

It was clear that his touching her hair had managed to disarm them both.

"No," Quinn said in a tone that brooked no argument. "I say that because it is true." Surprise flickered in her eyes and, for a moment, she seemed uncertain what to say.

Quinn did not intend to let the moment pass.

He lowered his head and captured her lips with his. To his delight, Melissande hesitated but a heartbeat before she placed her hand on his chest and leaned into his embrace.

It was precious little, but that was all the encouragement Quinn needed to intensify their kiss.

It was not the heat of the wine coursing through Melissande's veins this time and she knew it. Yet the languid sense of overwhelming pleasure, the loss of control—the loss of even the desire for control!—was much the same.

Quinn's kisses teased and tempted. They interfered with her power to protest, for each left her more hungry for the next. Melissande knew she would have been hard-pressed to determine precisely when each ended and another began. His lips teased and nibbled, tasted and cajoled in a ceaseless caress that melted her bones. Her resistance did not have a chance, especially as she knew this mating was destined to be.

Surely it was no crime if she permitted herself to enjoy her husband's seductive touch just this once? Quinn's hand slipped to her nape and the weight of his broad palm there weakened her knees.

She felt cherished. The expression of wonder on Quinn's face when he touched her hair could have meant nothing else. He had shown a weakness, if only for her hair, and Melissande felt herself suddenly less willing to fight with him.

If they were compelled to mate this night, this one and only time, she told herself that she should make the most of the moment.

Wanting to touch him, she laid her hand on the mat of curly russet hair in the middle of his chest. His skin was warm yet unyielding, and she felt the pulse of his heart beneath her hand.

It quickened its pace, right against her fingers. The sign that he was not unaffected by their embrace encouraged her and Melissande dared to lean closer.

Her breasts brushed against the lean strength of his chest in a most disconcerting manner. Melissande parted her lips and let her head fall back into the strength of Quinn's supporting hand. When his tongue meandered between her lips, she knew she could stand no longer.

In that moment, Quinn swept her off her feet. It was as though he guessed her very thoughts, and she felt a new link forged between them. Melissande's flesh came alive at the touch of his skin pressing against hers.

It was so intimate. And she was such a wanton to enjoy it.

Yet Melissande wanted more.

She was on the bed a moment later with Quinn looming over her, his lips on her cheek, her jaw, her earlobe and trailing down her neck. Melissande heard herself sigh and gripped his shoulders, liking how the hard curve of him fit beneath her hand. Quinn trailed a row of burning kisses along her collarbone, across the swell of her breast, and abruptly captured her nipple within his lips.

Melissande cried out in surprise. She clutched at his head, her fingers lost in the chestnut curls, but he suckled undeterred.

And she felt something new awaken within her.

Before Melissande could identify this sensation, Quinn's hand slid lower. She inhaled sharply as his strong fingers slipped through the tangle of curls, then she felt their warmth on her most private place.

She gasped. Quinn glanced to her and smiled.

"Lay back, my lady," he urged. "I grant you my word that this will not hurt."

Melissande did not even think to question her trust in his word. She had lain back for only a moment before his fingers moved gently and sent a wave of pleasure flooding through her. She gasped again and Quinn chuckled before he continued.

But there was little will left within her to protest. Melissande closed her eyes and named that dawning urge within her as desire. As Quinn suckled her other breast and the heat rose beneath her skin, Melissande surrendered to the moment.

And the pleasure increased a hundredfold with every caress of his fingertips. Melissande writhed but Quinn granted her no quarter. It was too hot in the room, there was too much tension beneath her flesh, yet there was no escape from the sweet torment of his touch.

Melissande grasped Quinn's hair in two fistfuls and drew him back for her kiss, her own embrace demanding as it had not been before. She slipped her own tongue into his mouth and explored his spicy warmth with abandon.

Melissande felt his hardness nudge against her hip and though her pulse inexplicably quickened at his touch, she could not bear to look upon him.

But Quinn's fingers cajoled her arousal, just as his lips teased her even more. He nibbled on her earlobe and the gentle pressure of his lips nearly sent her into a frenzy. Melissande arched against him and the tangle of hair on his chest tickled her aching nipples unbearably.

Yet she could not pull away. She wanted to sample him even more. His fingers nibbled at the sweet spot between her thighs and Melissande shivered anew. She twisted and Quinn casually tossed his leg over hers, the hair on his legs tickling her beyond all. She was too aware of him, of every sensation, of the velvet of the coverlet beneath her back.

"Drift with the tide, my lady," he whispered against her ear.

The fan of his breath made Melissande shudder from head to toe. Once begun, it seemed she could not stop her shivering. The heat radiated through her to burst from her fingertips. She clawed at Quinn's back, but still he caressed. She tangled her legs about him until they were entwined, his strength only feeding her pleasure.

"Follow it, follow it," he urged. Melissande gasped as her heart beat wildly and clasped Quinn to her chest as she followed his bidding.

Suddenly she gained some crest her body had intuitively sought. Melissande gasped aloud. Her mind's eye filled with colors and it seemed she had just stepped off a precipice. She was floating in a bottomless crevasse, yet sheltered within the warmth of Quinn's embrace. She felt everything tighten within and her very womb seemed to pulse of its own accord.

Melissande fancied that she cried out in pleasure, then was aware of nothing but the steady rhythm of Quinn's heart pounding against her own.

Quinn propped himself on his elbows, content to watch his flushed lady doze for a moment in the wake of her release. The fingers that had dug into his back reposed on his upper arms and he admired their slender delicacy. Sooty lashes fanned her pink cheeks and her ruddy lips had parted slightly.

Quinn could smell nothing but the intoxicating scent of her release. He reveled in the certainty that he had pleased his bride well. The glorious golden tangle of her hair writhed beneath her and spread itself across the linens. Quinn could feel its silkiness wrapped about his fingers.

Unable to resist temptation when she stirred, he bent and brushed his lips across hers. Her eyes flew open and he feared for an instant what she might first say, but she smiled with a lazy satisfaction.

"That did not hurt," she said.

Quinn grinned. "Did I not promise you as much?"

She nodded shyly, her gaze flying to his when he slipped his weight between her thighs.

"This may hurt, my lady, although I shall endeavor to be gentle," he warned.

A tiny frown marred her brow. "But I thought it was done?"

Quinn shook his head as he encountered her wetness. She was innocent and he had best move slowly. Quinn caught his breath and closed his eyes at the promise of her sweetness, willing himself to proceed with caution. "No, my lady, we have only half done the deed."

Melissande said nothing else but her grip tightened on his arms. He felt himself nudge at her portal and leaned lower, crossing his arms beneath her and cupping her shoulders within his hands. "Wrap your legs around my waist, if you are able," he urged, and heard the strain in his own voice.

He must proceed slowly, Quinn reminded himself, regardless of how long he had been alone, regardless of how much he wanted to embed himself within her in one thrust. Slow and careful, that Melissande might at least taste the pleasure mating could bring.

She complied with his request, the way she ran her toes up the back of his legs nearly undoing his control in one fell swoop. Quinn closed his eyes in pleasure, feeling cocooned within his bride's embrace.

She was warm, like satin left in the sun. And unbearably soft. Quinn knew he had never even dreamed that such sweetness might exist. He heard her gasp and halted guiltily, his eyes flying open.

Melissande smiled and wriggled her hips in a most inviting manner. "Just a twinge," she whispered. Her eyes danced with an alluring and newfound confidence. "I want more."

Her very demand enflamed him, then Melissande writhed beneath him. Never would he maintain his control under such a siege!

"My lady!" he protested, only to find an achingly soft fingertip pressed against his lips.

"Tell me how to please you," she urged, to his astonishment. "It is only fair that we each have our pleasure this night."

Quinn could not find the words. Melissande wriggled experimentally and he closed his eyes, willing himself to hold on for a few moments longer.

Evidently his response tempted his bride to guess.

She arched against him, pressing the fullness of her breasts against his chest. Quinn's hand slipped seemingly of its own volition to the indent of her waist and lodged there.

"Does that please you?" she whispered. Quinn did not know how he would endure. His pulse pounded in his ears, his chest was tight and still she coaxed him further.

With each heartbeat, he feared he would burst.

"Melissande...I..." Quinn could not form a coherent thought to save his life.

Melissande stretched up and rolled her tongue into his ear. The gentle touch of her tongue, the sensation of her breath there, the brush of her lips, all combined to make his blood nearly boil. He ran his hands over her skin and reared back. Quinn gripped her hips and rocked.

And Melissande granted him no mercy. Her legs tightened around his waist, her arms locked around his neck. Quinn was trapped within her, captured by her, enfolded and encircled by her warmth in a way he had never dreamed of before. She drove him to a frenzied height with a surety that stole his breath away.

Quinn's eyes flew open as her nails dug into his shoulders once more. In a flash, Quinn realized that she was reaching the crest again.

This woman was his bride and partner for all time. This woman he would pleasure until his dying day. This woman was his and his alone.

Quinn's own release swept through him in a torrent. He arched high and spilled his seed with a vigor he had never known before. He knew he groaned as everything within him strained, then he sagged against her in relief.

"Melissande," he whispered in surprise.

She opened her eyes and granted him a sleepy smile that warmed him through to his soul.

Melissande. He had sold the lady's potential short when he had expected this mating to be only a trial.

On the verge of sleep himself, Quinn nestled down beside her and gathered her close to his side. "Melissande," he murmured wonderingly into the delicate curve of her ear.

His bride said nothing, but she snuggled against him as her breathing deepened. Quinn de Sayerne had but one thought in the darkness before sleep wholly claimed him.

Clearly he was the most fortunate man in all of Christendom.

The blood on the sheets was a rude awakening the next morning.

Melissande blinked but the incriminating red spots remained. She rolled over, but Quinn was already tending the fire, wearing only his chausses, the golden light of the dawn picking out the glints in his hair. That he granted her a smugly self-satisfied smile did nothing to assuage Melissande's guilt.

She had broken her pledge to Arnaud!

Melissande felt the color drain from her face. How could she have forgotten? What manner of faithless wretch was she?

And how could she have savored the consummation of a match with another? She was not fit to sweep the ashes from the hearth if her solemn pledge was worth so little!

"Good morning, my lady," Quinn purred.

"There is nothing good about it!" Melissande snapped. She felt him recoil and her conscience twinged that she had hurt him.

But her word had been broken! Was that not of greater import than Quinn's feelings? She noted that Quinn halted uncertainly a few paces from the bed, but did not spare him a glance lest her determination be swayed.

"I thought that last evening would have made this morning a sunny one," he said carefully.

Oh, so that single deed was meant to make all well between them? Trust a man to find matters so simple! Melissande flicked Quinn a hostile glance, more than content to blame him for her troubles.

Was Quinn not the man at the root of it all?

"It is all *your* fault that matters lie as they do on this morning!" Melissande accused. "Had you not so desired Sayerne at all costs—had you not come home to fetch your precious, worthless estate!—I might have been happily at home this morning."

Melissande glanced up in time to see Quinn's jaw set. She had pricked his temper already but had no intention of backing down.

"Some might say that a woman is always at home with her man beside her," Quinn argued with obvious restraint.

"Then they are fools!" she returned. "Being a woman does not mean I have no wits or no place of my own right. My home is Annossy and I am content there *alone.*"

"Alone?" Quinn asked carefully. "It seemed to me that you enjoyed the fact that you were not alone last eve."

"I was seduced against my will!"

"No, my lady! I was not the only one who savored our mating last night!"

"Oh!" Melissande leapt from the bed. A glint lit Quinn's eye and she donned a chemise with savage gestures before she spoke, her anger unabated as she stalked him across the floor.

"Oh! That is an unchivalrous accusation to make of a lady who is regretting her impulsiveness! What manner of knave might you be?"

"Impulsiveness?" Quinn propped his hands on his hips and stared down at her with snapping eyes. "It was hardly impulsiveness that had you straining against me like a cat in heat!"

Melissande slapped his face. Quinn's head jerked hard to her left, then his gaze swiveled back to meet hers.

"Your slap does not change the truth," he growled. "You wanted me last evening and I know it. Nothing can change the truth of that."

"Truth?" Melissande demanded, her voice choked with outrage. He was implying she was playing the wanton, and she did not care for the insinuation. "What truth is there in my behaving in a manner alien to me? Why, were I not the wiser, I might wonder if *you* had had some doing..."

Melissande's chin jerked up and she glared at Quinn. His eyes narrowed, as though he suspected what she might say.

"It was the cursed wine," she hissed. She saw the truth when her spouse stepped warily away. Melissande followed him, her pointing finger at the ready. "You saw that my cup was never empty!" she accused. "You ensured that I was too besotted to avoid your intent!"

Quinn colored. "I thought it might ease your fears," he explained, his voice turning defensive as he continued. "And both of us had the same intent last eve, for we had agreed to Tulley's terms."

"Ha!" Melissande retorted. "You thought the wine might grant you an easy conquest!" She leaned closer and let her voice drop, wanting nothing else but to hurt him as he had hurt her in compelling her to break her word.

"Tell me, Quinn, do you always have to weaken women with drink to lure them to your bed?"

Quinn swore beneath his breath with a vehemence that made Melissande suddenly afraid of him. She had pushed him too far this time and when his eyes blazed like molten gold, she feared for her safety. Quinn abruptly turned and stalked across the room.

"The wine cannot make you act as you would not," he muttered as he stared into the flames. He took a deep breath when Melissande did not argue with that and she heard his breath shudder as it was released.

"You have told me only half of the tale," he said with eerie perceptiveness. "Maybe it is time you told me what really is at the root of your manner this morning."

Quinn's tone was even, his words compelling in their demand. Melissande knotted her hands before herself and stared at his back, suffused suddenly with guilt at her churlish manner. She felt like a poorly behaved child before Quinn's herculean self-control.

But no. She had been disserved by this match. She had every right to be angry. Even if Quinn showed an uncanny ability for both infuriating and disarming her. Melissande lifted her chin and stared at him as her guilt grew.

If nothing else, she owed Quinn the truth, she conceded. Better late than not at all.

"You should know that I had no interest in this match," she said quietly.

Quinn snorted. "Yet I did?" he demanded.

Melissande swallowed carefully, yet again uncomfortable with his reminder that he was less than pleased in his obligation of wedding her.

"Make no mistake, my lady," he added in an undertone. "You are fair to look upon, but I had always hoped to choose my bride and make a match to suit both my heart and hers."

He fired a glance over his shoulder that pierced Melissande's very soul.

"I was foolish enough to imagine last night that, despite the odds, we might have such an opportunity here." He held her gaze for a long moment, his own searching. "Was I so mistaken?" he asked quietly.

Melissande turned abruptly away. "Yes," she said simply.

Quinn snorted anew and kicked a stray piece of kindling into the flames.

"Tell me then, as you seem so inclined to do so," he said, his tone newly sardonic, "what precisely was your objection to this match? It cannot have been me, for you did not know me, although your first impression was apparently less than favorable."

She did not like to see this bitterness in Quinn and liked even less that she was responsible for his mood. Melissande bit her lip, the truth more difficult to declare than she had imagined it would be. She took a deep breath and forced herself to plunge onward.

"I am pledged to another," she said quietly.

"What?" Quinn spun on his heel and stared at her in shock. Melissande held his gaze determinedly.

"You heard me," she said, and lifted her chin proudly.

"Pledged to another?" Quinn ran one hand through his hair and scowled at the floor for an instant before he looked back to her. "Yet you did not imagine that this matter might interest me?"

"Tulley did not care."

His eyes flashed and Melissande knew well the storm that would come.

"I am not Tulley!" Quinn roared. "Do you think that I am such a selfish cur? Do you think that I would care nothing for a pledge you had granted? Do you think that I would not have walked away had I but known?"

"You would not have abandoned Sayerne."

"I would not willingly have wed a woman pledged to another. You owed me the truth before last evening and you know it."

Quinn's eyes narrowed suddenly and Melissande did not trust the abrupt change in the direction of his thoughts. He crossed the floor with angry steps and wagged a finger beneath Melissande's nose.

"Or maybe it amuses a fine lady like yourself to see a 'barbarian' unwittingly guarantee his own demise?" he accused coldly.

"What?" Melissande asked, her own indignation restored by his question. "Your demise? What are you talking about? Now I know that you have lost your wits!"

"Really?"

"Really! I would not see anyone choose their demise in ignorance. What manner of woman do you think me to be?"

"Either a very clever one or a fool," Quinn retorted. "What makes you imagine that the man to whom you are pledged will avoid seeking me out when he hears what I have done? After Tulley arrives, all will know that I have claimed your maidenhead and the tale will spread rapidly. I have no doubt that he will insist upon some manner of restoring his honor."

Melissande gasped. "He would not!" she declared. "I would not!"

"Then what manner of man might he be?" Quinn asked in a low whisper that made Melissande shiver anew. "I would take vengeance upon any who claimed what was mine."

Melissande took a deliberate step away from this determined Quinn. "You are a barbarian," she accused in an undertone.

"No," Quinn said with a resolute shake of his head. "I am honest and I stand by what is mine."

It was time that this discussion was back on familiar terms. Melissande knew that she needed once again to make her position clear, lest Quinn be falsely encouraged by her manner of the night before.

Curse the man for making her complacent with wine! What manner of knave would do such a deed to his bride?

Although Melissande could not deny that the night had been pleasurable. She would not even allow herself to think that it might have been so, with or without the wine.

"Honest or not, I will not permit you in my bed again," she declared proudly.

"Permit me?" Quinn demanded. "It seemed to me that you *invited* me last evening."

"And if I did so, that was only by your instigation!" Melissande accused wildly. "It was you who saw to it that I was drunk! It was you who seduced me! And it was because of you that I broke my most solemn vow! By my own volition, I did *not* invite you."

To Melissande's mortification, at that last she burst into tears.

Quinn retreated and eyed her warily from the shadows as she sobbed. Melissande dabbed ineffectually at her tears, but it seemed that he did not intend to offer her solace. She finally glanced up to find his gaze thoughtful upon her.

"What is his name?" he asked quietly. There was a coldness in his voice that made Melissande shiver.

"Why?" she demanded with false defiance.

Quinn's lips twisted in a wry smile. "Maybe I am curious about the manner of man who captured your heart."

Melissande opened her mouth to correct his assumption, then closed it firmly again. Her heart had nothing to do with this matter. It was her word alone that stood compromised, though maybe there was no need for Quinn to know that.

"I would have your vow in exchange," she said.

Quinn folded his arms across his chest and Melissande noted the sign of his rising impatience. But he had never hurt her, no matter how much she had pressed him. The thought encouraged her to continue.

"What vow?" he asked coldly.

Melissande lifted her chin. "To not touch me," she said as clearly as she could. "The match is consummated. Both you and Tulley have what you desire. Now I would have what I want."

Quinn's eyes blazed anew. "And you would have me not ever touch you as I did last night? You would not arch in pleasure ever again as you did just hours past?"

Melissande swallowed hastily. "No," she said boldly.

Quinn paced across the floor with relentlessly long strides. He closed in upon her and grasped her chin in his hand, tipping her gaze up to hold his. His flesh was warm against hers, his very touch sending a thrill through Melissande but she dared not let her gaze flicker.

Some trace of her weakness must have shown in her expression, though, for suddenly Quinn smiled.

"Liar," he whispered with pleasure, and dropped his lips to hers.

Gentle he was, coaxing and tender. It was frightening to Melissande how little difference the wine had made in her response and she noted how her body inclined toward him with horror.

"No!" she cried as she tore her lips from his. She planted both hands flat on Quinn's chest and shoved him away with a strength born of desperation. To Melissande's dismay, her tears began to fall again and she wiped them away with trembling fingers.

"Look what you have done!" she declared. "Not only did you compel me to break my word once, but you insist on forcing me to do so again."

"My lady, you err," Quinn said tightly. "I have never forced a lady in all my days."

"Well, to be the first is no place of pride in this," Melissande spat. She threw back her hair and squared her shoulders as she stared him down. "And make no mistake, sir. You will not so weaken me again. You are forbidden to cross the threshold of my chambers from this day forth, whether we be wedded or not."

There was a terse moment of silence.

"What is his name?" Quinn asked quietly again as though he had not heard her outburst. His lips were tight though, and Melissande knew well he had felt the bite of her words.

"I do not have your vow," she reminded him.

"I will touch you only when you so desire it," he declared.

Melissande met his gaze through the veil of her tears. "*Never* shall I desire your touch. I would have your pledge to not even so try."

Quinn shrugged, but Melissande caught a glimpse of resolve in his eyes before he dropped his gaze. "The pledge you have is all I will grant. Now, tell me the name of the man who holds your heart in thrall."

Melissande's lips tightened, but she guessed by Quinn's manner that he would grant her no more than he already had. "Arnaud de Privas," she said proudly. The name echoed with emptiness when it fell from her tongue and Melissande desperately tried to recall the face of the man to whom it belonged.

It had been so long. In all honesty, giving her word was all she recalled of the matter. Quinn repeated the name once under his breath, as though committing it to memory, then met her gaze steadily.

Melissande caught her breath, astonished yet again at his effect upon her. It was a lie to leave Quinn believing that Arnaud held her heart, but should it keep Quinn at a distance, she could not afford to tell him the truth.

At least not until she understood why he was able to turn her into such a wanton with his slightest touch. To be so vulnerable to another was not a sensation Melissande enjoyed.

Another barb might ensure that Quinn had no further ideas about their marriage. She drew herself up tall.

"I would expect even the most barbaric knight to respect a lady's vow," she said.

"With wine or not, you still rise to my touch, just as I rise to yours," Quinn asserted.

That he should see through her so readily and glimpse her weakness terrified Melissande beyond all. She deliberately let her lip curl. "Maybe you are not so experienced on the field of love as I might have thought," she said in as disparaging a manner as she might. "Could you not discern that I only pretended to share your pleasure?"

His eyes blazed at that and Melissande did not dare look away.

"Why would you do such a thing?" Quinn demanded.

"Did we not agree that the deed must be done? No need was there for unpleasantness." Melissande shrugged and made a sweeping gesture with one hand. That Quinn was furiously angered by her assertion could not be missed, but she feigned unawareness. "It is done. And I have your vow."

Quinn paced the length of the room and back, his hands clenched into fists as he confronted her anew.

"You lie!" he declared hotly. "You feigned nothing last evening and I know it! Do not insist upon this tale, Melissande. Let there be truth between us."

Melissande folded her arms across her chest and turned away, hoping against hope that it appeared his appeal fell on deaf ears.

She could not afford to be charmed by Quinn, she reminded herself forcefully, even as her heart urged her to do the opposite.

Annossy hung in the balance.

"I tell you no tales," she said softly.

Quinn crossed the floor at that and halted beside her. Melissande schooled herself against the scent of his skin, her heart racing when she saw his hand rise from the corner of her eye.

He meant to touch her again! To cup her face as gently as he had before and coax the truth from her lips. No! She could not permit him. Yet she could not move away. She swallowed in dread, knowing he would see the truth should he so much as touch her again.

Somehow she had to divert him.

Melissande swiveled smartly and planted the tip of her finger in the middle of Quinn's broad chest. "Is your word worth so little, then?" she challenged. "Does the pledge you have granted me mean nothing in truth?"

Quinn's hands balled into fists and he stalked back across the room.

"This, then, is what you desire? To be a wife in name only?" he demanded, disbelief and anger mingling in his tone.

"Yes! Yes, that will suit me well," Melissande declared, her voice becoming bold as she warmed to the theme. To keep Quinn at a distance was her main objective. "And if you had your wits about you, you would remain on Sayerne and away from Annossy."

"Fine!" Quinn roared, and flung out his hands. "I understand my place! And blessed I am to be spared the vexation of your presence in the future!" He jabbed an angry finger through the air in Melissande's direction. "But rest assured, my lady, the next time that I am between your thighs—and I will be—I will have been *invited!*"

Quinn would have stormed out the door had not a delicate knock echoed on that wooden portal instead. His gaze flew to Melissande and she inhaled hastily.

A familiar voice carried through the door. "I trust you are awake?"

Tulley! Melissande scooped up a robe and threw it over her chemise, her heart pounding in trepidation.

Had the lord heard their argument?

Chapter Five

Tulley cleared his throat delicately when Quinn opened the door. The older man smiled apologetically but did not move away.

Quinn cursed silently. His guts writhed with the certainty that Tulley must have overheard their argument. Melissande was responsible for goading his anger, for she stirred his fury as no one else could.

"Am I interrupting?" the lord asked mildly. His sharp gaze flicked to the bed and back to the couple. "Is there perhaps an estate or two falling forfeit this morn?"

Tulley's glib manner did not suit Quinn in the least. He cast an annoyed hand toward the bed and paced to the window. "See for yourself," he said tightly.

Melissande did not look up but folded her arms about herself, tears still glistening on her cheeks. Quinn, inexplicably to his mind, wanted to step close to her and ease those tears away.

Curse the lady! First she infuriated him, then confused him with an unexpected wave of tenderness. He gritted his teeth as Tulley crossed the room and gazed at the bed linens.

"Ah! Very good!" Tulley declared. "It is a pleasure to be mistaken on occasion." Quinn felt Tulley's speculative regard upon him but was not inclined to look up. Let the man think whatever he would. It would not be long before everyone knew the poor state of this match.

Tulley coughed in his precise manner once more and Quinn imagined that he was not immune to the atmosphere in the room.

"It seems to me that all is not rosy this morn," the lord commented.

No one responded.

"In fact," Tulley continued carefully. "I could not help but overhear your last comment, Quinn."

At that, Quinn looked up, not in the least pleased to find a frown on the lord's brow. Tulley fixed him with a bright blue eye and his brows drew together into a paternal scowl.

"Apparently, I have not emphasized the importance of this match adequately to the two of you." His lips tightened as he glanced to Melissande, who stubbornly stared at her toe. Quinn could not help but note that her golden hair spilled over her shoulder in a most bewitching manner.

"I understand that this was a matter of some interest to you," Quinn said.

The lord's eyes blazed.

"No! This is markedly more than a passing matter of interest!" he said, as he crossed the floor toward Quinn. "Surely I have made my intent clear to see this match become a full marriage."

There was an undercurrent of steel to Tulley's voice. He pounded his fist into his hand as he glanced between the uncooperative couple. "It is of the *utmost* import that this marriage be seen as unassailable. Finding the two of you fighting like shrews on your wedding morning is not fitting in the least!"

"The match is made and consummated," Quinn observed in poor temper. "You have seen the better part of your desire in that."

"No! That is not the half of it!" Tulley was clearly not swayed, even though Quinn believed he had made the ef-

fort to do what was required of him. "There will already be
talk in the kitchens, and such chatter will travel like the
wind. It doesn't take much imagination to divine that you
two intend to make your ways separately. That is not what
I had in mind at *all!*"

Quinn saw Melissande's hands tighten into fists and knew
that she too was fighting her impulse to argue. It was curious to find that they had in common their response to Tulley's manipulation.

"Not at all," Tulley repeated. "Can you not see that these
bandits will not be deterred from their pillaging unless your
match appears to be one made in good faith? What deter-
rent is a crusading warrior as Lord of Annossy if you,
Quinn, never set foot on the estate? Do not imagine for a
moment that people will not know the way of things."

"Lord of Annossy?" Melissande interjected hotly, Tulley's words apparently bringing her back to life. "Nothing
was said of Quinn becoming Lord of Annossy! I understood that this plan was to assure his succession to Sayerne!"

"And that it was, my dear, but surely you understood that
the two estates would be merged with this match?" Tulley
demanded impatiently.

Quinn did not appreciate the lord's manner with Melissande, for he spoke to her as though she were but a child.
Quinn knew that she was keen of intellect, and even he had
not made what Tulley assumed was an obvious conclusion.
He was to be lord of *both* estates?

For the first time, Quinn wondered whether he was adequately trained to administer a manor. Surely such a fact as
the merging of the estates would have been obvious to him
otherwise?

Was it possible that Melissande's doubts were well-
founded?

"Merged? Never did I agree for Annossy to merge with
any other estate, let alone Sayerne," Melissande snapped.

"And had that truly been your intent, you should have made the matter clear from the outset."

"Surely you did not imagine that the law would be changed for you, Melissande?" Tulley retorted with his sharp manner of the day before. "The title of Annossy has never been officially granted to you because of that law. Throughout all of Christendom, a woman cedes her property to her spouse upon her nuptials and you should not be so proud as to imagine that Annossy or you would be treated differently."

The lord straightened and glared between the two of his subjects. Quinn imagined they had not been as obedient as the older man might have hoped.

"In fact, as a result of your impetuous arguing this morning, Annossy will be Quinn's only holding for the time being," Tulley declared.

"What?" Melissande demanded in outrage.

"I beg your pardon?" Quinn asked in the same moment. Surely Sayerne was still to be his?

Tulley lifted his chin and met Quinn's gaze with frosty disdain. "I do not intend to grant Sayerne to you as of yet, Quinn," he said with uncanny calm.

"What is this?" Quinn demanded. "Surely you do not intend to break your word? The entire intent of this match was to assure Sayerne to my hand!"

Even Melissande's head shot up. "You cannot do this!" she charged. "You gave Quinn your promise!"

"I can do whatever I see fit to do," Tulley said firmly. "And I will see this match made in truth before I grant Sayerne. If you precisely recall my words, you will realize that I never did say *when* Sayerne would be invested."

Tulley's gaze narrowed as he glanced between the pair. "I would strongly suggest that you never accuse me of breaking my word again," he advised in a low tone. "You might find yourself sorely punished as a result."

Quinn's heart sank. He had been used by this wily lord, tricked into taking a wife that would drive him mad, and all for nothing. And now, Tulley was insulted, as well. The future could bode no darker fate for him than this.

Sayerne was lost. Quinn could hardly accept the truth.

Maybe it would have been easier if he had never had the promise of possessing Sayerne dangled before him like a glistening golden ball. Maybe it would have been better to not have been blessed by Dame Fortune on that day in the East and gone to his grave never knowing such disappointment.

Of course, then he would never have spent the night just past with a bride more fetching and feisty than he had ever expected to have. Quinn slanted a glance in Melissande's direction, noting how her cheeks were flushed with anger. They had flushed in passion much the same way, and the recollection was distracting.

"But mercifully for the two of you, I am not without compassion. Marriage is a state that requires adjustment and it is my fault that this change was thrust so hastily upon you both." Tulley held up a finger and shook it before them warningly. "One year I will grant you to see this a match in truth. You have one year to produce a legitimate heir and when you do—" he nodded to Quinn "—Sayerne will be yours."

His! A bubble of elation tripped through Quinn before it was suddenly flattened.

He would never have an heir by Melissande. There might have been hope in Tulley's promise, if Melissande had not taken such a stand against Quinn.

Even now, he knew he could not fulfill Tulley's condition. Although he might have been willing enough, the lady had made her demand, and Quinn, fool that he was, had made his own vow of sorts.

And there was the matter of the lady's heart having been granted to another. Quinn would not force Melissande, yet it still chafed that his chivalry would cost him so dear.

Sayerne was as good as gone. Quinn's anger rose yet again at Tulley's manipulation. The lord might at least have found Quinn a bride untethered by a betrothal vow.

"But, my lord . . ." he began to protest, only to have Tulley raise his voice to interrupt.

"But *nothing!*" he said savagely. "This matter is serious beyond all and if you both had listened to me yesterday, you would have understood that. My holdings are at risk due to the vulnerability of Annossy. *I will not tolerate such a risk!*"

Tulley spun on his heel and stalked across the room, hauling the heavy oak door open and pausing on the threshold to look back.

"Understand this," he said, his voice modulated once more. "It is beyond gracious of me to hold your estate in trust for an entire year and considerably more than your due in so thwarting me. You should thank me for the opportunity to prove yourself. See that you do not disappoint me again." With that, Tulley spun on his heel and left the room.

An awkward silence was left in his wake.

Melissande turned away with a most purposeful manner. As Quinn watched, she opened a trunk, discarded her robe and folded the garment into it.

"Could you see that my maid Berthe is summoned?" she asked him as casually as if nothing had just occurred.

"Your maid?" Quinn asked, confused by her manner. Surely she had heard Tulley? The man had raged loudly enough to be heard in Paris.

"Yes, please."

Still Melissande's tone was suspiciously devoid of emotion. It was not Quinn's imagination that she avoided his gaze, and Quinn wondered at the cause. "I have packing to do and she does a finer job than I."

Quinn pursed his lips thoughtfully, then decided to ask. "Where are you going?"

Melissande flicked a glance in his direction, which fed all of his suspicions. "Home," she said flatly, and turned back to the trunk.

Home? Where precisely did she mean?

"To Sayerne?" Quinn forced his voice to remain level.

Melissande shook her head hastily. "No. Annossy."

"Annossy!" Quinn could not check his response. "Why would you go to Annossy? Our home is at Sayerne. There is work to be done to rebuild the estate and the sooner that is begun, the sooner it will be done."

Melissande paused and turned to grant him a cool glance. "My home," she said very deliberately, "is Annossy."

Quinn folded his arms across his chest and eyed his defiant bride. "Are you suggesting that we make our home at Annossy?"

Melissande made a sound in her throat that might have been a laugh. "Have I invited you?" she asked mildly.

"I understood that a man did not need invitation to his own estates," Quinn retorted.

Melissande spun to face him, her eyes glittering. "Have you been invested with the seal of Annossy?" she demanded hotly. "No! And until you are so invested, no right have you to rule over that estate."

"You have not been invested with that seal either," Quinn argued. He flung out his hand in frustration. "From what Tulley says, you administer Annossy by his grace alone until he grants the seal to someone he finds fitting."

"No!" Melissande stormed. "Annossy is mine, by blood and by right, regardless of what Tulley says. I was born there. I was raised there and my parents died there. Do not imagine that I will so casually turn over its administration to one who knows nothing of such matters."

"It is not up to you what happens to the estate," Quinn said. "It is up to Tulley, since you were born a daughter."

"I know fully well that I was born a daughter!" She spun to face Quinn with tears glistening in her eyes. "Would that I could have been born a son and taken command of my family's holdings in the eyes of the law, instead of at a lord's convenience."

Her vulnerability undermined Quinn's anger. He took a deep breath and decided to try to settle the matter. "We could go to Annossy first, if you please," he suggested.

Melissande's eyes flashed fire. "I did not invite you to Annossy! I tell you I will go alone!"

What a vexing woman she could be! Quinn jammed his hand through his hair in frustration. "Did you hear nothing of what Tulley just said?" he asked. "We have to produce a child in the next year. If my memory serves, that leaves us less than three months to see the deed done. This is no time for you to go to Annossy alone and play such games!"

Melissande snorted under her breath, evidently dismissing his arguments, and turned back to her packing. Had ever he met such an exasperating woman? Quinn cleared his throat, desperately trying to find some way to convince his wife.

"Time is of the essence, Melissande, and we must begin immediately."

She spared him a glance that might have been pitying, and returned to her packing. "Your difficulties have nothing to do with me," she asserted coolly. "Tulley demanded that I wed you and consummate the match in order that I might keep some claim to Annossy. As far as I can tell, my obligation here is completed."

Ye gods, but the woman tested him! Had he ever known anyone more obstinate? If she had taken up the Cross and graced the field of battle in the East, Quinn had no doubt the Crusaders would have seen greater victory.

"You cannot do this!" Quinn bellowed. "You are my wife and our path lies together now."

Melissande slanted him a knowing glance. "That is true enough," she conceded with suspicious ease. "You may come to stay at Annossy then, but do not imagine that I shall permit you into my chambers. Remember we have made that agreement already."

Quinn's hands flexed. He could bear it no longer. He crossed the room in three long strides, clasped Melissande's shoulders within his hands and gave her a shake. "Are you quite mad? Did you not *hear* Tulley's demand? You cannot heartlessly abandon me to lose my estate."

"Sayerne is not my problem," she asserted calmly. "And you losing your title has nothing to do with me."

"Sayerne *is* your problem," Quinn gritted out. "Because Sayerne is *my* problem and you are my wife."

Melissande lifted her chin defiantly. "Clearly our opinions differ in this. Your battles are not mine simply because you say so."

"You should know by now that I do not intend to forfeit my legacy," Quinn retorted.

His wife's eyes snapped with anger. "Understand this, barbarian." Melissande jabbed her finger hard into Quinn's chest. He did not dare flinch beneath her assault. "Whether you forfeit your legacy means nothing to me, but I will not watch you destroy mine."

"I do not even *want* Annossy," Quinn snapped. "I want nothing but Sayerne, my own estate, and the time to rebuild it to its former glory."

Melissande's eyes narrowed and Quinn knew she had drawn a conclusion he would shortly hear voiced. "Your sire and his wishes are behind this," she accused abruptly. "Jerome made it clear that he intended to see Sayerne and Annossy merged to one property, one way or the other. I would not put it past him or you to have concocted this plan before his death!"

"Fool! My lady, you do not know what you are saying." Quinn gave Melissande another little shake, which apparently had no effect upon her. She tried to shake free of his grip, her emerald eyes shooting sparks.

"I know what I see and I am unafraid to name it. I will not be used by the likes of Jerome de Sayerne!" she declared. "You are the blood of his blood and cannot be trusted!"

"I am not my sire," Quinn roared. "Should it be the last thing I do, my lady, I will prove the truth of that to you."

Melissande wrenched herself out of Quinn's grip and her chemise tore in the process. The sound of tearing cloth silenced both of them, Quinn's gaze falling of its own accord to the tear and the ripe curve of her breast in the shadows revealed.

"Barbarian," she accused in an undertone. Quinn was shocked to see tears glistening in her lovely eyes, and was all the more shocked that he was responsible for their appearance. "Do not imagine that I will be readily convinced of your lofty intent," she added fiercely. "Have you not already made me break my word? Torn my garments? Stolen my maidenhead?"

Melissande sniffed and cast an arch glance over her shoulder as she turned away from an effectively silenced Quinn. "Blood is the thickest of all," she said, and her disdain would have been clear to the most casual observer. "I will not be easily convinced that you and your sire were not two cut from the same cloth."

Chastened and thinking it unseemly to take further issue with a lady, Quinn dropped his gaze to his hands. Was he doomed to be condemned by his father's errors?

Melissande seemed too ready to blame him for her woes, but he could not make a case in his own defense. It was only by his deed alone that she might see the differences between father and son, yet Melissande showed no signs of paying the most minute attention to Quinn.

He could not argue with her, but neither could he show her the truth. That was frustrating beyond belief. Quinn's gaze followed her retreat across the room and he hated how he noted the shadows of her slender beauty beneath the sheer chemise.

His body responded with enthusiasm and not for the first time, he wondered what tangle he had enmeshed himself in.

It was only after Melissande had disappeared behind the bed curtains and his mind had cleared that Quinn realized *she* had come to his defense before Tulley. *She* had been the one to first declare Tulley's new condition unfair. Quinn could not help but wonder at that and he looked toward his oblivious wife with new eyes.

Was it possible that she did not disdain him as she maintained? Quinn covertly watched her packing and noted the nervousness in her gestures. Could the lady have some scrap of regard for him?

He squared his shoulders and faced the reality before him. Sayerne was at risk and he had only three months to prove Tulley wrong. For such a prize, Quinn could not abandon the field. Should there be any chance of making this come right, Quinn had to try.

Three months. That seemed adequate time to woo his bride. Surely the lady needed nothing but a little time and attention? Women were sensitive creatures, after all, and Quinn's sire's greatest crime had been not treating them with care.

She had to have been as shocked as Quinn at these rapid nuptials. No, more so, for she had lost a betrothed in the process.

Quinn gazed out the window at the sunlight now making the snow sparkle like gemstones as he made a bargain with himself. In the three months until Sayerne was truly lost, he could only try to earn his lady's trust.

And should he not be able to gain his wife's regard in that time, Quinn vowed to himself, he would willingly ride away from Melissande, Annossy and Sayerne.

* * *

Quinn was up to something and Melissande knew it well by the time they reached the miller's abode that night. It was no coincidence that he had been charming since their argument. Quinn had made conversation, he had inquired after her comfort and every time Melissande had looked to him, he had granted her that engaging, crooked smile that made her heart lurch.

This was only a game to him and she was nothing but a pawn. She would do well to keep that in mind.

It did not help that his aid and attention throughout the day had left her confused. If he so much as touched her again when she was as tired as she was now, Melissande was afraid she might yield to his touch.

And that she could not afford to do.

Their party halted in the stable yard before the mill house. The ride had been quiet despite their numbers. In addition to Quinn and Melissande, Berthe and Bayard, the four squires of Quinn's rode with them, as well the six knights in Annossy's employ who had accompanied Melissande to Tulley.

The day had been unseasonably warm for this early in the year and snow had melted in rivulets across the path. It would have been easy to associate the false spring with the state of her marriage, but Melissande refused to think in that direction.

Once they stopped, Melissande watched Quinn throw his shapely leg over his saddle. He looked to her and she knew that his hands would be locked around her waist shortly. Panic rose within her. Anything but that!

"I can dismount alone," she informed him hastily. Her kirtle conspired against her, but still Melissande struggled to see herself on the ground without his aid.

Quinn frowned. "It is no trouble at all, my lady."

"My lady, it would be wise to await such aid," Berthe interjected in a most unwelcome manner. Trust that woman to have an opinion about this, as she did about most else!

Melissande did not wait for Quinn, regardless of the advice. She could not risk it. It was time to put distance between them while she still could.

She twisted hastily in the saddle, but while she was in the act of slipping to the ground, her untethered beast stepped forward.

Melissande's ankle twisted under her weight even though she grasped wildly at the stirrup strap. She caught her breath at the sharp stab of pain that fired up her leg.

"My lady, are you injured?" Berthe demanded.

"Have you not a scrap of sense in your head?" Quinn raged from too close behind her. Melissande felt the color drain from her face as she tried to stand as though nothing were wrong.

For the span of a heartbeat, she feared she would not be able to put her weight on the leg. Fear flooded through her as the limb wavered uncertainly and she was certain that she would fall and hurt herself anew. Then Quinn was there, the strength of his arm around her waist reassuring in a way Melissande knew it should not be.

"I am fine," she insisted, knowing that her vehemence was due to his proximity, not any certainty in her own abilities.

"You are?" Quinn asked with thinly veiled impatience. He released her with an abruptness that was unsettling. "Then walk to the portal."

Melissande closed her eyes and willed herself to do the deed. Reluctantly she released her grip on the palfrey's saddle. She could not show this man any weakness. Melissande took a step forward with the injured foot and had barely put any weight upon it when she felt her leg crumpling in pain.

"It hurts," she gasped, but Quinn had already scooped her easily up into his arms, chiding all the while.

"Who was the fool who taught you to dismount before your horse was tethered?" he demanded. His amber eyes flashed with concern. "And who trained your steed? What possessed you to take such a feisty creature to be your own mount? A plague on finely bred steeds who cannot be trusted to hold their ground!"

If Melissande had not forced herself to recall Quinn's objectives, she might have been fooled that he cared about her welfare. It was only the question of her fertility that concerned him, she reminded herself firmly, and that only until Sayerne was secured.

"Are you all right?" he asked in a whisper. The man's charm was dangerously disarming.

"You may rest assured that my womb is undamaged," Melissande responded acidly, taking refuge in retaliation. Quinn's eyes narrowed and a nearby Berthe gasped.

"Well," the maid declared, "I have never seen you in such sour temper, even when you were so ill years ago. Even your parents' passing did not bring out such venom from you."

Melissande heard the maid draw in a disapproving breath and knew the woman straightened self-righteously behind Quinn. "My lord, I do apologize for my mistress's manner. Usually, she is of a most pleasant temperament."

Melissande peeked through her lashes to find a very considering light in Quinn's golden gaze.

"Really?" he said, but she knew he had guessed that he lay at the root of her testiness.

"Where does it hurt?" Quinn asked quietly.

That was a reasonable question. Melissande knew she had to give an answer or appear more churlish than she had already.

"My ankle." Melissande's voice was uneven in a most curious manner, but she quickly attributed that to the surprise she had had.

It could have nothing to do with Quinn holding her close. The unsteady hammering of her heart could only be the result of her unexpected landing and the surprise of the pain.

"Did you twist it or is the bone broken?" Quinn crouched down in the straw, balancing Melissande in his lap in a most familiar manner.

But his touch was soothing. For a moment, she was tempted to pretend that nothing was wrong between them, that she had merely met this charming knight under other circumstances, that she had the luxury of letting him care for her ankle.

Melissande leaned back against Quinn's strength despite herself and closed her eyes, refusing to watch his response. The warm press of his fingertips was on her ankle, and Melissande knew it was only the inappropriateness of such an intimate touch in the forum of the stable yard that made her catch her breath.

He was surprisingly gentle. "Does it hurt when you move it so?" His hand enfolded her ankle in a way that made Melissande feel quite delicately made, even though she was not a small woman.

"No."

"Like this?"

"Aïe!" Melissande cried out despite herself, only to have Quinn gather her reassuringly close. Her hands were on his shoulders, though she was certain that she had not deliberately placed them there.

Quinn pressed a kiss to her brow, but Melissande refused to open her eyes. She would not let him take advantage of her weakness.

"I believe it is just a twist and not a break. Your inestimable Berthe can probably wrap it adequately for now."

"I certainly can, my lord, for I was trained by one of the most prominent herbalists in—"

"Michel!" Quinn called to one of his squires, his words silencing Berthe. Melissande heard the boy's footsteps approach even as Bayard snorted with barely restrained laughter at his companion's deft interruption.

"It seems that I am not alone in trying to evade your chatter," Bayard commented, an undercurrent of laughter in his tone.

"Well," Berthe huffed. "At least, *this* knight has the justification of seeing to his lady's care and not simply the excuse of poor breeding to his credit."

Melissande peeked through her lashes to find the pair facing off again.

"Ha!" Bayard snorted. He lifted his leg so that his spurs glinted in the sunlight. "What would you know of fine breeding? A man must earn the right to even train for spurs such as these."

"And though he might win them, he could still know nothing of etiquette, as your own manner makes clear," Berthe retorted.

"Etiquette? I know more of courtly manners than you could even guess." The knight leaned down, his dark eyes snapping with mischief as Berthe held her chin high and ignored him. "In fact, my fine maid, should I decide to turn my charm upon you, you would be smitten with me in no time at all."

Berthe's dubious expression was eloquent. "That is unlikely."

Quinn cleared his throat, his gaze hawk-bright on Michel as though he did not even hear the bickering of Berthe and Bayard. "We will need hot water and a length of cloth for Berthe to bind my lady's ankle," he instructed the boy.

He looked to Melissande and she immediately closed her eyes tightly again.

"Yes, my lord."

The boy stepped away, his footsteps scratching in the gravel, and Melissande heard the bustle of Berthe's skirts as she followed in his wake.

"And make sure that it is freshly woven linen!" the maid called out, her voice fading as she bustled away to make preparations. "I will have nothing second-rate for my lady!"

"Come, boys!" Bayard called. Melissande was amused by how readily the pair ignored each other's presence and hastened to their tasks. "It is time we saw these steeds settled and fed."

Footsteps again carried to her ears, interjected by the creaking of the stable door being opened. Melissande licked her lips carefully, knowing that she and Quinn were effectively alone.

She wondered what he would do and did not know whether to dread or anticipate it. She felt him lean closer and her heart began to pound.

Melissande squeezed her eyes tightly shut, certain that Quinn had turned that bone-melting gaze upon her. She could feel its effect without even looking, for a tingle of awareness launched over her skin.

"I shall tend my wife myself this night," Quinn purred.

Melissande's eyes flew open. It was no consolation to see the quirk of amusement that twisted her spouse's firm lips. "You will not!" she declared hotly. "Berthe will tend me, as is right and proper."

"Berthe," Quinn observed with apparent satisfaction, "cannot lift you into your bed."

Melissande flushed, seeing the direction of his thoughts. "You promised," she accused tightly.

It was no consolation that Quinn appeared perfectly at ease in her company when she was unsettled in his. Melissande had a childish urge to poke him for not being as disturbingly aware of her as she was of him.

Quinn leisurely arched a brow. "No, that was not the vow I made," he reminded her. Melissande nearly ground her teeth in frustration.

Quinn seemed completely undistressed by her disapproval. He stood up with her weight easily cradled in his arms and inclined his head toward the mill house.

"Do you think that you can walk all the way without my aid?" he asked conversationally.

Melissande longed to hit him for his smug assurance. Never had anyone incited her to such a violent response as this man. Surely this could not be natural?

Instead of indulging herself, she eyed the distance and knew she could not manage it alone. She had not been able to take a single step and it would take a good thirty to the house. Irritation rose within her that Quinn was right, as well.

"Berthe could help me," Melissande suggested.

Quinn shrugged. "Yes, if you hobbled. And that will do nothing but make the ankle swell even more." His gaze dropped to meet hers and Melissande did not trust the mischievous twinkle that appeared in the amber depths. "Of course, that might keep you in bed much longer," he suggested, his tone low and intimate.

"Your thoughts are in the gutter!" Melissande snapped.

"The matter of an heir is of great concern to me these days," Quinn responded evenly. "And you know the reason for that."

"And I am to be nothing but a means to an end." Melissande's tone was savage. Quinn looked slightly alarmed, but she was not prepared to let him escape the truth. "Trust me, my lord, if I could but give you my womb and be untroubled with you and Tulley and your plans, I would willingly do so."

"You have no desire for children?" he asked carefully. He seemed puzzled.

Melissande snorted. "What does my desire matter? Do not tease me with the possibility that my opinion is of any importance at all."

"But you had given your pledge to another to be married," Quinn mused as though she had not spoken. "Surely you intended to have his children?"

Melissande caught her breath and lifted her chin, knowing that it would not be easy to satisfy an intent Quinn that her lie was the truth. But she had no choice. Her only escape from him was to insist upon her love for Arnaud. She took a deep breath and looked her husband squarely in the eye.

"What I might have done for the man I love has nothing to do with our marriage," she declared. Quinn's eyes narrowed, and Melissande feared for a moment that he might drop her on her rump and leave her in the yard for her sharp words.

Surprisingly, a part of her felt that he would have been perfectly justified to do so. Had she ever been such a shrew? Berthe had been right when she said that Melissande was usually of good temperament. Was she making the worst of this match by showing an unknown and unpleasant side of herself?

But surely any woman would respond with similar alarm in her circumstance?

Quinn lifted his head and frowned, leaving her wondering what he had seen in her expression. "I must admit, my lady, that it is hard to believe that you love anyone or anything other than Annossy," he said with remarkable calm.

Curse his sharp gaze!

"But even that is stolen from me now," she retorted before she could reconsider. "Did Tulley not promise to invest you with the lordship of Annossy?"

Quinn said nothing, and Melissande again feared that she had pushed him too far. He strode toward the miller. The man waited nervously with a smile that was both anxious and welcoming. When Quinn spoke, his voice was low enough that only Melissande could hear.

"We have made enough of a show today. Tales of the state of our match will travel far and fast," he said. "Would you agree to a bargain here and now?"

"What manner of bargain?" Melissande asked irritably.

Quinn's glance flicked to hers and away. "You have made it clear that you desire nothing but Annossy. I want only to claim Sayerne. Give me the child Tulley requires and I will forswear any claim Tulley might grant me on your estates."

Melissande's mouth dropped open in surprise, but Quinn, she saw immediately, was perfectly serious.

"Really?" she asked.

"My word, my lady, is my bond."

Melissande swallowed. That would fulfill her own desire to live independently at Annossy, and she had only to grant Quinn an heir. And she could insist on raising the child herself at Annossy—it was merely the fact of its existence that concerned Tulley and Quinn. Melissande knew that Tulley would not let defiance of his will go without punishment for either herself or Quinn.

They both might lose their holdings over this. Melissande slanted a glance through her lashes to Quinn. Her heart skipped a beat when she found his gaze locked on her and she hastily looked away.

It was too easy to remember the pleasure she had felt in his arms. And something within her made her want to experience that again.

She might never have another chance to secure Annossy for herself, she told herself wildly, although Melissande knew that was not the only reason for her impulsive decision.

"What are your terms?" she asked tersely.

If Quinn was surprised by her agreement, he did not show it. "We shall mate daily until we are successful," he said tonelessly.

"Daily?" The word burst more loudly from Melissande's lips than she intended. "Daily? Surely that is excessive?"

The potbellied and balding miller was close, so close that he might overhear any comments between them. Melissande's ears burned that he might have understood the meaning behind her words, but his expression was uncomprehending.

His gaze darted quickly from left to right, like that of a bird on the hunt. Melissande knew that this man would be a great source of reliable gossip within the community.

As though he had made a similar conclusion about their host, Quinn leaned down and whispered directly in Melissande's ear. The flurry of his breath made her shiver.

"I would suggest we play the happily wedded couple tonight and dispel any rumors already started."

"A wise thought, husband," Melissande murmured, well aware of the miller's indulgent eye. She stretched up and pressed a kiss upon Quinn's firm cheek, feeling the heated flush that stained her own face as a result. She raised her voice slightly that the miller might not miss her words. "I thank you for your aid, Quinn."

Quinn fixed her with a glance that was surprisingly intense, almost as though he had not expected her to be so agreeable so quickly. Melissande enjoyed the fact that she had surprised him and found her lips curving into a smile.

"It was my pleasure, my lady," he murmured.

The miller beamed. "Welcome again to you, sir. I trust all went well with my lord Tulley?" He looked expectantly to Melissande and she understood that the little round man knew precisely who she was and what her relationship now was with Quinn. He waited politely, though, to be officially informed.

"Yes, very well," Quinn said. His gaze slid sidelong to meet Melissande's and he smiled in a confidential manner that made her heart leap. "I have been entrusted with a beautiful bride by Tulley's own hand. Together we shall administer both Sayerne and Annossy.''

''Really?''

''Really.'' Quinn made introductions, as well as apologies for Melissande's ankle, and the miller bobbed out of sight. She heard him summoning his servants, Michel's voice raised in clarification, and the sound of scurrying feet inside the mill house.

The miller's tousled head ducked suddenly back out into the fading light. ''Might I be so bold as to assume that two so newly married would prefer...some privacy?'' he asked. His birdlike gaze darted between Quinn and Melissande.

Quinn looked to Melissande and she knew he was allowing her to give the final word on the matter. Melissande was not convinced that Quinn was not simply trying to gain her confidence, but still his gesture was chivalrous.

''My lord is welcome in my chambers tonight,'' she said. The words fell more readily from her lips than she might have expected.

Melissande felt some tension ease out of Quinn's muscles, just as Berthe sniffed indignantly behind them. She had not known how the maid had managed to trail behind and wondered what that sharp-eared woman might have heard.

''One might hope that one's spouse was welcome there *every* night,'' Berthe muttered.

Such cheek deserved a reprimand but Melissande did not have the urge to do so on this night. She avoided Quinn's gaze, still not completely comfortable with this agreement and the intimacy it promised. She thought that Quinn smothered a smile and her doubts blossomed.

Had she made a fool's bargain? she wondered irritably as her ankle began to throb. Was he laughing at his success in fooling her? Melissande was not sure whether she had agreed too quickly to have the child he desired.

No wonder he smiled.

But she had to trust Quinn to keep his pledge that he would decline any claim to Annossy. His easy talk to the miller echoed in her mind and made her uneasy.

What did Melissande know about the values of Quinn de Sayerne? He had kept one vow in her brief experience of him, but that for less than a single day. Had it been Jerome with whom she had struck this agreement, Melissande knew she would have had grave doubts about the other man's intent. Jerome had deceived her too many times over matters of property. The reminder did not ease Melissande's doubts.

The fact that Quinn had waited until a moment of weakness to suggest his plan sounded more like the manipulative techniques of Jerome than Melissande might have preferred. Her lips tightened with the certainty that sire and son were two of a kind.

Quinn had been invited to her chambers, but Melissande had yet to invite him between her thighs. She doubted now that she would do so until she knew much more about Jerome de Sayerne's son.

Chapter Six

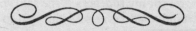

Something was wrong. Quinn did not like that he couldn't identify the problem more precisely than that. Melissande was more of an enigma to him than he might have liked.

But he knew her well enough to distrust her silence.

As they ate simple but hearty food at the miller's table, Quinn struggled to pinpoint the moment when her mood had changed. He failed to see the problem. They had made an agreement, he had kept his pledge. All had seemed to be progressing well.

And now this. He glanced to his bride to find her eyes uncharacteristically downcast and fidgeted inwardly. Her manner could not be a good sign. What was she thinking?

Perhaps it had nothing to do with him. He dared to hope.

"Does the ankle trouble you?" he whispered to her. She shot him a venomous glance that eliminated any uncertainty that he was responsible for her mood.

"Yes," she said tersely.

Now Quinn did not know what to think. He stared at the remnants of his stew as though the answer might be found there.

"Perhaps my lady would like to retire," he suggested with the care of a man who confronted an unpredictable creature.

Melissande's green eyes shot sparks in his direction. "Yes," she said simply, when Quinn was expecting an angry torrent of dissent.

When had he become so poor a judge of a person's thoughts? She turned to the miller and conjured up a smile so charming that Quinn was dumbfounded. The woman seemed determined to keep him confused.

"I do apologize for my rudeness," she said with a sweetness Quinn certainly had never seen directed to him. "My ankle is painful and I apologize for having been a less than gracious guest as a result."

"Oh, Lady Melissande, do not trouble yourself on our account," the miller said. He pushed to his feet and bustled toward her. "I can only think of your misfortune in having such an injury so early in your journey. Perhaps you should have taken your meal in your chambers, at your leisure."

"I could not have been so rude," Melissande demurred as Quinn watched in amazement. In his experience, this lady had defined "rude," but Quinn suspected this might not be a good time to make such an observation.

He wondered if she was trying to make him aware of some inadequacy in his suggesting earlier that she retire to her chamber to eat. Indeed, this business of social niceties was more complicated than Quinn recalled, and once more, he felt a rough man-at-arms.

The miller's chest puffed out. "We have been honored by your presence and your valiant effort to make conversation despite your pain. But come, your chambers are ready and it will not do for you to tire yourself. Come, come."

"I thank you so much for your hospitality."

"It is nothing, nothing at all." The miller folded his hands together and granted Quinn an inquiring glance. "Maybe the lord could aid you...?"

"Certainly," Quinn growled, and pushed to his feet.

If nothing else, he was good for brute labor. Bayard smothered a grin but Quinn had nothing to say to the man. In poor temper, he picked up his incomprehensible wife and followed the miller toward the stairs.

She did not even look toward him, her chin held high and her body stiff. Her pose was deliberate and Quinn knew it, although he still could not understand what he had done.

How he would love to give this proud woman a shake! Or even better, a kiss that would have her winding herself around him, much as she had the night before.

The thought made Quinn more aware of the curves of his burden than he might have liked. He nearly missed a step on the stairs as his imagination busily conjured up tempting images.

But he had given the lady his word. In anger, but it was a pledge nonetheless and Quinn would stand by his word.

Even if the denial killed him. Quinn closed his eyes for a moment and prayed that hers was really the weaker gender.

He ruefully admitted that his experience to date seemed to indicate the contrary.

The miller carried a candle that lit the hall with a fitful flicker. They climbed to the second floor in silence and Quinn was grateful that the broad wooden stairs were even and well made, for he could not see his feet. The miller waved them through a doorway with a flourish and fitted the candle into a wrought iron sconce mounted on the wall.

The room was of more ample proportions than Quinn might have expected, the mattress broad and plump. The walls were whitewashed between the dark timbers, and the wooden roof sloped away from the wall with shuttered windows. The numerous shutters made Quinn conclude that the window concealed must be unusually large. The floor was solid hardwood, a few sweet herbs strewn across its gleaming expanse.

Quinn wondered if the miller had a companion who tended his hearth so neatly.

"My own room," the miller said with no small measure of pride. "And the finest I can offer a bride. The linens have been changed and there will be hot water in the morn that your maid can bring to you. The view from the window is quite a lovely one in the morning." He smiled and looked between Quinn and Melissande with a paternal air.

"I thank you for your thoughtfulness," Melissande said graciously.

The miller nodded and bowed. "If there is anything you need, please do not hesitate to call." With that, he ducked out of the room and closed the door.

The instant they were alone, Melissande squirmed. "Put me down, if you please," she said with evident annoyance. "And please have Berthe come to help me."

"Maybe I do not please to do so," Quinn said with an evenness he was far from feeling. Melissande glanced up with evident hostility. "Maybe I would like to know first what has changed your mood."

"Nothing has changed my mood."

"I would argue with that. You seemed quite agreeable to the terms of our bargain." Quinn gave her a little toss in his arms, the closest he could come to giving his uncooperative wife a shake. "Yet suddenly, you are eyeing me as though I were the spawn of the devil himself."

"The spawn of Jerome de Sayerne is close enough to that!" she declared hotly. "Now, put me down and leave me be."

"What did my father do to make you so bitter?"

Melissande glared at him for an instant before her lips thinned. She folded her arms across her chest. "While my parents were alive, he abused his vassals by taxing them too much, feeding them too little and working them too hard. He bedded every woman he could get his hands on and when they had the misfortune of conceiving his child, he cast them out."

She flicked a venomous glance to Quinn and he remained silent as he listened. He knew this was not a tale he would enjoy, but it was important to hold his objections. "Jerome spotted a maid of mine on a visit to my father, a nobleman's daughter lent to our service. She was abducted by your sire later and cruelly used. My father stood by her when she returned in rags and tears, even when her state was obvious to all." Melissande swallowed and her eyes narrowed. Quinn thought he saw the glisten of tears there. "She had been my nursemaid when I was a child and was much loved."

Melissande caught her breath as though she could not speak. Quinn did not know what to do to ease the hurt of her recollection, but wished that he did. He remained stoically silent.

"She died in labor," she said huskily, and Quinn's heart wrenched in sympathy. Sadly, he was not surprised by this tale of his sire. "Your father never acknowledged the child or provided for it. It sickened and died the next winter, despite our efforts."

Melissande cleared her throat and blinked quickly before she fired a glance at Quinn. "When my parents died, your father began his campaign to forcibly join our two estates. When Tulley protested, Jerome became more subtle. He moved border markers, he stole the harvest and sowing seed from our storage barns."

She laughed harshly when Quinn could find nothing to say. "And you ask what I have against your father," she said bitterly. "Now he is dead but the attacks on Annossy still continue. And you have come home to claim your father's lands. Is it any surprise to you that I have suspicions?"

Their gazes locked for a long moment. There was accusation and pain in her eyes that Quinn longed to erase. It burned within him that she thought he was like his father.

"I am different," he said simply. "Give me the chance to show you."

Melissande took a deep breath and looked away. "Put me down," she said finally. "I would prefer to be alone."

Quinn's anger flared that she would not even give him a chance. If he left now, he was certain this rift between them would only grow. He appreciated that she had told him part of her story and that the telling had been difficult, but did not want there to be space between them.

"I was invited here," Quinn reminded her.

"In a moment of weakness that I now regret."

"Do you also regret making our bargain?"

"Yes," Melissande said stubbornly, but Quinn noted with interest that she did not meet his eyes. Her voice, though, was resolute. "Yes, I do."

She was trying to deceive him. Her lips said one thing, but her eyes said another. Quinn's anger rose again that Melissande would not continue to be honest with him and he decided that he was not above playing her games.

"So your word is worth as little as that," Quinn mused, knowing that his comment would infuriate her. He knew that she took pride in her sworn pledge, as any decent person should. "You gave me your vow, and now that it is no longer convenient to your means, you would forget your pledge. How like a woman!"

Melissande slapped him harder than Quinn had thought she would be able to. He permitted himself only a blink of surprise.

"Beast! You took advantage of me in a moment of weakness! You used me for your own ends, precisely as your sire might have done in this place. I am not convinced that you are made of different stuff than he, despite your claims."

"My father is dead," Quinn said flatly.

"But his wiles live on in his son."

"I told you that was not so."

"But you have not proven it to me," Melissande countered. She lifted her chin and met his gaze challengingly. "If you are as much of a gentleman as you would maintain, then put me down and leave me tonight."

"I was invited," Quinn reminded her again.

"Into the room, but not into my bed or between my thighs," Melissande countered firmly. She braced her hands on his shoulders and pushed. Her gaze lifted to his and her eyes glittered angrily in the shadows. "Prove to me the kind of man you are," she whispered.

"And what about the kind of woman you might be?" Quinn asked in a low voice.

"You know that already," Melissande retorted.

Quinn permitted himself a slow smile and noted how her gaze rose to watch his lips, as though she were powerless to do otherwise. Her eyes were wide and green, making her appear both heart-wrenchingly innocent and slightly afraid.

He thought of how fiercely protective she was of those she cared about, how hard she had fought against him, how rigid her standards of right and wrong were, yet how vulnerably sweet she was once she let down her guard. She was the kind of woman any man would be proud to call his own. Quinn longed to gather her close, to cherish and protect her.

"Yes," he said carefully as she watched. "Yes, I know the kind of woman you are." His voice dropped lower and he watched her breath catch. "Do not imagine that I shall soon forget our wedding night."

He meant more than their mating. He meant the way she had trusted him and shown him her softness, but Quinn did not know how to explain that to her. Melissande gasped but Quinn could think of nothing but kissing her. He wanted to taste the sweetness hidden within her once more. He bent lower and brushed his lips across the softness of hers.

She trembled. Her breasts heaved within the confines of her kirtle and he wanted suddenly to free them that they might fill his hands.

He wanted Melissande this night. His body showed the one unmistakable sign and, with her hip pressed against him so, Quinn knew that she knew the truth.

But she was afraid he would break his pledge.

Quinn took a deep breath and fought for control. He was tempted to follow Melissande into bed and coax her into submission, but he knew that was precisely what she expected of the barbarian she had decided he was.

Though she might enjoy their mating while it occurred, later she would hate him for it. Quinn wanted none of that. This was his chance to prove her expectations of him wrong.

And it was about time the lady had a surprise of her own.

Quinn deposited her gently on the bed. He felt her stiffen as she braced herself for his assault, but he only brushed his lips across her brow. She froze, her eyes narrowing in distrust.

"Sleep well, my lady," he murmured. Quinn knew that he should leave this very instant, but he could not deny himself one tiny indulgence.

He held her incredulous gaze for a long moment, then leaned closer and slowly slid his mouth across her lips once more. She trembled again but did not pull away. Quinn dared to be encouraged by that minute sign. Maybe the lady did not hate him as much as she would have him believe.

"I shall summon Berthe for you," he whispered.

Before Melissande could summon a question—or before Quinn could change his mind—he straightened and strode across the chamber, stepping back out into the hall and closing the door behind himself.

He heard her mutter a vehement curse in the privacy of her chamber and smiled as he leaned back against the heavy door. This battle might not be as lost as he would have thought. Quinn grinned outright with delight before composing his expression as he descended to the warm kitchen again.

"Quinn!" Bayard declared with some surprise. "I thought that you and your bride had retired?"

"Ah, the lady has pain and is in need of sleep." Quinn beckoned to Berthe. "She asked for your help, Berthe. I wonder if you might prepare a sleeping draft for her."

"Yes, my lord. It shall immediately be done," Berthe responded crisply.

"And what of you? Surely you do not forgo your marital due?" Bayard demanded with a conviviality born of good ale.

"Ah, I just wanted another draft of the miller's fine brew," Quinn said as he sat down again at the board. Michel placed a filled tankard before him almost immediately and Quinn lifted the unwanted ale to his lips with apparent satisfaction.

"Surely you jest," scoffed the observant Bayard.

"The lady needs her sleep," Quinn said firmly.

"And a fine acknowledgment is that for a man to make for his wife," Berthe said, and granted Quinn an approving smile as she sailed past, although he had only a moment to wonder at the oddity of that. "I'm glad to see that *some* men understand how to treat a lady with respect."

Quinn blinked, but the comment made no sense to him until he noticed the ruddy hue of Bayard's ears.

"That is unnatural," Bayard muttered into his ale, almost as though he hoped none might hear.

"I heard that!" Berthe called from the foot of the stairs. "And you may rest assured, Chevalier Bayard, that it is not unnatural, but *civilized!* Pay attention and you might learn something from your well-mannered companion."

"I have no need of such manners," Bayard growled, but the other men were laughing aloud at the maid's chastisement.

Quinn sat back and sipped his brew, unable to keep his imagination from teasing him with the vision of Berthe slowly removing Melissande's garments in the golden candlelight upstairs. The very fact that he remained downstairs showed his determination to earn his wife's trust to be stronger than even he might have estimated.

Of course, it was all for Sayerne, Quinn told himself stubbornly, though he guessed that was not the whole truth.

The sunlight was warm on her bare flesh.

Melissande rolled to her back with satisfaction, feeling well rested. It was early and her ankle had ceased to throb.

The household dozed in silence. Melissande imagined that even the animals had not been tended yet. She stretched and encountered a solid wall of muscled flesh.

With a tangle of curly hair in its midst that she knew without opening her eyes was russet.

The scent of masculine skin surrounded her like a cocoon. An excitement that was decidedly inappropriate danced through her veins and made her flesh tingle to life.

Melissande listened to the sound of Quinn's deep, even breathing before she dared to open her eyes. He was asleep. He had a nerve to invite himself into her bed while she slumbered!

Yet regardless of how annoyed she might be with him for his audacity in sharing her bed, Melissande was curious.

And he *was* asleep.

She had seen very little on their wedding night, admittedly because she had been too nervous to look. Surely it could not hurt to peek now, before the man awakened? Curiosity, her mother had always said, was a healthy attribute.

Melissande took a deep breath before she opened her eyes. Her gaze flew to Quinn's face, something within her softening at his peaceful repose. He looked less imposing in sleep with his chestnut hair tousled and his lips twisted in a half smile. Melissande reached up before she could stop herself and touched one fingertip to his lips.

They were soft, like her own, despite the hardness of the life he had lived.

She realized then that she had not asked Quinn about his past. What had Tulley said? That he had taken up the Cross? Had Quinn been to Jerusalem then? Melissande watched him sleep and wondered what he had seen, where he had been, what exotic flavors he had sampled. He had seen the world while she had stayed home and administered Annossy with breathtaking predictability, from one season to the next.

Melissande felt suddenly very sheltered.

Her finger strayed through the prickly stubble of beard on Quinn's chin, across his cheek and traced the outline of his jaw. He was a handsome man, Melissande could admit to herself when no one else might guess her thoughts. Her other fingertips joined the first as she let her hand trail down the corded strength of his neck.

And felt the puckered length of a scar.

Her fingers halted uncertainly, hovering above the heat of his flesh. She had not noticed this on their wedding night. The wound was old and long healed, although its mark still marred his shoulder. It was lengthy and she guessed the wound had been deep.

This was vivid evidence of how different Quinn's life had been from hers. Melissande wondered how he had been wounded, where he had been, who had stitched up his flesh.

Her gaze flicked to his face, but he still slept.

Her shaking fingers tentatively touched the puckered flesh. It could not have been an easy time for him. Melissande could not imagine that this strong and resolute man would take kindly to being at less than his full capabilities. She traced the length of the scar and knew it must have taken a goodly time to heal.

And he had likely been far from home. Melissande knew that she would have been hard-pressed to endure such an ailment away from everyone and everything she knew. The discovery gave her a new appreciation of the strength of Quinn's character, and of the gentleness he unfailingly showed her.

This was a man who had seen and done much. Melissande knew that she could never have been bold enough to walk away from everything she knew to seek her fortune abroad.

At least not without a compelling reason to do so.

What had driven Quinn away? Was it possible that he had not seen eye to eye with his sire, as he maintained? Or was she seeing an explanation where there was none?

He grunted and frowned suddenly in his sleep. His hand brushed at hers as it might at a troubling fly. Melissande's heart skipped. She snatched away her hand and regarded him with wide eyes, certain she would be caught looking.

But Quinn merely rolled to his back, apparently satisfied that the "fly" was gone. His breathing deepened as Melissande watched, and she propped herself up on her elbow to watch him.

His continued slumber made her even more bold. There was a great deal that she had not really seen. Carefully, Melissande drew back the linens. The sunlight filtering through the shutters marked his chest in bands of gold and shadow.

He was a warrior and his body showed the evidence. His muscles were developed to hard curves, there were small nicks and scars all over his flesh in addition to the large one she had already noted. His flesh was tanned to a bronze hue.

Melissande's overwhelming impression was one of strength and vigor. Here was a man who had earned his way with his hands and his blade. A code of honor was hinted at in that choice and Melissande found herself intrigued with her spouse.

She wanted to know more about Quinn de Sayerne and the realization surprised her.

But she would see something first, she decided before modesty could stay her hand. Her fingers fell to his flesh again and she touched the dark circle of his nipple, surprised to find it like her own. Her hand followed the trail of hair that swept toward his navel. Below his navel, a matching russet arrow swept upward from his masculinity.

The linen rested about his hips, but she saw the silhouette beneath the cloth.

She wanted to see more.

Melissande swallowed, uncertain that she dared. She flicked a glance to Quinn, reassured that he slumbered peacefully despite her exploration.

Carefully Melissande lifted the linens. Her eyes widened in surprise at the arousal she revealed.

Was it always like this? The recollection of its strength within her prompted Melissande to explore further. Fascinated by him, she pulled down the linens and examined Quinn in the sunlight.

Melissande gazed upon him and wondered what he felt like there. Was the surrounding hair wiry or soft? Was the flesh truly as hard as it appeared?

Quinn slept on and Melissande took heart from his obliviousness. She reached out and touched him. There.

That part of him lifted to her hand, as though welcoming her touch.

How absurd! She swallowed a squeak of alarm and scooted backward. Melissande eyed Quinn and that part of him suspiciously, but neither moved.

His chest merely rose and fell as he slept peacefully.

Melissande's lips twisted in indecision. She looked at him again. Surely she had been mistaken. Surely he had just moved in his sleep.

Surely there was no harm in knowing for certain.

She swallowed and reached out once more. As soon as her fingertips brushed against Quinn's hardness, it rose slightly.

This time she did not pull away. Melissande nervously laid her hand across him and felt the slight swell beneath her touch. Her fingers closed gently and quite naturally around Quinn's strength. Shocked at her own audacity and uncertain how to proceed, Melissande flicked a glance to Quinn.

Only to find his warm amber gaze locked upon her.

He smiled and Melissande knew she flushed scarlet.

"I am sorry," she began in a fluster.

When she might have pulled away her hand, the weight of Quinn's hand landed atop hers, capturing it there.

"Do not apologize," he said with reassuring calm. "Curiosity is a healthy trait, and only natural."

"I do not mean to give offense," Melissande began again, but got no further.

Quinn chuckled and he rose beneath her hand in a most curious manner. "And none is given, my lady. Rest assured of that." His thumb slid across the back of her hand and Melissande looked away when the hue of his eyes had deepened to a rich amber.

"If this is the way civilized men awaken, you may consider me converted," he commented with amusement.

Melissande pulled her hand abruptly out from under his. "You mock me," she accused tightly, certain she would never be able to look the man in the eye again.

"I do no such thing," Quinn countered. So quickly did he respond that Melissande was tempted to believe him. She flicked a skeptical glance in his direction, only to find his expression sincere.

The sight made her heart flutter in a disconcerting manner and she wondered whether she had caught some malady traveling in these cold months. Certainly that could explain the oddity of her own behavior of late.

She took refuge in accusation.

"What kind of knave are you to invite yourself into my bed?"

"A knave who desires his lady's name to be unsullied," Quinn said. Melissande scowled, certain he teased her, and glared at him. Quinn shrugged.

"There is no pallet here and the floor is far too cold alone. If I had asked for a pallet, you can imagine that rumors would have spread."

His explanation made such good sense that she could scarcely argue with him about his choice. Melissande's lips pursed with irritation. How she hated when Quinn was right!

"Still, you could have awakened me to ask."

Quinn smiled a most disarming smile. "And disturb your much needed sleep? That would have been unchivalrous." He leaned closer and Melissande eyed him warily. "And tell me honestly, my lady," he whispered, "did my presence disturb your rest in the least? This is a broad mattress and I imagine that you did not even know I was here."

Melissande's flush heightened with the awareness that she had known he was there. She remembered only too well how cozily warm she had felt after desperately trying to warm the feather tick alone. She could probably pinpoint the very moment Quinn had joined her.

"You presume too much," she snapped, and made to rise.

Quinn caught her wrist in his gentle grip. "And you will catch your death should you arise when the house is still cold," he murmured.

He lifted the linens invitingly and smiled. There was a dangerous seduction in his voice and in his smile, yet Melissande was tempted to burrow into the warmth beside him. She nibbled her lip uncertainly.

"Come and be warm," Quinn coaxed. "I promise to keep to my word."

Melissande did not question her impulse to trust him. She slipped into the bedcover's warm embrace and settled into the mattress a distinct distance from Quinn.

"You will be too cold there," he said. His arm locked around her waist and Melissande gasped as he pulled her resolutely against him. He was invitingly warm, but she closed her eyes that he might not see her response to his touch.

"Go back to sleep. It is still too early to be awake," he murmured against her hair. Melissande nearly laughed aloud at the thought, for every fiber of her being was alive as it had never been before. Sleep was the furthest thought from her mind, but she kept her eyes closed in the hope that Quinn would torment her no more.

Instead, his hand lifted from her waist. Melissande waited with dread, only to be flooded with mortification when his fingertip dropped unerringly to her lips.

He could not have been awake when she touched him, she told herself wildly. It was only a coincidence that he touched her where she had first touched him.

But Quinn's finger relentlessly retraced the path her own had taken, though across her flesh instead of his.

Melissande felt his finger's warmth slide across her cheek, around her ear, down the length of her jawline. She swallowed when his other fingertips joined the first in sliding down the length of her neck.

She caught her breath when his fingers eased beneath her chemise and gently traced the silhouette of her collarbone.

"You mock me again," she whispered. She felt Quinn lean over her and reluctantly opened her eyes to find his eyes gleaming with intent.

"No, my lady," he murmured. "I would simply know you as you now know me."

Melissande might have protested, but she could not find the words when Quinn's hand closed tenderly around her breast. She gasped and her back arched of its own accord.

All she saw was Quinn's easy smile. It was reassuring, though that made little sense. A heat unfurled in her loins as she felt her pulse pound beneath his palm and Melissande recalled clearly the desire he had fired within her.

Their gazes held as she realized that she wanted him again.

"You are beautiful," Quinn told her, and the awe in his voice as he glanced down to his hand could not have been contrived. He impaled her with his bright gaze again and Melissande could not summon a breath into her lungs.

She was trapped, but she knew in her secret heart that she was pleased to be so. That was a shocking thought, but she did not move.

Quinn's lips quirked in a smile. "Surely you do not imagine that I am much more familiar with the makings of ladies than you were with that of knights?" he asked.

He was teasing her. This was only a game. Melissande flushed and tore her gaze away, but Quinn bent to give her one of his temptingly light kisses.

"I would just look," he assured her.

Melissande licked her lips. He was her spouse. After what she had just done, she could hardly deny him. After all, *she* had not asked. She nodded and opened her chemise with shaking fingers. She looked away, half dreading what he would say.

"Beautiful," Quinn breathed.

Melissande dared to look, only to find his eyes glowing amber. His hand moved slowly from her breast and she knew she did not imagine that his fingers quivered.

His very uncertainty reassured her as nothing else could, and Melissande rolled toward him. Quinn's other hand cupped her nape and she reveled in the strength of his fingers tangled in her hair. His hand swept lower in an endless caress, his attention diverted from her face as he avidly watched its progress.

Melissande looked at his lips and considered how she would like to kiss him. She would take his strong jaw in her hands, just once, just to see how it felt, and press her lips

resolutely against his. She would arch her back so that her
breasts rubbed in that tangle of russet hair and Quinn would
open his mouth to her.

The thought stole her breath away.

Then Quinn flicked a glance to her and grinned mischievously. Melissande did not know what to expect, but suddenly he wriggled his thumb within the enclave of her navel.

It tickled outrageously. She squealed and laughed, even as she writhed to escape him. Quinn chuckled and his other hand joined the fray.

"Quinn!"

"Ticklish, my lady?" he demanded as he tormented her.

"Oh, yes! Oh, stop!" Melissande could barely catch her breath from laughing. She twisted desperately, pushing at Quinn's hands in an effort to escape. "No! Stop, please! I beg of you!" she gasped.

Quinn stopped suddenly, his hands locked around her waist, his fingertips too close to her ticklish spot for her to relax. He loomed over her and Melissande did not trust the unruly twinkle in his eyes.

"I will stop for a kiss," he whispered wickedly.

Melissande's heart leapt. "You are a devil," she protested lightly, more because she thought she should than because she had any particular objections.

Quinn laughed and the merry sound tempted Melissande to join him. "A devil?" he demanded with an arch of his brow. "Only a saint would demand so little from such a beauty."

Though he jested, it was clear the compliment was meant honestly. The thought that this man found her pleasing to look upon warmed Melissande deep inside.

She held up an imperious finger. "One kiss," she dictated.

Quinn's grin broadened. "Unless the lady desires more," he murmured as he leaned closer.

That the lady was already considering the matter did nothing to reassure Melissande.

She inhaled sharply as Quinn leaned over her, deciding that it wouldn't matter if she slipped her arms around his neck. Her fingers fanned out of their own accord around his shoulders and Melissande would have been shocked to know the vision of willingness she granted Quinn just before he kissed her. She arched her back without intending to, closed her eyes and parted her lips.

Then Quinn was kissing her. His kiss was everything she had longed for just moments before. His arms enfolded her, he braced his sinewy thigh between her legs. Her pulse quickened as his lips withdrew, then his mouth closed resolutely over hers. His tongue explored and Melissande greeted it with hers. His hands slipped from her waist to spread behind her, one at her nape again and one cupping her buttocks.

Still she wanted more of him.

His touch enflamed her as nothing else could. Melissande wound her fingers into his hair, she arched against his strength, she loved how gently he touched her. She wanted to know him, to touch him, to taste him as she had never before. She wanted to explode beneath him, she wanted to feel the weight of his strength within her.

Quinn dragged his lips from hers, and for the first time, Melissande was aware of the evidence of his arousal. She instinctively rubbed the softness of her belly against him.

"My lady," he gasped. "If you do not stop, I will not be able to stop with one kiss."

But Melissande did not want to stop.

She stretched up and rolled her tongue in Quinn's ear. He quivered, much as she did beneath his touch, and that evidence of his vulnerability emboldened her to new heights. She wanted to disarm him, she wanted to make this supremely self-controlled man lose control.

She wanted to feel him explode within her again.

Melissande's fingers were moving through his hair, caressing his ears, stroking his jaw, his neck, his lips. She framed his face within her hands and stretched up to press her lips to his, just as she had envisioned doing.

Quinn sagged against her. "My lady," he protested raggedly.

Melissande pulled him down and rolled atop him, sprawling across his chest as she kissed him again. "The lady desires another kiss," she whispered against his throat. Quinn clutched her buttocks with his hands and seemed to stifle a groan.

"My lady, test me no further," he murmured, and the strain of maintaining his control was evident in his voice.

Melissande kissed him relentlessly. Her hands roved over him, savoring the warm satin of his skin beneath her touch, until her fingers landed upon that part of him. She looked up to his face as her hand closed around him. He was larger and harder than he had been before.

Quinn's eyes fluttered closed and Melissande marveled that he could be so affected by her touch.

"I want you," she confided.

Quinn's eyes flew open, his expression rapt as he scanned her face. "Really?" he asked in evident surprise.

Melissande smiled a small smile of uncertainty. "Yes."

Quinn inhaled and his strength grew within her hand. He leaned back against the pillows, his voice strained when he spoke.

"I am not invited."

"Yes," Melissande whispered. She slid over his chest and reached to run her free hand over his face. "Yes, on this morning, my lord, you are."

He eyed her cautiously, but Melissande managed to smile.

"We had a bargain," she whispered.

It took no more than that.

Quinn hauled her atop him and pulled her lips down for his impassioned kiss. Melissande felt his restraint fall away like a tangible thing and reveled in the surety of his touch. He cupped her buttocks and lifted her high above him, his gaze locked with hers.

"I would see you," he murmured in a voice as languid as honey in the sun. Melissande did not understand until he settled her weight atop him. Her knees were on either side of his waist.

"Oh!" Melissande's eyes widened as she felt him slide within her. She trembled deep inside and she felt her pulse quicken.

Quinn chuckled, launching a most curious vibration within her. "Oh!" he mimicked good-naturedly. His hands dropped to her waist and his eyes glinted with a warmth that fed Melissande's confidence. "It is all up to you this time," he informed her.

Melissande did not know what to do. She recalled Quinn's movement from before, so she lifted herself tentatively above him, then let him slide within her again. Quinn's little moan of pleasure and the sensation pleased her so that she embraced the task before her with enthusiasm.

And Quinn responded in kind.

It was not long before she was clutching at him and he was holding her close. Their hearts pounded as one as her breasts were crushed against his chest, their rhythms in perfect synchronization. Melissande felt the heat rise beneath her flesh. Quinn's breath rasped in her ear and she tasted that elusive release on her horizon.

When the wave broke over her, she reared back and threw her arms toward the ceiling in ecstatic release. She heard Quinn gasp her name and felt his strength surge beneath her.

Moments later, she slipped into the bliss of sleep. She knew that she smiled, for she was cradled against the solid heat of Quinn as his lips moved against her hair.

* * *

As soon as he was certain she was asleep—and that he would escape unscathed for the moment, at least—Quinn carefully extricated himself from Melissande's embrace.

He had tricked her and knew that he would pay the price.

Quinn had not done so out of any devious intent, but that would not matter. Melissande had simply been there, seductively warm and soft when he awakened. That she explored him secretly enflamed his passion and matters had seen their own way from there.

Still Quinn felt horribly guilty. He knew that the lady loved another and knew that she had a high code of ethics. He should have stopped, though he wondered in all honesty whether he could have.

Although now, he wondered whose arms Melissande had imagined were locked around her. The thought sickened him.

Too late he realized what a fool he had been.

"Aha!" Bayard's merry voice made Quinn jump as he cautiously descended the stairs.

"What possesses you to startle an old friend?" Quinn demanded.

Bayard laughed aloud. "What kind of newly wedded man are you to avoid the pleasure of awakening with your lawful wife?" He winked and nudged Quinn companionably. "Does the lady resist your charms?"

"No." Quinn dropped to a seat and accepted a draft of cold ale. It would clear his head, if nothing else. "It is not so simple as that."

Bayard sat opposite him and grinned engagingly. "Care to talk about it?"

Quinn spared his companion a suspicious eye. "What makes you so merry? What manner of mischief have you been making?"

"Me?" Bayard pointed to himself with feigned surprise. Quinn chuckled despite himself. "You accuse *me* of making mischief? Surely, Quinn, you must be jesting. You should know that *I* have done nothing but slumber before the hearth.''

"Alone?''

Bayard choked slightly, before protesting his innocence anew. "How could you think otherwise of me?''

Quinn snorted, not in the least convinced, and took a draft of ale. Bayard leaned forward, undeterred, his eyes glinting with curiosity.

"So, tell me the whole tale,'' he urged. "Your secrets are safe with me. Does the lady spurn you?''

"No,'' Quinn said again. He met Bayard's eyes and recalled that this man knew much more about the vagaries of women than he. Maybe Bayard could help him in this puzzle.

"You see—'' Quinn leaned forward, dropped his voice and Bayard followed suit "—it seems the lady had pledged herself to another.''

"No! It could not be so!''

"But it is so. She insists upon it.''

"But what about Tulley? Surely he would not have forced her to break her word?''

Quinn sipped his ale with dissatisfaction. "Apparently that is precisely what he did.''

"*Aïe.*'' Bayard leaned back and ran his hand through his hair. "And when did she tell you of this?''

"When she wept, the morning after the match had been consummated,'' Quinn admitted grimly.

"This is not good,'' Bayard informed him sagely.

Quinn arched a brow. "Thank you.''

"But tell me this,'' the other knight asked. "Does she have any regard for this man?''

That was a reminder Quinn did not need. "She says she loves him with all her heart,'' he admitted tightly.

Bayard gave a low whistle. "What do you intend to do?''

"I do not know." Quinn frowned. "What is worse, Tulley overheard our arguing that morning. He demands an heir within the year and before he invests me with Sayerne."

"So, should you do the chivalrous thing, you lose all."

"Yes."

Bayard pushed his glass across the board. "Then, it seems to me that you have little choice." His voice was low and thoughtful, a tone that gave Quinn hope that he had a plan.

"Yes?"

Bayard looked directly into Quinn's eyes. "You must compel her to love you," he said. "You must make her forget this other man and see no one but you."

The plan was too like his own poorly formed idea to be reassuring. Quinn spread his hands out in frustration. "I do not know how to begin."

"Have you loved her again?"

Quinn flushed and fidgeted awkwardly on the hard bench. "This very morning," he admitted. "But I fear what she shall say about it."

"Was she not willing?"

"Yes, but not entirely awake yet."

Bayard leaned forward intently. "Did you see her pleasured?"

"Of course!"

"Has she ever called you by name in that moment?"

Quinn's heart sank and he could not hold his friend's gaze. "No," he admitted.

Bayard frowned and tapped his finger on the board. "It seems you have a daunting task before you," he mused. "But the prize of Sayerne is well worth the effort."

"Not to mention that of a marriage without strife," Quinn interjected sourly.

Bayard grinned. "You care for this lady, unless I miss my guess."

Quinn resolutely did not meet his companion's perceptive gaze and when he spoke, his voice was gruff. "We have similar values," he said stiffly. "And it pleases me to see her smile."

"Aha!" Bayard's voice was gleeful. "The truth will out!" He leaned forward suddenly and his voice dropped in confidence. Quinn met his mischievous gaze doubtfully. "That is an advantage unlooked for! Women *adore* a man who has a weakness for them. It flatters their vanity and I cannot imagine that your Melissande is different. Do not worry, Quinn, we shall see the lady enamored of you yet."

"My lord Quinn!" Berthe's voice rose sharply from the concealed kitchen. "I should advise you strongly against taking the advice of this ruffian for clearly he knows nothing of what pleases a lady." Quinn looked to his companion to find Bayard's ears glowing a dull red.

"Surely you have not tried to make sport with my lady's maid?" Quinn asked indignantly.

It was not reassuring that Bayard's ears turned an even brighter shade of red. Instead of responding to Quinn, he raised his voice, no doubt so that Berthe could hear. He sighed in a most affected manner.

"Ah, Quinn, the pleasure of avoiding this lady's sharp comments buoyed my spirits this morn, but now the day is lost," Bayard said, then grinned unabashedly.

"I heard that!" Berthe cried from the room beyond. "My mother warned me against your kind and I was lucky to keep my wits about me right from the first, despite the gilding on your tongue."

Quinn's brows rose in surprise. "You did not try to charm her, did you?" he asked, not in the least certain that his companion had not.

Bayard shrugged. "And what if I did?"

"Melissande will have much to say of the matter."

"And it is neither her business nor yours," the other knight retorted with a vehemence that seemed uncalled-for.

"This is the pursuit of pleasure, pure and simple. No more than that."

Though his assertion was bold, Quinn could not help but note the way Bayard lowered his voice that Berthe might not catch these words. And Bayard's gaze brightened a little too readily when she appeared to lend credence to his claim.

Berthe tried to spare a stern glance to Bayard, but Quinn noted that her gaze was snared once she dared to look. Bayard smiled a slow, sensual smile. Berthe flushed as she twisted her hands before herself and the other knight's eyes sparkled.

Bayard was smitten. Quinn saw the signs and was heartily amused. For that reason alone, he held his tongue.

"She is this close, despite her chatter," Bayard murmured, holding his thumb and finger an increment apart. Quinn stifled a smile, but Bayard had eyes only for Berthe. The kitchen was warm with the silence of their gazing at each other and Quinn knew he was less than welcome.

"I should check the horses," he said firmly. Bayard glanced up with a start.

"I will aid you."

"No. It is still early and I would walk alone."

Bayard shook his head before he grinned outright. "Have no fear, Quinn," he whispered. "Once I have shared with you my skills of seduction, your lady will not even permit you to leave her chambers. You will not be walking alone in the morning to soothe your desire then."

Quinn could not resist the opportunity. He leaned down that Berthe might not hear him. "I would see the evidence that your so-called skills are as effective as you claim first," he teased.

Bayard took the comment with less than his usual good humor. "And so you shall," he declared boldly. "Without delay." He rose and Quinn quickly left the kitchen.

"Do not imagine, sir, that I will fall victim to your overrated charms...." Berthe began as Quinn shut the door firmly behind himself. He took a deep breath and watched the sun glitter on the morning snow.

Quinn stepped into the yard, ignored the giggles behind him and fancied that this golden sunlight could make anything come aright.

Even the sweetening of Melissande d'Annossy.

Chapter Seven

He must think her shamelessly wanton.

Melissande dreaded seeing Quinn after the way she had behaved. She burrowed into the bed, determined to avoid that moment as long as possible.

Her maid, however, had other ideas.

"Good morning, my lady!" Berthe enthused. She threw open the shutters with abandon and Melissande hated her cheerfulness.

It seemed quite incredible that Melissande's mood was not immediately evident to one who knew her as well as Berthe did. She granted the other woman a glance, but Berthe merely smiled brightly.

"Good morning!" she repeated with a joviality that was already annoying. "And a lovely morning it is. Are you not terribly excited about seeing Sayerne this day? When I told Bayard how interested I would be in seeing it, he told me all about it. It is going to be wonderful to live at Sayerne and I, for one, cannot wait."

"No one said anything about *living* there," Melissande grumbled.

Berthe clapped her hands together. "But, of course! What could be more perfect?"

"Living at Annossy, which has not fallen into ruin, would be decidedly more perfect." Melissande was certain that the blame for her current troubles could be laid squarely at Sayerne's door, for it was Quinn's desire for that place that was at the root of everything.

"Ruin? My lady, you have not even seen Sayerne lately. I am certain that it will be wonderful."

"I doubt that," Melissande said sharply. "The estate has been mismanaged for many years and you already know that the villeins fled to Annossy in the last year." She sighed and sat up, running a hand through her hair. "I shall be surprised if there is so much as a stick of tinder left there."

"But even so, will it not be exciting?" Berthe asked. "Will it not be romantic?"

Melissande looked to her maid warily, certain the woman had taken leave of her senses. What could be exciting about living in a decrepit estate in the winter?

Berthe seemed to have taken some curious affliction, for she was acting very strangely. Melissande was certain that the flush on her cheeks must be a sign of some fever.

There could be no other reason for her sudden enthusiasm to see Sayerne.

"Exciting?" she asked as tonelessly as she could manage.

"Oh, yes, to rebuild Sayerne is such a romantic idea." Berthe rolled her eyes dreamily. "It will be exciting to help your lord, to stand stalwart by his side and bring his estate to its former glory."

Clearly the woman was stricken ill.

"It will take a good quantity of hard work, likely without reward." Melissande's lips twisted at the very thought. "And it is not even his estate yet," she added.

"Ah, I see that I have awakened you too early, my lady," Berthe clucked before she laughed gaily. "Did that handsome groom of yours keep you awake all night creating an heir? I imagine that he is adept beyond most at the art of love." Berthe smothered a giggle. "I should not have slept, either, in your place," she murmured mischievously.

Melissande felt her face heat at the unexpected teasing, but Berthe continued undeterred. To Melissande's astonishment, the maid even winked at her.

"I can imagine that you would not protest his attentions. You must have fairly melted at his touch." She inhaled deeply. "Such a man. So handsome. So noble. Those hands. And those eyes." Berthe rolled her own and shivered with delight. "They are like amber, or fine old eau-de-vie. To have his attention would be enough to turn a woman's knees to butter."

Melissande felt a nudge of irritation at the maid's familiarity. That her knees responded in precisely that manner to Quinn's gaze was not reassuring in the least.

Quinn was *her* husband, after all.

"Do you not think that you are being overly familiar this morning?" she asked archly.

Berthe smiled sunnily as she shook out the blanket Melissande wished she had left snuggled atop the bed. The air was chilly with the windows open and, without the linens, Melissande would be compelled to rise and dress.

And see Quinn again. Her heart sank to her toes at the thought of the accusations he would make.

She would die of mortification.

"Surely, my lady, we know each other well enough to talk of such matters."

"What has taken possession of you this morning?" Melissande asked suspiciously. "And why this sudden interest in Sayerne?"

Berthe sat abruptly on the bed. "Let me see your ankle," she demanded pertly. She was changing the subject and though Melissande knew it, she let the matter be for the moment.

The maid looked as excited as a child who knows a gift is in the offing, and Melissande could make no sense of it.

The ankle was less swollen this morning and Melissande imagined she might be able to walk upon it. Berthe smiled with proprietary pride at the improvement, but did not release her mistress's ankle. She leaned closer and her voice dropped confidentially.

"Tell me, my lady," Berthe urged. "Tell me how you feel when your lord touches you." She leaned closer and her voice dropped to a breathy whisper. "Tell me how it feels to be in love."

"Berthe!" Melissande hauled her ankle out of the maid's grip and rose hastily to her feet. "This is inappropriate and you know it! If you have affection for my husband or his estates, you should at least have the good sense to keep such nonsense to yourself!"

With that, Melissande dragged a kirtle over her shoulders, feeling more disgruntled than she certainly thought she should.

What if Quinn had tender feelings for Berthe? What if he kept the maids and serving wenches with child as his sire had done? How on earth would Melissande deal with such indignity?

And how would she lure Quinn to her own bed?

The thought came unbidden and was certainly unwelcome. Now she even *thought* like a wanton! Melissande laced the sides of her kirtle with a vengeance. Berthe apparently was not inclined to help. The maid lay back across Melissande's linens and closed her eyes, her smile dreamy.

"Do not worry, my lady. It is not your lord who fills my dreams," she confided. "I would only know whether love makes my heart pound like this."

Melissande looked to her maid in surprise, refusing to acknowledge the relief those words prompted. "Then, who?"

Berthe closed her eyes and ran her hands over the rumpled linens, looking like a cat reposing in the sun. "His companion knight," she murmured as though she could not even allow herself the luxury of saying his name.

"Bayard?" Melissande was skeptical until her maid closed her eyes rapturously.

"Yes, Bayard de Neuville." Berthe sighed. "Do you not think he is handsome beyond all? And amusing? And such a dangerous charm. A woman could readily lose her head when he speaks."

"But you chide him so."

"It is all I can do to keep my wits about me." Berthe shuddered delicately. "If he ever guessed that I have any regard for him at all, imagine what that awareness might do to his pride! He should be bent on seducing me then, and I would be powerless to protest." Berthe smiled, as though the prospect was less than dismal.

"I had no idea."

"And hopefully he does not, either." Berthe sighed again. "He is so handsome." She squinted up at Melissande and her eyes widened slightly, as though in surprise. "Not more handsome than your lord, of course," she corrected hastily.

Melissande smiled thinly. "Bayard is a rogue of the first order," she stated. "His charm is too quick for a lady of repute to take him seriously. I would expect you to be more immune to the charms of his kind."

Berthe's smile thinned. "I think you judge him too harshly," she said with uncharacteristic sullenness. "Last night he told me of Sayerne, and it was magical. I could see the hills as he described them and the place sounds romantic beyond all else."

Melissande reached out and laid her hand over the other woman's. "My concern is only to not see you hurt," she said quietly. "And Bayard might have no heart to grant. He might pursue a woman with sweet words and promises, but he is the kind my own mother warned me against."

"Why?"

Melissande saw that Berthe was listening to her and was relieved. "Because he will pursue you only until you yield to him, then disappear. You will lose your chastity and your honor, and have nothing left for another who might treat you well.''

Berthe turned abruptly away and Melissande was suddenly afraid her words were being disregarded. She leaned over the other woman and her voice dropped urgently. ''Tell me that you have not yielded to him.''

Berthe smiled and her fingers tangled with Melissande's in a most companionable manner. ''I also had a mother, my lady, who was wary of charming men,'' she said. ''But there is a gentleness about Bayard that touches my heart. Though he jokes with the others, he can appreciate finer things and be quiet when we are alone. I believe there is more to Bayard than meets the eye or I would not so permit my heart to stray.''

She pushed to her feet and fastidiously brushed off her kirtle as Melissande watched. ''Though even he may not guess as much.'' Berthe met Melissande's gaze with a smile. ''Yet.''

Melissande smiled, her mood lightened by the other woman's confidence and wished, for a fleeting moment, that matters could be so easy between herself and Quinn.

But he wanted her only for the child she could bear him. And she, Melissande realized to her disappointment, was proving herself all too ready to play into his hand.

Quinn was not in the kitchen when they descended, and Melissande bit down on her disappointment. The sound of his voice in the stable yard quickened her pulse. Though she dreaded his response, she was curiously anxious to see him again.

She probably just wanted to put the worst behind her.

She broke her fast beneath the miller's eye, finding the bread as palatable as dust. She hoped that no one guessed how anxious she was to leave the house and join Quinn, but she was not to be so fortunate.

"My lady," Berthe chided. "You must eat at a more leisurely pace." Melissande glared at her maid, but Bayard had already slid onto the bench beside her while the miller clicked his tongue chidingly.

"Yes," the miller added. "It is poor for the constitution to eat in haste. You will regret it throughout the day."

"Ah," Bayard interjected. "The lady is only in haste to see her new home."

Melissande flicked an arch look in his direction. "New home?"

"Yes," Bayard said easily. "Sayerne beckons us across the miles this day."

"I have heard nothing of Sayerne becoming my home."

"But where else would one live?"

Melissande frowned thoughtfully. Had everyone forgotten that Annossy had not been abandoned this past year while Sayerne had? She looked at Bayard's innocent smile, remembering readily Berthe's comments along similar lines.

Had they all lost possession of their wits? Why was everyone suddenly so convinced that not only would she and Quinn live at Sayerne, but that it would be marvelous to do so? Despite today's sun and the early thaw, it was too soon to expect spring without another snowfall.

Quinn stepped into the kitchen and Melissande decided to hold her tongue for the time being. Her heart leapt at his appearance, but he granted her no more than a polite smile before turning to the miller.

"I fear it is time we left your hospitality," he said, glancing to Melissande again. "If my lady has broken her fast?"

"Yes, yes. I have finished."

"Then we should depart. The road will be long this day with the mud from the thawing snow."

Quinn thanked the miller as they left and Melissande was disappointed that he spared no more attention to her. Though he assisted her into her saddle, his touch was formal and fleeting, leaving a wedge of dissatisfaction lodged within her.

As they rode out of the miller's yard, only the miller's call disturbing the silence of the morning, Melissande knew her first instinct had been correct.

Quinn was disgusted with her. That was the only explanation that sufficed.

She had behaved most inappropriately. Her mother had taught her that a lady should be reserved, aloof, disinterested, yet Melissande had ignored all of that. It was bad enough that she had looked upon Quinn's nakedness while he slept, but she had even been so forward as to *touch* him there.

Her cheeks burned in shame.

The worst thing was that there was nothing she could say in her own defense.

They rode in silence throughout the day, the entire party drawn into an uneasy quietude. The sun was delightfully overwarm for the season and the lack of wind made the ride one that might have been pleasant under other circumstances. The snow that had been thick when Melissande and her party had ridden to Tulley was left only in occasional drifts, the rest of the countryside muddy.

Even the hills around them seemed unusually quiet, as though the countryside took their mood, as well. The sound of trickling water carried to their ears from all sides, muffling the noise of any wild creatures that might be about. In some places, the puddles on the road were enormous, and elsewhere the road was soft from the melted snow.

At dusk, they crested a rise and Melissande wondered whether they should not be drawing close to Sayerne.

"There!" Quinn said with satisfaction. His voice sounded unnaturally loud after their quiet ride.

He glanced back to Melissande as the party halted and she knew she was being invited to look. She swallowed nervously, aware of every eye upon her, and urged her horse forward. She reined in beside Quinn, aware that this was the closest she had been to him all day.

She should endeavor to be the dutiful wife. After all, if Quinn decided to request an end to the marriage from Tulley, she could still lose Annossy.

"Isn't Sayerne beautiful?" he asked with pride.

Melissande blinked and forced herself to look at the land arrayed before her. Even from here, she could see that the estate was in a shocking state of disrepair. The mud and puddles did the sight no favors.

She deliberately clamped her lips closed so that her expression of dismay could not burst forth. Melissande's heart twisted at Quinn's evident pride in the shambles his sire had seen fit to leave him. Her eyes danced professionally over the site.

The land had not been tilled in at least a year, for the winter-deadened remains of weeds were thick where crops or clear soil should have been. The fences were broken, the gates untended.

There were no fresh hoofprints or footprints in the mud and nothing moved in the village ahead. Sayerne was abandoned and she could not help but think that it was rightly so.

Melissande looked again, feeling Quinn waiting for her comment. She did not know whether any amount of work could bring this estate back to profitability again. And should Quinn endeavor to do so, Melissande was afraid he would burden Annossy so heavily with debt that even that estate would lose its solid financial footing.

It was certainly only fair to tell Quinn the truth. After all, he had little experience in such matters.

She cleared her throat carefully and flicked a glance to her spouse. His face was expectant, as a child awaiting approval. Melissande's heart twisted that it was her approval he so obviously desired.

And she intended to tell him to walk away from Sayerne. It was beyond cruel that she should have to do this.

She hesitated and looked back to the estate. Clearly this place mattered to him more than was logical. Surely there was something of merit about Sayerne? Surely she could soften the blow with some kind comment? She eyed the estate again, determinedly pushing her prejudice against Jerome and his deeds from her mind.

"The site is excellent," she said finally.

And that was true.

"Really?" Quinn's features brightened. "Why is that? I must confess, my lady, that I know nothing of such matters of the earth."

"The slope of the hills," Melissande told him with honesty. "The estate is a large valley, sheltered from the wind and serviced by a fleet river. That is advantageous. There is adequate water for the crops and additionally, one could expect the soil to be rich and fertile around the river.

"And there is more." She gestured to the surrounding hills. "See how the foothills fold around on the north and west sides?" Quinn nodded eagerly. "That will keep the wind to a minimum so that the valley will be more sheltered. It will be warmer for the crops. Maybe the site would even allow cultivation of crops not often grown so far north. You might be able to have a vineyard. Or cultivate figs."

"Ah." Quinn eyed Sayerne with a pride of ownership that Melissande did not feel was entirely justified. He granted her a cocky grin and her heart sank that she had now given him false confidence. "Then we will be prosperous soon with such gifted land," he said blithely.

She could not let him think all was rosy, for that was far from the truth.

Melissande frowned and eyed the ramshackle town. "The estate has been much neglected," she said firmly, hoping Quinn understood the fullness of what she meant. "It will take much work. I do not even know whether anyone could build a profitable manor from what is left here."

"Work?" Quinn scoffed. "We are not afraid of hard work. In no time at all, Sayerne will make you proud," he assured Melissande.

"Yes, we shall live here and work together," Bayard contributed merrily. Quinn slanted a puzzled glance in his companion's direction. Melissande noted the look and wondered about it, but she had more pressing matters before her.

"An estate of this size cannot be run, let alone repaired, without numerous villeins." Melissande cleared her throat, knowing she had to continue. "Sayerne no longer has any tenants."

Quinn, to her surprise, smiled. "Then we shall find some," he said blithely. "Didn't many of them come to Annossy? We shall simply ask them to return."

"But most did not stay," Melissande added. "There was not enough land available at Annossy, so they moved to other estates."

Quinn did not seem overly troubled by this news, either. "Then maybe my wife could lend me some labor," he suggested, the teasing glint in his eye making it increasingly difficult to cling to what Melissande knew was true.

"Annossy is hard-pressed to see its own labor done in time, for the fields are extensive." Her voice was tight and she closed her eyes as Quinn looked away. Bayard and Berthe looked at her as though she were beyond cruel to be negative in this, but she could not lie to Quinn.

The task was impossible and only a fool would think otherwise.

Which did nothing to explain the hopeful expressions on the faces of her three companions.

Melissande sat straighter in her saddle as she endeavored to make her point once more. "In my experience," she said carefully, "there is too much to be done here for the estate to be readily redeemed."

Quinn went still, his eyes dancing over her features. "What are you suggesting?"

There was nothing for it. She had to speak her mind.

"That you should maybe leave Sayerne be," Melissande said in a breathless rush. Quinn's brow darkened slightly but she plunged on nonetheless, anxious to have her say while she could. "I would not see you pour all your funds into a property that might not yield you dividend."

"You think Sayerne cannot be rebuilt?" His voice was silkily calm and Melissande knew he was insulted.

Melissande looked Quinn squarely in the eye. "I would not lose everything on a fool's wager."

"That is your fear? That I will gamble upon what is mine and lose everything?"

"Yes." There. She had said it. Melissande folded her hands before herself and waited.

"Never have I owned anything in my life beyond my steed and armor and the blade in my hand. This legacy is beyond precious to me." Quinn's voice was low and sincere, although Melissande knew he did not understand the challenge before him, should he try to rebuild Sayerne. He leaned closer, but she could not meet his gaze.

"I cannot walk away from this," he whispered.

Melissande gritted her teeth. "You cannot risk Annossy in this foolhardy task."

Quinn shook his head and looked away. "It is always about Annossy with you, is it not?" he asked.

Melissande flushed. "Annossy is everything to me," she said tightly.

Quinn eyed her for a moment. "So I see." Before she could say anything, he grinned confidently. "But I will not fail in this. I grant you my personal guarantee, my lady, that you will risk nothing in this endeavor."

Melissande eyed him uncertainly as she wondered whether her spouse had taken leave of his senses. Did he have any idea how large was the task before him? How much coin he would need? And supplies? Labor? Seed?

And what value was the vow of any man on something he readily admitted he knew nothing about?

But Quinn seemed merely amused by Melissande's attitude. He wagged one finger before her, his playful assurance restored. "I shall rebuild Sayerne, even if I have to do it alone and with my bare hands. You shall see, my lady."

With that, he gave his beast his spurs and rode down what might have been the unplowed road, making way with his charger. Melissande watched him ride away as her mouth dropped open.

Clearly she was married to a mad dreamer.

Melissande exchanged a glance with Bayard, who grinned outright in a manner unnervingly similar to Quinn. Had they both lost possession of their faculties?

"What ho, Quinn! Let us break a path together!" Bayard cried as he rode in pursuit, the mud flying wildly in his wake.

"Completely mad, the pair of them," Berthe clucked in a reassuring echo of her mistress's thoughts.

The words rang curiously, though. To Melissande's surprise, she realized that there was little censure in the other woman's tone. The maid looked after the men with what might have been an affectionate smile playing over her lips.

Make that three who had lost their wits.

"It will never be profitable," Melissande muttered, knowing the truth when she saw it. "Never."

Berthe granted her an arch look. "Do you not believe your own husband's word?"

This was ridiculous. This was not a question of belief, but a reasonable assessment of what could and could not be managed. The truth was clear to any who bothered to look.

"The task is too large," she snapped.

Berthe tossed her hair. "And your lord's determination is larger. I believe he will see the task done." She gave her palfrey her heels and the beast trotted away. "And with the aid of all of us," Berthe added, "how could he fail?"

The other riders stirred impatiently and Melissande's mouth dropped open at her maid's words.

"The aid of all of us?" she repeated. "All of *whom?*"

Berthe was *her* maid. The knights accompanying them were in the employ of Annossy. Surely Quinn did not intend to elicit workers from her very household? And without her permission? Melissande would never permit that!

Berthe did not answer though, leaving Melissande to try to catch up with the three of them despite the mud. The warriors and squires rode behind her, their silence fueling her fears.

"All of whom?" she shouted. "Quinn de Sayerne, surely you do not intend to take labor from my own household? You cannot do this without my permission!"

They ignored her, so Melissande rode hard in pursuit, ignoring the mud that splashed on her kirtle. Such a travesty could not pass unchallenged!

The château was worse than she had anticipated.

Snow lingered in the cold shadows inside the hall. Melissande stooped to examine something on the stone floor and her lips thinned in recognition of rat dung.

"This is a lovely building," Berthe enthused. "I can just imagine how it will look when we have put it to rights." Bayard grinned and openly gave the maid's hand a squeeze. She smiled at him in a manner that made Melissande question the maid's earlier assurances. "Just as you said," she murmured with eyes for Bayard alone, "this is so romantic."

"Yes, and wait until it is clean," Bayard said.

Clearly Melissande was immune to romance. She wanted nothing but to be home at Annossy, warm, sheltered and well fed. She shivered as the wind crept into the hall and swirled around her ankles.

It was barbaric to be expected to live here.

Quinn appeared before her with a ready grin. "What do you think?" he demanded with enthusiasm. "Isn't the keep finely made? Imagine once the fire is lit in the grate how inviting it will be."

"There is no tinder," Melissande observed.

"Ah, but there is! Tulley granted us supplies, knowing that Sayerne was somewhat less than completely prepared for our arrival."

Now there was an understatement.

Melissande put her hand on Quinn's sleeve. He turned immediately to her, his gaze bright. "Quinn," she said in a low voice. "It is unsuitable for us to live here." She licked her lips, knowing he would not appreciate what she was going to say. "Maybe we should proceed to Annossy and stay there while you rebuild Sayerne."

"No! Annossy is too far to travel on this night, and it will be easier to complete the work if we are here." For Quinn, the matter was apparently resolved, but Melissande could not leave it be.

"You mean to live here, then?" she asked, her polite manner slipping in a most decided manner.

Quinn grinned. "I cannot see why not."

That was enough. She was cold, hungry and tired and Sayerne offered no solutions to any of those ills.

"Are you mad?" Melissande demanded. She flung out her hands to gesture to the abandoned hall. "This place is beyond filthy! No one could live here. No one should be compelled to live here before it has been thoroughly scrubbed. Have you not eyes in your head? That is rat dung on the floor and goodness knows what other wild creatures have taken haven within these walls."

"I thought we could make it suitable...."

"Suitable? Make it *suitable?* Quinn, do you understand nothing at all? It is not the place of the lord and lady to scrub the floors! Or have you not *noticed* that there is no one here to do your bidding?"

"The squires could—"

"Squires are but boys. They may know plenty about horses, but here we speak of a manor, a home, an estate. Have you no idea how much labor awaits you here? You cannot do this alone!"

Quinn's lips set stubbornly. "Then I shall find aid."

"Oh, yes. The line forms at the gate even now." Melissande propped her hands on her hips. "Or maybe you are unaware that it is still winter and that your stores are empty. This may surprise you, but those who labor often expect some guarantee that they shall be fed in exchange for their work."

Quinn folded his arms across his chest now and Melissande knew his temper was rising. "Are you saying you will not lend me labor from Annossy?"

"Of course I am saying that! How could I send my tenants to work where they might be fated to starve? That would be beyond irresponsible of me."

"Whereas refusing to aid your spouse would not be?" His tone was low and dangerous, but Melissande did not care.

"When he has lost possession of his wits, I cannot say that it would."

They stared at each other angrily and Melissande was aware of the others watching with bated breath.

"So, now I am a lunatic," Quinn mused. "Is this the excuse you will take to Tulley?"

Melissande spat. "I take nothing to Tulley."

"Then what do you want?"

"I want to live at Annossy, not Sayerne."

Quinn arched a brow. "And I?"

Melissande took a deep breath. "It would be rude of me not to invite you to Annossy, as well," she admitted tightly.

"Invite." Quinn muttered the word under his breath. He exhaled, then fixed Melissande with a glare. "And I, as your lord and spouse, say we shall remain here." He paused and it seemed his glance became significant. "At least until our bargain is fulfilled."

Melissande exhaled in a hiss at the reminder, knowing she could not press him on this, at least not before the others.

"Do I have your agreement?" Quinn asked smoothly when she said nothing.

Melissande's lips tightened with a defiance she was not free to express. "Yes," she said almost inaudibly because she had no choice.

Quinn smiled victoriously, evidently taking her agreement at face value. "You may be surprised," he assured her. "Sayerne is a gracious place to live and, should you try a little, you will enjoy it."

"And we shall rebuild," Bayard added with a significant glance to Berthe. That woman clasped her hands together and smiled.

"It is like something from a chanson," she murmured with delight.

Melissande eyed the three of them dubiously. Clearly they were as mad as could be. And nothing she could say would change their minds.

But one did not reason with the mad.

One lulled them into complacency and fled to Annossy while they slept. And so Melissande would do, regardless of any bargain she had with Quinn. She owed nothing to a man gone mad.

And if she had to make love with Quinn half the night to ensure that he slept soundly, that was the price she would have to pay to be safely home again.

"Your enthusiasm in this is unexpected," Quinn commented as he and Bayard returned from seeing the horses settled. The other men and squires trailed behind, murmuring to each other companionably.

Bayard snorted and shrugged in a manner most alien to his usual assurance. "The lady thinks it romantic," he said gruffly. "If she enjoys the illusion of our building a home with our own hands so close to Annossy, it would be churlish to observe the opposite."

"You showed no such restraint before," Quinn teased. "Maybe this is serious." Bayard shot him a glance of loathing and hauled open the door to the hall.

"I told you otherwise," he muttered.

Quinn smiled at the sight of the ruddy flush on Bayard's ears before the sight within stole his thoughts away.

The room was transformed. Though the squires had carted Tulley's grant of goods into the hall, two of them remaining to help the women, Quinn had never expected such progress.

The fire had been kindled with Tulley's tinder and a part of the hall near the hearth was made cleaner. It had been accomplished so quickly that Quinn was reassured about his task here.

Melissande sat before the fire, on a stool also supplied by Tulley, the very image of domesticity. Berthe crouched before her as they reviewed the supply of foodstuffs, and Quinn eyed his wife's slender shape with appreciation.

Maybe he had been too hard on her. Her life had been different from his and she could not know how regal Sayerne was, even in its current state, compared to the other places he had bedded down these past years.

And it was only fair for a woman to have doubts when there were so many changes made quickly after her nuptials, especially when those nuptials had been unexpected, as well. He could forget her outburst in light of that, but was not certain she was prepared to do the same. He gained no clues from her manner, which did not reassure him.

Quinn resolved that she would not regret his choice that they remain here.

"You have worked hard," he said with genuine appreciation, heartened when Melissande granted him a smile. Bayard lingered behind Quinn like an ungainly shadow and he wondered what had taken possession of the usually charismatic man. The knight was rapidly becoming annoying, particularly in the company of these women.

"The boys have helped a great deal," Melissande acknowledged. "But we only tried to make adequate space for the night."

"The place looks transformed."

Melissande laughed. "My lord, you are too quickly impressed." Quinn glanced to her, uncertain whether she teased or mocked him, and was reassured by her mischievous smile.

"Better that than a taskmaster never satisfied. What did Tulley send for our meal?"

"Simple fare. Bread and cheese, a good quantity of wine and some cold meat."

Quinn grinned. "Simple fare suits me."

"As it does me," Bayard added from behind him. Apparently he had merely been waiting for an appropriate opening to the conversation. "Especially if the company should be fair."

"There is plenty of food for all this night," Melissande said.

When she said nothing else, Quinn dared to hope that she had abandoned her earlier doubts.

Emboldened, he called the squires to him. "Before we eat, what say we make arrangements for the night? You know that I would prefer you boys to stay in the stables with the beasts, so take adequate blankets there now. The lady and I will remain before the hearth."

Quinn held his breath, but no reprimand came. Could she be amenable to his plans? Did he dare to hope that they might make another attempt to conceive this night? He had told her he desired to couple daily, but never had Quinn imagined that Melissande would so readily comply.

But her face showed no protest.

"I think that we should bed down with the steeds, as well, my lord," one of the knights suggested.

"Good sense does that make," Quinn agreed quickly, not in the least averse to having his lady to himself. The squires nodded and departed with a load of blankets before Melissande's quiet voice broke into Quinn's thoughts.

"I must insist that Bayard sleep in the stables, as well." Quinn was so surprised that she did not protest the arrangements for themselves, that he did not immediately understand.

She smiled with a softness that disarmed him. "It would be inappropriate for Berthe to be compelled to share close quarters with a man," she chided. Her glance was filled with import and Quinn knew she had noticed Bayard's amorous pursuit, as well.

"Ah. Ah, yes." Quinn felt a fool for not thinking of such formalities himself. He had spent too long in the company of men alone. "Bayard, the lady's request is my own."

Bayard frowned for an instant before he smiled amiably. "But I would not have Berthe be chilled on this night," he protested with all his usual smooth charm.

His engaging manner was completely lost on Berthe.

"Chilled?" She leapt to her feet and swatted him across the shoulder. Bayard yelped as he jumped. "As though the likes of you would ever care whether a lady would be chilled! It is your own comfort you consider and nothing else."

She swatted him again and Bayard stumbled beneath her assault as Quinn winced sympathetically. "And what manner of man are you to assume that I would be the kind of woman who might readily agree to such nonsense? I was well raised and any man with an eye in his head ought to be able to see it.''

"I merely thought..." Bayard tried to protest, to no avail. Quinn glanced to Melissande to find her smothering a smile. Their eyes met for a moment and his own lips quirked as he realized their response was much the same.

It was as though they shared a secret. The words spoken earlier in anger were forgotten in the intimacy of this moment.

Berthe landed another strike on Bayard. Although Quinn could not imagine that the knight was hurt, being so much taller than her, Bayard still backed warily away. He even held an arm up as though to protect himself.

Quinn barely restrained himself from laughing aloud to see the knight defending himself against a slip of a woman.

"Think?" Berthe demanded. "Ha! You would not know the meaning of that should you trip over it in the bailey. *I* have morals." Berthe punctuated each "I" with a swat, slowly but surely backing Bayard toward the door. "*I* have values. *I* am not some scullery wench or worse, some tavern whore, ready and willing to welcome you between my thighs."

They slipped through the heavy wood doors, Berthe's voice still carrying to their ears. "*My* chastity is a gift to be granted to the man who places a ring upon my finger alone, and you, sir, would do well to recall that simple fact."

Quinn looked to Melissande, unable to quell an impish grin. "If I didn't know better, I might conclude that she liked him," he said.

Melissande chuckled. "And you would not be far wrong," she agreed readily.

Quinn could only take her response as encouragement. "Really?"

Melissande shook her head. "Those she cares for most are the ones who gain her longest tirades." She shrugged and her lips twisted with mirth as her dancing green eyes met his gaze. "Bayard has been granted the longest lectures I have yet heard."

Quinn chuckled as he settled himself at his wife's feet. Did he dare hope that his meager charm was appealing to her? "And he has been persistent in this pursuit."

"Is her regard for him returned?" There was a trace of concern in Melissande's voice that touched Quinn's heart. Not every lady would be concerned for the tender feelings of her maid.

He reached up and took her hand, encouraged that she did not pull away. "Bayard has a good heart, although it is securely hidden beneath his light manner." He turned his wife's hand within his own, marveling at the softness of her skin. "I suspect that he is quite smitten with Berthe."

Quinn glanced up in time to see Melissande smile. It was a bewitching sight, especially when she noted his attention and flushed slightly.

Things seemed to be proceeding quite well.

Maybe Quinn had not been wrong to hope for the outcome of this evening. Quinn's heart took an ungainly leap as he endeavored to keep his voice level.

He must find something else to talk about. Somehow he must keep the conversation flowing between them.

"Would you care to try Tulley's wine?" Quinn invited abruptly, not knowing what else to say.

Melissande nodded. "Yes, I would."

"As would I."

Although reluctant to release her hand for even a moment, Quinn did so and delved into the pack. He removed a pair of goblets with an exclamation of victory that made the lady laugh lightly. A moment later he had retrieved a wineskin and filled both goblets with the ruddy brew.

"To new beginnings," he toasted impetuously, feeling quite flushed with the possibilities himself. Melissande said nothing but laid her hand upon his as she lifted the goblet to her lips.

Quinn could not believe his fortune and heartily wished that Berthe and Bayard would not return soon.

They sat silently for a few moments and sipped as they stared into the flames. Quinn cleared his throat, knowing he had a question to ask her. He wanted to understand how she thought. He wanted to know everything about her and decided the place he would most like to begin.

"You are as protective of the welfare of your maid as that of Annossy," he observed carefully. "Are you always so protective of what you hold dear?"

Melissande swallowed, her gaze snared by his own. She stared helplessly back at Quinn as though he had seen something within her that she hoped none might glimpse.

That he had seen into her secret heart was no small thing and Quinn treasured the moment.

Melissande nodded silently before her gaze dropped to her goblet once more.

Anxious to reassure her that she could trust him with this confidence, Quinn leaned forward and covered her hand with his. Still she did not look up.

"What must I do to enter those ranks?" he murmured.

Melissande's lips parted in surprise as she looked to him again. Uncertainty lingered in her eyes and Quinn wanted nothing more than to dismiss her doubts.

"I would have you defend me as you defend them," he whispered with all sincerity. "I would have my wife hold me in such steadfast regard."

Melissande shook her head in what might have been wonderment or confusion. "I do not know," she said finally, though her voice was strained. "I do not know how it happens, only that it does."

Quinn leaned closer and he could smell the perfumed heat of her skin. He licked his lips before he spoke, knowing the risk of what he asked. "Do you have any objections to my trying to gain your regard?"

His words hung between them. Her eyes widened in surprise and Quinn could see the flecks of gold that the firelight made dance within the green.

An eternity later, she shook her head hastily, then averted her gaze as Quinn's heart pounded in his ears.

No objections. She was prepared to consider abandoning the man who held her heart and her broken pledge.

It was more, far more, than Quinn had expected.

He studied his wife's profile for a long moment, taking strength from the fact that she had not immediately denied him. It was beyond brave of her to even acknowledge that she might be able to love after the loss of this Arnaud who had so thoroughly captured her heart.

And Quinn would not steer her false. This he knew without doubt. He would earn Melissande's love. Just as he would rebuild Sayerne.

"Then I shall do so, my lady," he whispered in the darkness. "And you shall not regret it."

Still Melissande did not look to him, but Quinn saw the single tear trace a path down her cheek. It was a tear for love lost and Quinn knew it, just as he knew he wanted to gather her close.

"I wish," she said unevenly, "that matters might have been different for us."

Quinn swallowed. He ached to ask her for details about this Arnaud, to know what manner of man had captured her heart, to know why she was so certain he would not take vengeance upon Quinn. Was Arnaud dead? Had he not returned from a Crusade? Had his loss filled her with an ache inside?

Quinn did not know. He wanted to have Melissande's confidence, to know her thoughts, to feel free to touch her as they sat companionably like this.

But it was too soon. And he would not risk losing her over

his own impatience. This was a lady well worth the contest and Quinn would not readily abandon this field.

She had granted him encouragement. On this night, that was all he needed to trust in the allure of his own charm.

Chapter Eight

Quinn had not counted on his wife's own charm having its effect upon him.

They sat together long after the men had retired to the stables and Berthe had chosen to sleep in a nook nestled against the back side of the fireplace. They said nothing for the longest time, but their hands remained entwined as they stared into the flames.

"I must leave for a moment," Melissande said suddenly.

"But why?" Quinn glanced up to find her cheeks stained pink. Her gaze flicked demurely away and he chuckled under his breath in understanding. "Make sure you hurry back," he urged, and her color deepened as she rose. She nodded, looked directly into his eyes, then stumbled.

"Whoops!"

Quinn reached up to grasp her hand. Melissande smiled as she clutched his fingers and regained her balance. He noted how the wine had stained her lips more red than usual. She frowned as though having difficulty putting her words together.

"You have an uneven floor here at Sayerne," she said.

Quinn stifled a smile that the wine was troubling her so and endeavored to appear serious. "That will be the first task of repair," he assured her solemnly.

Melissande smiled again then eyed the distance to the garderobe.

"Do you need my assistance?" he asked but Melissande shook her head.

"No," she said simply before taking a deep breath and launching on a crooked path in that direction.

Quinn watched her progress with a careful eye, not in the least convinced that he would not be required to intervene. His lady seemed most vulnerable to wine's influence and in the future he would take care with how much she was granted.

Although the result was certainly a much softer Melissande.

The fire crackled amiably in the hearth as it settled to glowing coals. Quinn extinguished the candles to save them for another time, and the hall was cast into shadow. Only this corner was lit and for all the hall's size, it appeared no more than a cozy room by a trick of the light.

Quinn laid blankets before the hearth where the flagstones had gained some warmth. The thought of nestling close to Melissande warmed him through and through. He noted that his fingers were less adept than usual at his task and acknowledged the nervousness rising within him.

Would Melissande let him touch her again?

"Oops!"

Quinn's heart lurched as the lady in question tripped on the threshold of the room on her return. She stifled a giggle and glanced to him guiltily, as though wondering whether he had seen her misstep. When she caught his eye, her smile broadened into a mischievous grin and Quinn knew his heart had been thoroughly captured.

Melissande had enchanted him.

He strode toward her, liking the way her eyes widened at his approach. He stopped before her and propped his hands on his hips, noting that she clung to the edge of the door leading to the garderobe. "It seems to me, my lady, that you are unfit for walking."

Melissande flushed slightly as she chuckled. "The task is considerably more difficult than I recall," she acknowledged. "It must be this ill-fitted floor."

Nothing was wrong with the floor and Quinn saw now that she knew it, as well. Her eyes sparkled with mischief and Quinn could not help but tease her. He guessed that she wanted his aid to cross the floor but didn't want to ask for it.

He pretended to be stern. "Are you feeling the wine?"

Melissande feigned surprise. "The wine? No, these cursedly crooked floors of Sayerne are tripping me up."

Quinn chuckled himself. "Ah, but that could not be the result of the wine?"

"No!" Melissande lifted her fingers to her lips in a playfully shocked manner. "That was *wine* you served me? You knave!"

She aimed a swat at his shoulder and missed. Her swing threw her off balance. She gasped as she spun awkwardly, then laughed when she dropped soundly to her rump.

Undeterred, she shook a finger up at Quinn. "Knave. Trying to seduce me with your wine."

Quinn's lips twisted as he squatted down beside her. "But what did you think you were drinking?"

He had her there. Quinn watched with amusement as she thought furiously, then folded her arms across her chest. "I thought that you tempted me with some delicacy from the East. The juice of pomegranates, or some such. Is that not red?"

"I don't know," Quinn admitted. "I never tasted any."

"But you were there."

Quinn shook his head. "It was not a voyage of leisure, my lady," he said sadly, recalling only too well the horrors he had seen there.

He thought of the many young men so filled with optimism on the route to the East who never would see home again. He thought of dust and heat and flies. He thought of those long days and nights that Bayard had tended him while his mind had wandered in the darkness.

"No." Her hand landed on his knee and Quinn looked down to find her gaze sharpened. "It must not have been."

She did not even know the understatement that she made.

Quinn looked to his wife, with her wide green eyes so full of innocence. His gaze danced over her hair, softer and finer than anything he had seen for years.

He realized two things in that instant. First, that he was beyond fortunate to be home, to be blessed with a wife and on the path of being granted his legacy. To have roots was no small thing.

Second, he knew that he wanted to protect this woman from knowing about the evil he had seen. The world could be a terrible place, but Quinn wanted to keep Melissande precisely as naive of its horrors as she was in this moment.

Their gazes held for a long moment, and he wondered if she guessed anything of what he thought. Then Quinn bent down, unable to think upon it anymore, and scooped Melissande into his arms.

"Let us talk of sweeter things this night," he suggested.

She smiled and twined her arms around his neck, kicking her feet like a young girl. "Hmm. What shall we talk about? Maybe your secret motive in pouring me such a goodly quantity of wine?"

"Me?" Quinn acted insulted. "It was only my lady's desire for wine that I attempted to satisfy." He glanced around the hearth with mock concern. "But sadly, there was not enough to please her desire."

"You!" Melissande poked him in the chest. "It was you who drank it all and left none for me!"

"Me?"

"Yes, you! And you will not convince me that you did not have a scheme in mind." She grasped his ear and gave it a short tug. Quinn winced, as he was certain was expected. Melissande chuckled. "Now, confess," she whispered.

Quinn rolled his eyes as though making a great concession. "Well . . ." he began.

"Tell me, tell me, tell me."

He bounced her weight in his arms as he stood before the hearth, liking the way she smiled up at him. "Truthfully, I did have a small goal in mind."

"Aha!" Her eyes flashed with victory. "Confess your devious objective!"

Quinn sighed. "I hoped for one kiss so that I might be lulled to sweet dreams."

"A kiss." Melissande folded her arms across her chest and pursed her lips as though weighing a request of great magnitude. The twinkle of her eyes gave away her true mood, however. "And you thought that I would bestow such a kiss willingly upon you?"

Quinn shrugged. "A man can only hope for as much from his wife."

To his astonishment, Melissande threw her arms around his neck and pressed herself against him. He could feel her heartbeat crushed against his own and taste her breath on his lips. "Truly," she said in a low voice, "I should think a man could expect more from his wife."

Quinn blinked uncomprehendingly once before his wife stretched to touch her lips to his.

She was as soft and warm as he recalled, the taste of the wine heady on her tongue. She gripped the back of his neck and urged him closer so demandingly that Quinn was dizzy.

He had never imagined that *she* might initiate their embrace. Quinn refused to question his good fortune as desire roared to life within him.

He dropped to his knees on the blankets he had laid out. Quinn hesitated for a heartbeat as he laid Melissande on the wool, afraid that she would spurn him even now.

Instead she smiled softly at him and, holding his gaze resolutely, unlaced the sides of her kirtle. He saw in her eyes that she knew the import of what she did, but her fingers did not falter.

It could only be a good sign for their future together and Quinn, willingly, shed his own garments beneath her watchful gaze.

Would she truly let him touch her?

Quinn felt suddenly awkward and hesitated, but Melissande merely took his hand in hers, laying it then upon her shoulder. She urged his hand to push her kirtle away, baring her sheer chemise to his gaze. Quinn swallowed at the sight. The firelight lovingly outlined the silhouette of her breast through the sheer fabric and Quinn could not look away.

"Surely you have not forgotten our bargain, husband?"

Quinn swallowed. "But this morning..."

"Now it is past the witching hour, though, and tomorrow might be busy." His wife smiled a seductive smile and Quinn was overwhelmed by his good fortune. He had never imagined that such a beautiful bride would be his own.

When she reached up to frame his face in her hands and drew him down for another kiss, Quinn knew he was lost.

It was long hours later that he dozed with Melissande nestled against his side, satisfied and sated as never he had been before. Quinn felt her fingers meandering over his chest and smiled, secure in the knowledge that he was a good way along the path of dismissing that other intruder from his wife's heart.

Victory would seem to be in the wind.

She traced the outline of his scar and Quinn instinctively stiffened.

"Does it hurt?" Her tone was laced with concern.

Quinn shook his head. "Only the knowledge that it is there and the recollection that it prompts." He did not need to look to know that she was watching him. Quinn kept his eyes closed, hoping she would drop the subject.

But Melissande pressed onward.

"What recollection?" she asked softly.

Quinn frowned and tried to pull her closer against his side that she might sleep. Melissande resisted, and propped herself up on one elbow to regard him. He could guess that her hair was spilling over them both—he imagined that he could feel its softness on his own bare shoulder—but he would not look and be weakened by the sight.

"That is not a tale that a lady should hear," he said, hearing the gruffness in his voice.

"Why?"

Quinn swallowed, then opened his eyes. Melissande's gaze was bright with curiosity, as he had known it would be. Her lips were slightly swollen from his kisses, her hair was unfurled and there was a softness about her that made him want to comply with her request.

"I would spare you such sordid tales. It is too different from the life you know here."

Melissande dropped one fingertip to his lips and traced their shape in a most disconcerting way. "I would know about your scar," she urged. "I suspect from its size that the wound was deep. Surely there is a tale of valor to be heard in your survival."

Her lashes swept over her cheeks, which tinged with pink before she continued. "I would know the tale, then sample that valiant warrior yet again before I sleep."

Quinn caught his breath, then forced himself to be dismissive. "If there is a tale of valor here, it is not the tale of my own."

Melissande smiled anew. "You are overly modest," she accused gently, matching the words with a tap on the end of his nose. Quinn smiled in turn before her gaze locked with his again. "Tell me," she urged. "Please."

He could not deny her after the intimacy they had just shared. Quinn frowned into the shadows above as he chose which parts of the story to tell. He folded his hands behind his head, his memories making the past come to life for him again.

"Seven years past, I answered the call to the Crusade," he began slowly. He flicked a glance to an attentive Melissande and shrugged helplessly, trying one last time to avoid telling her this. "I do not know where to begin."

"Tell me how you gained the wound."

Quinn sighed and settled back against the blanket. "It happened in battle long after Jerusalem was taken, although we fought so many times in so many places that I do not even recall the name of the fortress. Maybe I never knew its name." He frowned again. "It does not matter. The fortress was held by the Muslims and our commanders decided we should storm its gates and take possession.

"That was something we had done before, with a relatively good record of success. All were agreeable to the idea and plans were made."

Quinn paused to clear his throat, the smell of the dust before those gates in his nostrils once again. He smelled the fear of the horses mingled with the scent of their sweat. He heard the young men who would never ride home again cry out for the last time.

When he spoke, his voice faltered. "But the attack was a failure."

Quinn closed his eyes against the remembered screams. Horror unfolded anew in his stomach at even the recollection of the barrels of hot oil being dumped on the invaders. They were so far ahead of him and it seemed the oil flowed down at the speed of molasses in winter.

It had all happened in achingly slow motion, but he had been powerless to intervene. Men he knew, men he had fought with, had disappeared beneath the gleaming morass and there had been nothing he could do.

His recollection was so vivid that the very same sight seemed before him again.

Quinn could smell their skin burning. He saw the flashing curved blades of the surrounding army that surprised them from the rear. He heard the horses bolt and men scream for mercy as the circle of their opponents tightened and forced them ever closer to the spilling oil.

He swallowed with an effort, recalling that his wife awaited his tale. "We were surprised from the rear," he heard himself saying, his voice as dispassionate and distant as though it came from another.

"But surely there were sentries," Melissande asked. Quinn gripped her shoulder, appreciating her understanding of warfare.

His lips thinned with the recollection, though, and when he spoke, his voice was tight. "We were betrayed."

Melissande gasped, her outrage but a faint shadow of his own. "Surely not?"

"Yes," Quinn said grimly.

"But who would do such a thing?"

"One with no soul or conscience. One of our very own."

"No!"

Quinn nodded once before his wife's amazement.

"How could they?"

"I do not know." He paused, struggling once more with the certainty that someone had set the ambush in motion against those of his own kind.

"Did you know who it was?"

"They told us later." Quinn blinked. "I understand he did not live long after that battle. It was said he was set upon by bandits when he rode alone one day, but I suspect some survivor of that day took his own due."

He paused and cleared his throat, knowing how hard his tone would become when he spoke again. "And rightly so.

Betrayal is a crime of the worst order. There is no punishment foul enough to counter the deed."

Quinn fancied that his wife fidgeted in that moment, but then Melissande's hand touched his gently.

"The battle was bad?" she asked, her voice filled with a soft concern that undermined his determination to be strong in the telling.

He felt his tears rise and fought them desperately. She must not see him so weakened.

Quinn looked away, willing the vision of his memory to leave him be. "We were surrounded," he murmured. "Although we fought valiantly, all of us were either captured or killed."

Melissande touched the scar again and Quinn felt as though it burned his flesh, so great was his guilt that he had been one of the few to survive. "That was where you were wounded?"

"Yes. I imagine they thought me dead at first, but I was not. Bayard was wounded, as well, and when they imprisoned him, he insisted that they take me along." Quinn closed his eyes. "They probably thought him mad to take a corpse."

"You were imprisoned?" There was an awe in Melissande's voice that would have turned to horror had she known the fullness of what Quinn had experienced. He resolutely ignored his hazy recollections of that fetid cell.

"Yes, and I suspect that was much the same as most prisoners face." He endeavored to keep his voice matter-of-fact, knowing that the opposite was the truth.

"At least you were with Bayard."

"Yes." He turned and looked into Melissande's eyes. She was so soft, so innocent of such ugliness, that his heart twisted. He had to protect her, he had to reassure her.

He had to make her understand about Bayard. "And that is how I know his heart is true," Quinn said, his voice hoarse in the darkness. "That man even had the chance to be released once his wound was healed, but he refused. Instead he chose to remain with me, not knowing whether we would later be permitted to leave or not."

Her green eyes were sober. "You were badly wounded."

Quinn turned away from her perceptiveness without answering. "It is to Bayard, twice over, to whom I owe my life."

He lay very still in the darkness but Melissande did not move. He could not guess what she was thinking. Quinn cleared his throat again.

"And this place," he said, feeling his tears rise but powerless to stop them. "Sayerne." He had to tell her the rest now that he had begun.

"I kept the memory of Sayerne bright in my mind. It was a talisman of where I might go if I survived. The memory of its beauty gave me strength."

"Then I can understand why Sayerne is important to you," she whispered.

Quinn could not look to her as he felt the warm salt of a tear make a path over his cheek. "Yes."

He took a deep, shaky breath before he continued. "Tulley's man found me at Ascalon, shortly after I had been released. Bayard and I made our way home as quickly as we could once we had heard the news. It seemed impossible that Sayerne could be mine so shortly after our release, especially when I had thought about it so much."

Now she knew as much of the tale as Quinn was prepared to grant her. He waited for her condemnation, her outrage, her judgment, but she did not say a word.

Instead she leaned over him, her hair pooling on his chest like silk and her fingers light on his flesh. "I think that is indeed a tale of valor," she whispered. "And not one of Bayard's bravery alone."

With that, she kissed him on the lips again. Quinn's tears broke over his cheeks and he gathered her close, savoring the perfume of her skin and the warmth of her slight weight across his chest. He buried his face in her hair to make his final confession.

"No one knows that tale but Bayard and I," he whispered.

"And no one else shall," Melissande assured him softly. "Thank you for telling me."

And her lips were on his again, tempting him to forget the past and look only to the future. Quinn's heart swelled fit to burst as he clasped his bride in his arms. A new determination to lose himself in her sweet compassion flooded through him and he did not care whether he slept even a wink before the dawn.

Melissande had underestimated the effect of the wine.

Or maybe it was the effect of Quinn she had underestimated. She slanted a glance to the man sleeping soundly beside her and she almost smiled. His hair was tousled and a small smile played upon his lips.

She ached with satisfaction from his loving.

Curse him for swaying her conviction so! Curse him for being so endearing. Curse him for asking how to win her affection. She gazed down at his sleeping features and her heart twisted.

Curse him for confiding in her.

Melissande never imagined that she would have doubts about her decision to flee to Annossy, but with one simple tale, Quinn had filled her with uncertainty.

It was no small thing to entrust another with a tale of such pain. Melissande did not doubt that Quinn had told no one else. She guessed that he had not even told her half of what he had seen. His voice had been too grim and the pauses had been too long between his words.

She suspected that he had tried to protect her from the foulness he had seen. That gesture and the thoughtfulness behind it made her wonder whether he really could be the same as his father.

If he was as he appeared, Melissande knew that she could have lost her heart to a man like Quinn, if their circumstances had been different.

Melissande reached out and stroked a chestnut curl back from his brow before she realized what she was doing. She stared at her hand, amazed that she had touched him with such affection.

Another glance to his face and her resolve to leave him faltered. Wouldn't fleeing to Annossy, especially after he trusted her with that story, be a betrayal?

Melissande's stomach churned with the certainty that Quinn would see the matter that way. She could not willfully hurt him.

She looked away and gazed about the deserted keep. But the conditions here were primitive, the task impossible. She had no certainty that Quinn's enthusiasm would waver enough to let him see the truth. She could not risk jeopardizing the security of Annossy.

But would it be so terrible to remain here with him? Melissande never anticipated the doubt that assailed her, making her reluctant to slide away from her husband's side.

The door creaked suddenly and Melissande instinctively huddled beneath the blankets.

She eyed the widening sliver of light and knew her eyes did not deceive her. Someone entered the hall! Should she awaken Quinn? Her heart pounded in her ears as she pressed against him, willing him to awaken by himself.

The door creaked again as it was closed, then a voice whispered in the darkness. Melissande could see nothing, but knew the intruder must be able to hear her thundering pulse.

Why did Quinn not wake up?

"Berthe?"

It was Bayard. Melissande exhaled unsteadily in her relief and rolled to her back, closing her eyes as the tension flooded out of her.

Indignation quickly replaced her relief. What kind of knave came to a woman in the middle of the night?

"Bayard?" Berthe demanded in a hoarse whisper from the adjoining room. "Is that you?"

"Yes." He walked cautiously a little farther into the room and Melissande watched his shadow progress with interest.

Berthe snorted and Melissande saw her silhouette appear in the doorway to the other room.

"Berthe!" Bayard declared, and his shadow approached Berthe's shadow with haste. "I could not sleep," he confided in a low tone that Melissande could still hear. "I was thinking of you and was concerned that you might be cold huddled alone before the hearth in this place."

Berthe's hand snapped out. Melissande guessed by the movement of the shadow and Bayard's smothered yelp of pain that the maid had grasped his ear again. Melissande stifled a giggle as Berthe launched into a hushed tirade.

"You! How could you think such a thing? You worry about nothing but your own sweet pleasure and I told you already that I am an honorable woman."

"You will awaken them," Bayard protested, to no avail.

"No, you will have awakened them with your inopportune visit. And maybe it would be a good thing if they did awaken and my lady might see the manner of mischief you try to make while her gaze is averted. I imagine the punishment she might measure out for you."

"Punishment? What punishment is more painful for a man who has lost his heart than to have his lady love deny him?"

"Lost his heart," Berthe scoffed. "I doubt that you even have a heart, for I know it is not that part of you which brings you here tonight."

"Berthe!" Bayard's tone was pained, though whether that was due to the maid's grip on his ear or his injured pride, Melissande could not say. "How can you say such a thing about me? I want only to court your favor."

"In the midst of the night? In the dark? No, Bayard, you plan only to steal my chastity away and leave me with nothing! Take your silver tongue away before I awaken my lady and tell her of your deeds."

"But..."

"But nothing." Berthe's shadow moved and Bayard made another sound of pain. "I bid you leave me be immediately."

Berthe snapped her wrist and the released Bayard shuffled to the door under her watchful gaze. "Your judgment is harsh," he said, "and most undeserved. If you would grant me just one opportunity, I shall prove your conclusions wrong."

Berthe sniffed. "I shall consider the matter."

Bayard bowed, perhaps sensing accurately that he could make no better case for himself at this time. "Then I bid you good-night," he said, and ducked back into the night.

Berthe clucked her tongue and shook her head. "Charming rogue," she mused. Once again, Melissande heard affection in the other woman's tone. "How much longer can I resist him?" The whispered question fed Melissande's protectiveness.

Despite Quinn's assurances, Melissande had no doubt that Bayard would abandon Berthe as soon as he had what he desired. Loyalty to a companion knight was different from loyalty to a woman, especially when one was on familiar turf.

And what of Quinn?

Melissande looked to her sleeping husband, uncertain what to think. How similar were these two men? And how bent on their personal objectives were they to the exclusion of everything else?

Quinn had confided in her and softened her heart, but had that been merely a trick to gain her trust? Melissande's lips pursed with indecision.

Had he not said that Sayerne was important to him above all? And did he need Melissande—or at least the child she could bear him—in order to ensure his legacy? If Melissande left and did not grant Quinn that heir, he would lose all that he confessed to hold dear.

She could see that he might go far to make sure that did not occur.

Hadn't everything these past days been about conception of that child? The bargain was about that, as were Quinn's sweetly seducing kisses. The telling of his tale had resulted in lovemaking. Melissande fidgeted as she admitted that that was necessary to the conception of the heir Quinn desired.

Was he as self-serving as his father? She could not say.

It would not be difficult to make the argument that she, too, was being charmed in a most calculated matter. Quinn wanted Sayerne, at all costs. He had said as much himself.

Melissande sat up hastily, suddenly convinced that Quinn's tale had been deliberately told. She wondered if it was even the truth or whether it was a lie contrived to win her sympathy.

Melissande rose abruptly and dressed with jerking hands, sparing a glower for her sleeping spouse. How dare he manipulate her so? How dare he want her for no more than her womb?

Well. She would show him that she was not so easily made biddable. She *would* flee to Annossy. And she would convince Berthe to accompany her—for the sake of that woman's honor.

Melissande would see to it that Quinn could not follow her. She would see the gates of Annossy barred against him. If he was so enchanted with this hole of Sayerne, he could rot here.

Alone.

* * *

The moon was bright overhead when the two women had made their plan. After much convincing, Berthe finally agreed to help Melissande. They slipped out into the courtyard, leaving Quinn sleeping contentedly before the hearth, and Melissande did not let herself look back. They clung to the shadows as they made their way across the bailey, uncertain who might be awake and watching.

Melissande hung back as her coconspirator peered into the darkness of the stables. Her heart thudded in her chest, but Berthe appeared remarkably calm.

"Bayard?" she whispered sweetly.

There was a rustle of straw within, then the pale oval of the knight's face appeared in the opening. It was almost comical how disheveled he looked. To his credit, Bayard appeared quite astonished. "Berthe?"

"Yes, of course." The maid leaned closer and whispered hastily, sparing a few sharp glances over her shoulder as though she feared being followed. "I have been thinking since you left and I have decided to give you a chance." Bayard's brows rose and he opened his mouth, but Berthe raised a cautionary finger. "Say nothing. We must hurry if we are to have a few moments to ourselves and still return before our absence is noted."

"Absence? But why not remain here?"

"No, no, no." Her tone was curtly dismissive and Melissande smothered a smile at how naturally Berthe coaxed Bayard back to the path of their plan. "I would have you all to myself."

"I cannot argue with that." Bayard straightened proudly and flicked a worried glance across the bailey to the hall. He was unconsciously adopting Berthe's attitude of secrecy. The plan was working better than Melissande had hoped.

The maid continued in a hushed voice. "I think we should ride a little beyond the walls—the village is deserted, after all—where we can talk without interruption. We could find a little cottage out of the wind and share some privacy. What do you think?'' Her voice turned pleading in a very feminine and decidedly uncharacteristic manner. ''Could you saddle a pair of steeds while I get a blanket and some wine? We could meet at the gate house.''

Bayard hesitated, but Berthe reached out and ran a finger over his cheek. ''I would hear you argue your worthiness,'' she whispered fervently, then planted a quick kiss across his lips.

''I shall do it!'' Bayard declared. ''Give me but a moment and mind you stay out of sight. I would not want anyone to cast a shadow on your reputation over this.''

''And I shall be waiting for you,'' Berthe murmured, her voice low with a promise that sent Bayard scurrying back into the stables.

She turned to face the place where Melissande was hiding and smiled victoriously. Melissande smiled in return, although they were only half-done. They hastened together toward the gate, the muted sounds of the horses' trap carrying to Melissande's excited ears.

How she hoped no one else heard Bayard at his task. She could not risk awakening the knights, because one would surely insist on advising Quinn of what she did. Melissande was certain that she and Berthe could get to Annossy safely on their own.

As long as Bayard brought them the horses.

''That fool of a man,'' Berthe muttered. Whatever trust she had had in Bayard had apparently dissolved with his ready acceptance of her suggestion. ''How could he believe that I would change my mind and even *suggest* such an assignation? He sees no further than his own desire, for anyone who knew anything about me would not so readily believe I would do such a thing. I was a fool to believe he might think otherwise. You were right, my lady. It is best that I leave.''

"Maybe he just hopes," Melissande suggested. "Or thinks his charm irresistible."

"Ha!" Berthe snorted. "I shall show him how irresistible he is. The knave! I will help in barring the gate of Annossy against him myself."

It was not long before Melissande heard the horses. She saw their silhouettes, two palfreys with Bayard striding between. As he approached the gate house, Berthe stepped out and Melissande saw the flash of Bayard's smile.

"You changed your mind just as I knew you would," he mused with satisfaction.

"Yes and I have changed it again," Berthe retorted. "I will take the horses now and you will return to the stables."

"What?" Bayard looked understandably confused.

Melissande realized that this part of the plan had needed slightly more work. She stepped forward to add her voice for it was imperative Bayard be convinced to release the horses before he raised his voice.

Bayard saw her, his gaze dancing over the riding cloak about her shoulders before his mouth tightened. "You mean to leave him!" he accused hotly.

Now Melissande saw that this particular part of the plan had serious flaws. What would they do now?

Bayard stepped forward and raised an indignant finger. He meant to stop them! "Surely you realize..." he began in outrage, before he suddenly gasped aloud.

Too late, Melissande saw the horse leavings on the cobblestones. They were not yet frozen from earlier in the day and Bayard had stepped squarely into them. His feet flew out from under him with alarming speed. He swore viciously. Berthe gasped.

Then Bayard thunked his head on the stones and fell ominously silent.

"Oh no!" Berthe gasped.

The horses nickered to each other and one snuffled the silent knight's hair as the women stared at each other in horror.

"I never dreamed..." Melissande breathed, but Berthe was already on her knees beside Bayard. The maid ran her hands over his face and he murmured something.

"I am so sorry, Bayard," Berthe whispered. "I should never have deceived you. It was not supposed to work out this way."

Melissande crouched beside her maid. "At least he stirs," she whispered. Her fingers slipped into his hair and she felt the lump rapidly rising on the back of his head.

"What if he does not wake up? What have I done?" The women's eyes met again and Melissande saw Berthe's fear.

"I think he will be fine," Melissande assured her. "He still breathes regularly and the lump is not that bad. A headache, maybe, will be the worst of it."

Berthe's lips worked silently for a moment. "Bless fortune for granting him a head as hard as a rock." Melissande noticed that her voice was less strident than usual.

Bayard stirred again and both women looked to him in alarm.

"What if he awakens now?" Melissande demanded.

"What if he tells my lord of your plan?" Berthe whispered urgently. "My lord Quinn will be furious. He will pursue you and you will never reach Annossy."

Melissande pushed to her feet, her heart still pounding with uncertainty. So close and yet so far. "We must go this very moment, while we yet can."

To her surprise, Berthe shook her head, her hands still on Bayard's face. "I cannot leave him like this." She cleared her throat, then looked back to her lady. "You go," she urged. "Go now while yet you can. I will keep him from telling your lord for as long as I can."

"I cannot leave you," Melissande said.

Berthe shook her head. "Go. I will be fine." When Melissande yet hesitated, her voice turned pleading. "You must go, my lady. I beg of you. You must get away from your lord before his seed is planted within you." She granted a glance to Bayard and her voice lowered with determination. "I can deal with this one alone. Do not worry about me."

Melissande's decision was made in that moment and she reached for one horse's reins. "I will send for you," she promised.

"I know. Now flee while you can." Berthe frowned and flicked a glance to the stables. "You should awaken one of the knights to go with you."

"No. They will tell Quinn. Annossy is not far." Melissande summoned a brave smile for her maid. "I know the way back to the main road and from there to Annossy. I will be fine."

Berthe bit her lip, then nodded. "Then go."

Melissande did precisely that.

"She did *what?*" Quinn roared when he heard the news.

Berthe had not expected this interview to go well. She had avoided telling the truth for as long as she had been able to, out of loyalty for her lady, but there was no longer any escape. Bayard had awakened and told what he knew. The knight glared at Berthe with red-rimmed eyes while Quinn looked fit to explode.

Berthe lifted her chin. "She has returned to Annossy."

"Alone?" Quinn demanded. The surrounding knights shuffled their feet in consternation.

Berthe swallowed. "Yes."

"You permitted her to leave alone?"

"She insisted upon it, my lord."

Quinn paced a distance, folding his hands behind his back as though he pondered a grave matter.

"And it did not occur to either of you that such a choice might not have been wise?"

Berthe blinked. "We have ridden from Annossy to Tulley without difficulties just several weeks past."

"We!" Quinn bellowed. "*We* is rather different than the lady riding alone! You rode to Tulley with these six knights alongside!" The knights nodded in vigorous agreement. "Could neither of you manage to remember that there are bandits attacking Tulley's periphery estates? Estates like *Annossy?*"

Berthe looked to Bayard for reassurance and found none. "I suppose it was not the best-contrived plan," she conceded. "Although I could not leave once Bayard was injured...."

"Ha! You deliberately tricked me," that man muttered with a dark glance. Berthe fidgeted uncomfortably before she straightened with defiance.

"This was your own fault," she boldly informed Quinn. "You should never have demanded that my lady bear to you a child. Marriage alone must be a challenge to her pride, let alone the insistence that she immediately produce an heir."

Quinn was disarmingly still. "She discussed this with you?"

"Of course not! But I am not without eyes in my head."

"Even if you are without a heart in your breast," Bayard muttered.

Berthe spun on him in outrage. "And a fine one you are to talk! At least I stayed with you, but neither of you give me credit for my compassion. My lady did I leave to ride alone, and you stand here and argue about her welfare without doing anything about it!" She flung out a hand to Quinn. "What manner of man are you that you do not ride to see her safe?"

"I am a man betrayed by one he trusted," Quinn said in a dangerously low voice. "My wife has left me and I can only interpret that as a sign of her disregard."

Berthe was incredulous. "But surely you will ride in pursuit? Surely you will see that she is safe?"

"I have no use for faithless men and women," Quinn said calmly.

"We will ride in pursuit of our lady," one of Annossy's knights declared firmly.

"Fine." Quinn's lips thinned. "I have a message to send to Annossy with one of the squires, and he may accompany you."

With that, he turned away. The knights prepared to leave. Berthe gaped for a moment, before she ran after Quinn and clutched at his sleeve. "But, my lord, she is your wife."

He turned to her and she fancied she saw hurt in his eyes before his expression was shuttered. "No," he said in a flat voice. "She is that no longer. A lady only has to spurn me once to see me gone from her side."

Then Quinn bent to rummage in his saddlebag. He retrieved a sheaf of parchment and a quill, speaking over his shoulder to Bayard as he did so. "Find the boys and have them make ready to ride. One shall ride to Annossy with a missive, the others to the remaining compass points. We have need of villeins to rebuild Sayerne and it is time to see whom we might find."

"Yes, Quinn." Bayard did not even look to Berthe before he turned away. Her heart sank that he had turned against her, but she did not know how to make this come aright.

Quinn flicked a somber glance to Berthe. "You also are welcome to return to Annossy."

Berthe lifted her chin. If she left this night, she and Bayard would probably part for good.

And Berthe had decided that she wanted Bayard. Seeing him hurt had made everything clear to her. She had only one choice then, if she wanted him to soften toward her. "I have already chosen to remain here," she said.

"Spare us your favors," Bayard muttered. Berthe blinked back a tear but resolutely held Quinn's gaze.

He arched a brow and she feared his pronouncement. "Then you shall have to work to earn your keep, as well."

Berthe caught her breath. She had feared much worse from this quietly determined Quinn, but this option gave her at least the hope of regaining Bayard's trust.

"I am not afraid of earning my way." She nodded once quickly. "I shall begin with cleaning out the kitchens."

Chapter Nine

The second dawn showed the smudge of dark smoke of a fire on the horizon. It frightened Melissande, for it was too close to where she knew Annossy lay. The brightening sky did not bring good news. The billows of dark smoke rose so thick and black that Melissande knew the fire had not been put out.

And every step the palfrey took made it more clear that the fire burned close to Annossy. Melissande could not even think the worst, but when they rounded the last curve in the road, the bottom dropped out of her stomach.

It was true. Annossy itself burned.

Melissande's gaze danced assessingly over the damage as she rode closer. For a heartbeat, she let herself wish that she had arrived with Quinn. He would be cool and thoughtful, instead of nervous and frightened as she was. It would have been reassuring to be with someone calm in the face of adversity.

But Quinn was not here. She spent several moments feeling nervous and afraid, sick at heart, but after that passed she knew she could solve this dilemma alone, as she always solved dilemmas alone. She sat tall in the saddle as she rode closer, so that any villein who saw her might be reassured.

The mill burned. The spring wind blew in gusts and made the flames spread unpredictably. The fire must have been set deliberately, but it was clear that any invaders were already gone. Melissande could see no sign of forced entry into the keep.

Everyone was concentrated on putting out the flames. The low, thatched roofs of half a dozen homes in the village were burning. A cluster of small children stood watching with wide eyes. The château was untouched and Melissande breathed a sigh of relief.

"Lady Melissande!" the gatekeeper crowed. Melissande knew she did not imagine the relief in his voice. "But, my lady, why do you travel alone?"

"My circumstance is not important. What has happened here?" Melissande deliberately made her voice crisp, as her father had taught her would command respect. The gatekeeper scurried to open the gate, his words spilling over one another in their haste to be heard.

"They came just before the dawn. We had extra sentries on the walls, at your direction, but were taken by surprise. We heard nothing before the mill began to burn and by that time, the intruders had fled."

Melissande's gaze danced over the damage within the walls surrounding the village. The villeins had formed a line from the river, each passing a bucket to the next. Blackened roofs smoked on either side of the mill. Another flaming roof hissed beneath an onslaught of water as she watched.

"How many were there?" she asked.

The gatekeeper shrugged. "Some think only one."

"No one saw?"

"One sentry was hit on the head. He has yet to awaken. The others were distracted by a cry from before the gates."

"And that cry proved to be . . . ?"

"Nothing, my lady." The keeper looked sheepish. "It was evidently a distraction, but it was too late by the time we realized that."

Melissande nodded. "I would speak with the sentry when he revives."

"Yes, my lady. I shall have him sent to the hall on his awakening."

"Very good."

An older woman from the village glanced up and smiled when she saw Melissande. "The lady has returned!" she cried, and all pivoted to see. "Dame Fortune is with us when the lady is in residence!"

There was a ragged cheer from the villeins as Melissande rode into the small crowd. They closed ranks about her, each confiding some fragment of what they had seen. Melissande clasped hands and touched cheeks, reassuring her tenants as best she was able.

"Have any been injured?" she asked. To her relief, her tenants shook their heads in unison.

"We thought the entire village would burn!"

"They came in the night."

"My lady, when will this stop? Who would do this to us, and why?"

"It is over for now," Melissande said as reassuringly as she could. "You have done fine work in tending the fire so quickly."

"The mill is still burning."

"And so it will," Melissande agreed. "The fire will have reached the timber trapped between the stones by now. That will burn as long as it can. Leave it be, and keep everyone out of the mill. At least the ground is too wet for the flames to spread that way."

"Yes, my lady. It could have been much worse." Annossy's chatelain was at her side. Melissande smiled at the older man who had served her sire before her. Roger was more sensible than most and she appreciated his clear thinking.

"Excellent, Roger. As usual, you have matters well in hand."

He bowed in acknowledgment of her compliment and the sunlight gleamed on his bald pate. "Yes, my lady." He took the reins of her palfrey and led the beast through the press of the crowd to the gates of the château itself.

"But these children," Melissande said as she passed them. "Do they have anywhere to sleep?"

"The roofs on their homes have burned, my lady."

"Then send them to the hall immediately. No reason is there why they cannot help in the kitchens while their homes are repaired."

The children's eyes brightened at the prospect of making the main hall their home and Melissande exchanged a smile with one cute little cherub, her long-lashed eyes a shining blue.

The idea that she and Quinn could produce such a child sent a pang through her. The thought had appeal, more appeal than Melissande was prepared to accept, for she could easily imagine Quinn as an attentive and infinitely patient father.

She stubbornly blinked away her tears, reminding herself she had been charmed by a man who had only his own objectives in mind.

"A wise choice, my lady." Roger snapped his fingers and several of his aides scooped up the children to bear them to the château. "I must apologize for the welcome you have received this day, my lady."

"It does not matter, Roger. There is work to be done before we can sow this spring." Melissande dismounted within the bailey and Roger handed off the steaming palfrey's reins to the waiting ostler. "Nothing else is damaged but the mill?"

"No, my lady. Just the roofs and the mill."

Melissande's lips thinned. "But it is still too much. Have some salvage what they can of these homes. Others can find new thatch for the roofs. We will probably have to send a wagon to Lyons for new millstones if they are too charred to use. We will have to check their condition when the mill stops burning.'' Melissande gazed about herself, in her element again now that she was within these familiar walls.

She thought suddenly of Quinn and wondered whether he would pursue her. And what would he say if he did? What would she say? Melissande could imagine that Quinn would not be pleased with her decision to leave him, let alone her newfound determination not to bear him a child.

''Bar the gate. Let no one enter without my express permission.'' She turned a sharp eye on the chatelain. ''Can the wall be repaired today?''

Roger bowed. ''It shall be done, my lady.''

''Good. We must be prepared for the possibility of more intruders tonight.'' She turned to walk toward the château gates, pausing to pat the palfrey on the snout. ''See that she has some oats,'' Melissande advised the ostler. ''She has run hard for me.''

''Yes, my lady.''

Melissande glanced back to her chatelain. ''And, Roger, please be sure that the sentry is brought to me when he awakens. I would like to hear his tale.''

''Yes, my lady.''

Melissande walked through the crowd of her villeins that had followed them to the bailey.

''Those whose homes are damaged should come to the kitchens for their meals,'' she invited, raising her voice so that Roger could hear her. They exchanged a glance and he bustled away to do her bidding.

The miller was invited to sleep in the hall until the mill was repaired. Melissande shook the hands of men whose faces were streaked with soot and gave her assurance again that the mill would be operational soon.

It was only when she climbed the stairs to her own solar and looked out the window over the damage to Annossy that Melissande wished Quinn might have been here to see her pride and joy. Even damaged as it was, the estate was a fine one.

She told herself that she only thought of him because it would do Quinn good to see a well-run estate—and ignored the fact that Quinn had already seen the prosperous estate of Tulley. Melissande's gaze traced the path of the road, her heart sinking when she saw nothing move along its length.

She straightened her shoulders determinedly. She did not care whether Quinn followed her. She knew what kind of man Quinn was and time away from him would cure her of any whimsical thoughts about him. She had been charmed, but that would not last.

She would argue with Quinn at the gates should he arrive, and forbid him to enter her home. Though Tulley might have promised Quinn the lordship of Annossy in a year, as long as Quinn did not have the seal in his possession, he had no rights here.

If Tulley was going to hold Melissande to the letter of the law and refuse to invest her with her hereditary estate solely because of her gender, then Melissande would play the same game. Quinn only had a promise of being invested with Annossy. Until he was declared the lord by Tulley, she would treat him as an invader.

Maybe Melissande could have her pride, her independence, her Annossy.

And her lonely solitude.

Melissande lifted her chin stubbornly and looked over the men scrambling to repair the outer wall. Soon enough the sun would sink, leaving Annossy vulnerable to attack yet again.

As she watched from the silent solar, Melissande admitted to herself that the prospect of arguing with Quinn seemed flat. She folded her arms across her chest and fought back unexpected tears, not in the least relieved to realize that she would rather make love with him.

Regardless of his ultimate intent.

The man had charmed her more than she had even guessed. It was fortunate that she had put space between them before it had been too late to hold on to her common sense.

Although, in this moment, Melissande felt far from fortunate.

"Why do you not ride to Tulley?" Bayard's question surprised Quinn, since they had worked in silence all the morning. He settled the last stone of the fence in place and doffed his gloves to eye the other knight.

He shrugged. "Why would I bother?"

Bayard snorted. "Do not play games with me, Quinn. Tulley could intervene to see your stubborn wife back by your side. Why not ask for his assistance?"

"It seems much more likely that he would disapprove of me." Quinn frowned as he scanned the fence, making every appearance of being preoccupied with its repair.

He would never admit, even to Bayard, how much Melissande's departure stung. He had trusted her with a tale of his past, a story he had told to no one, and she had abandoned him. She knew how damning he believed betrayal to be.

And her departure was a betrayal. Melissande had walked away not only from Sayerne, but from marriage and from Quinn himself. All that despite his efforts to make something good out of this enforced match.

A faithless woman like that could rot alone at her precious Annossy. Quinn knew he had never met a woman so cold and self-serving.

"Come on," Bayard urged. "Didn't Tulley declare this marriage to be important to him? I think he would intervene."

"Nothing can be done without the cooperation of the lady. A marriage cannot be made single-handedly, even with the insistence of Tulley behind it." Quinn brushed off his chausses and pushed away from the wall. "This fence looks fit to contain the livestock we will buy this spring. We should repair some of the houses, in the hopes that the boys have found some interested villeins.''

Quinn avoided his companion's inquiring gaze and deliberately turned to walk away. It felt good to work with his hands again. And they were already making progress.

He would rebuild alone, if necessary.

"Quinn." Bayard fell into step beside him. Quinn did not look up. "You cannot ignore this matter. You need an heir within the year in order to gain Sayerne. Why work like this when your labor may not be rewarded?''

Quinn slanted his friend a glance. "You have as much faith in me as my departed wife.''

Bayard rolled his eyes. "You are undertaking a lot of work here, as well as spending a princely sum.''

"And now that Berthe and you are no longer cooing at each other, your interest has cooled, as well?'' Quinn asked, unable to keep an edge of bitterness from his voice.

Bayard's hand landed heavily on his shoulder and pulled him to a halt. Reluctantly Quinn looked up to find concern in Bayard's gaze.

"I believe that you can rebuild Sayerne," that man insisted quietly. "And I will help you. Just consider that Tulley is a man of impulse. I would not have his impulse steer you false.''

Quinn straightened. "Tulley is a man of honor. He is also a holder of numerous estates, all of which mean more to him and his treasury when they are profitable and secure. I cannot believe that he will do me a false turn if I restore Sayerne.''

Bayard did not look reassured. "You trust too readily, Quinn.''

Quinn's lips thinned in recollection of Melissande and her flight from him. His voice turned grim. "Maybe you are right.''

"And you are quick to lock the gates when you think you have been ill served."

Quinn glanced quickly to Bayard. "You think I am wrong?" he asked incredulously.

Bayard shrugged. "I think you have not considered the lady's side."

Quinn took a deep breath and folded his arms across his chest. "I invite you to make her case then."

"Now who is doubtful?" Bayard asked with a grin.

Quinn shrugged but did not soften his expression. He was right and he knew it.

He waited.

"All right," Bayard began. He propped one leg up on a fence and looked out over the hills. "All right. The lady wished to return to Annossy to live. One cannot say that she was without reason, for this place is not as hospitable as it might be."

"This is the finest place we have seen in years, outside of Tulley's residence," Quinn countered tightly.

"Yes," Bayard agreed. "But we are not the Lady Melissande. I would suspect that she has known only the likes of Tulley's estate. Probably that miller's abode was the most simple she has seen in years."

Quinn winced at the possibility of that, but said nothing.

"I can only imagine the shock Sayerne would give to someone of that experience."

"The maid seemed to take well to the place."

Bayard grimaced. "Maybe at first, but not any longer. Clearly there is no romance in Sayerne's air for Berthe anymore."

"You want me to repair my marriage so that you might continue to pursue the maid," Quinn accused. "Surely your pleasure should not be that demanding on me?"

Bayard winced. "I wish you would refer to Berthe by name. I would not see her feelings hurt by your disregard."

Quinn's brows rose high at this difference in the other knight's concern. He had never known Bayard to care about any woman he pursued, beyond the moment of pleasure that she might give him.

"This sounds serious," Quinn dared to say.

"Do not look for feeling where there is none. No man of sense would waste his time on a deceitful woman," Bayard retorted with more irritability than Quinn had seen in him for a long while.

"Now, I ask you to see the lady's side."

Bayard glared at Quinn and turned abruptly away. "It is not the same."

"The lady seems to be trying to win your favor," Quinn suggested.

Bayard grimaced. "The lady should return to Annossy."

Quinn chose to leave the matter of Berthe be. "I am still not convinced that my welfare is at the root of your concern," he said.

"Quinn." Bayard fixed him with a glance that Quinn could not shy away from. "I saw that the lady's approval mattered to you. It seemed to me that you two were well suited. Just tell me that you had no interest in her, that you do not care that she is gone, and I will leave the matter be."

Their gazes held for a long moment and Quinn saw the concern in his friend's eyes. He sighed and frowned anew.

"Yes, you are right," he admitted. "The lady charmed me. I had hoped to make the match work. Her response encouraged my faith that it was possible. She was willing that last night and charming beyond all." He felt a thickness in his throat and had to look away. "She leaves no small wound by showing that that was no more than a way to escape."

"You do not know that!"

"Of course I do!" Quinn responded with frustration. "Clearly she initiated our lovemaking that night so I might sleep soundly. Otherwise, she would not have left."

Bayard's voice dropped. "You believe that she betrayed you."

"Yes! I know that she did."

"But maybe she did not realize the heavy price you put on betrayal." Bayard's voice was filled with appeal but Quinn steeled himself against the argument. "Maybe she did not guess that you would be so dismayed."

"She knew," Quinn said tightly. "That night I told her the tale of the battle."

Bayard was silent for a long moment and Quinn knew the other knight understood what battle he had meant. "And about the traitor?" he asked quietly.

Quinn merely nodded. Then he took a deep breath. "I had never trusted anyone with that tale. The lady knew exactly what she did."

Bayard straightened and pushed away from the fence. "I see," he said finally, his voice uncharacteristically sober. "So, we remain at Sayerne."

"Yes."

"What about her safety on the road?"

Quinn snorted. "Had any bandit a whit of sense, he would run from her sharp tongue." Quinn immediately felt like a knave for making such a remark. He hastily shook his head and stood beside his old friend. "The lady has no need of me, Bayard. I cannot imagine that there is any situation that she cannot manage on her own."

"What about Tulley granting you Annossy? You could ride to him and demand investiture, then she could not deny you."

Quinn shook his head. "Tulley hinted that he would invest me with Annossy in a year, but I have no interest in those estates. The lady has her Annossy and that is all she wants. She is welcome to keep that prize."

Bayard gave Quinn's shoulder a reassuring squeeze. "Well, then, we shall have to see that you have Sayerne."

Quinn nodded and they headed off to examine the houses together. There was a shadow across his heart, though, and Quinn knew that even the promise of rebuilding and holding Sayerne as his own was not enough to brighten the bleak outlook of a future alone.

Three days passed before anyone called at the gate of Annossy. The wind had wailed from the west all the day long, sending clouds rushing across the sky in a portent of a storm. It had gotten colder and Roger had predicted that they would have snow covering the ground again by morning.

This arrival had to be Quinn! Melissande flew through the hall before she could check her response. The chill in the air when Melissande stepped into the bailey recalled her composure. She must not look anxious. She must appear aloof and disinterested. She must be prepared to do battle.

Even though she wanted to do nothing else but drag Quinn up to her solar and do things to him that made his eyes darken to the shade of amber. How she had missed the man's touch!

"Who calls at the gate?" she demanded with a crispness she was far from feeling.

"A party from Sayerne," the keeper said.

Melissande's heart skipped a beat in anticipation. She forced herself to stand tall and lifted her cloak over her shoulders as though supremely disinterested in the news.

"I shall speak to them at the gate."

Melissande tried to take her time walking through the village, but her steps hastened despite her intent. Her gaze kept flicking to the tall gates ahead as though she might discern Quinn's tall silhouette from this distance, though she knew it was not possible.

He was here! He had come! He would roar and bellow and drag her off to the solar to ravish her, in order to keep their bargain. Melissande could hardly wait.

She wanted to skip all the way along the road through the town and restrained herself only with the greatest difficulty. It still took too long for her to reach the gate and peer through the portcullis.

Only to find a cold Michel shifting his weight from one foot to the other. And her own six knights behind him. There was no familiar figure lingering behind the group.

Quinn had not come.

"Michel!" Her voice echoed her shock.

The boy's gaze brightened at her voice and he ceased his shuffling. "Yes, my lady."

"But what are you doing here? Is your lord not with you?"

"No, my lady."

"But why? Where is your lord Quinn?"

Michel looked puzzled by her question. "At Sayerne, my lady." His words sent Melissande's heart plummeting. "He is busy rebuilding. Surely you know?"

"Yes, yes, I know." Melissande heard her disappointment echoed in those few words. Why had Quinn not come?

Michel waved a scroll of parchment. "I bring a missive from him."

"A missive?" Melissande's anticipation rose again. Quinn had sent her a letter? Her fingers itched to peel it open.

"Yes. It is for your villeins. My lord bade me request your permission to have it read to them."

For the villeins.

Quinn had not pursued her. He had not sent word. He had not even asked after her welfare.

He only cared for Sayerne. Even knowing she had been right did not make the revelation welcome.

Melissande summoned a polite smile and gestured impatiently to the keeper. If nothing else, Quinn would have no cause to complain of her treatment of his squire. "Please, open the gate. The men are cold and their beasts need tending. Come in, Michel. You all look to be in need of a hot bowl of soup.''

"Oh, yes, my lady. That would be welcome, indeed.''

Melissande's disappointment turned to outrage when Roger read Quinn's missive to her villeins.

"This young squire brings to you an invitation from Quinn de Sayerne, heir apparent and acting lord of the estates of Sayerne," Roger said. The villeins muttered to each other and Melissande had no doubt they were recalling the reputation—and in many cases, their experience—of Jerome de Sayerne.

Roger cleared his throat and the group fell silent as he began to read. "'Good ladies and gentlemen of the estates of Annossy, I, Quinn de Sayerne, have an invitation for you. You all know that my sire, Jerome de Sayerne, has passed from this world. Many of you will know, too, that the estate of Sayerne has been in poor condition these past few years. I have come home to my legacy, only to find it abandoned and in disrepair.

"'But I have a vision of Sayerne, as prosperous as it once was. To achieve this, I need help to rebuild the estate. I would ask all who listen, especially those who fled my sire's abuses, to give me the opportunity to prove to them that I am not the same kind of man as he.'"

Quinn was making an appeal to her villeins that they might desert Annossy before the sowing! Melissande seethed at Quinn's affront. She had gathered her people in good faith to listen to this travesty!

But it was too late to intervene without anyone noticing, so she stood, listened, and fumed. Roger flicked a glance in her direction, then read on.

"'Sayerne's soil is rich, her site well chosen, and I know that I am not the only one who recalls her past glory. There is bounty in this land, if I only had more hands to release it from the soil. It is almost time to sow and I would invite any who have interest to come to Sayerne and share in the new life we can build.'"

Ha! *She* had been the one to tell him that the land was good. How dare Quinn use such information against her to lure her own villeins away?

But Melissande could see the tenants' disbelief and knew that few would heed Quinn's call. So few actually had the right to even do so. She settled back and folded her arms across her chest, curious to hear by what words these honest people would return to the son of Jerome de Sayerne.

"'Should you be freemen, you have only to bring your worldly goods to Sayerne and become a part of this endeavor. Bring to me a declaration of your holding's size and I shall grant to you a larger parcel here at Sayerne.'"

Melissande nearly choked on the generosity of the offer. Her tenants murmured to each other and she saw desire light more than one face. To grant more land was a major concession and one that Melissande could not match. Annossy's tilled land was fully granted.

"'And if you are serfs with a desire to similarly respond,'" Roger read on, "'you have only to give your name and status to my messenger. I am willing to purchase any serf interested to lend a hand to my efforts. I grant to all such men my solemn vow that upon my investiture with Sayerne's seal one year hence, I will set him and his children free after serving that year to Sayerne.

"'At that time, he will be granted land for his family to tend, like any other villein, and his serf status will be forgotten as he joins a company of equals. If I do not gain the investiture of my family estates, it will be written that that man shall be free to leave Sayerne and seek his fortune wherever he will.'"

What was this? The very idea was unheard-of! This was preposterous!

But it was an idea with appeal to the villeins. They murmured excitedly to one another, a few tossing surreptitious glances to Melissande. She noted more than one family discussion break out in the wake of the offer.

"When?" cried someone in the crowd.

"Come before the land is to be tilled," Michel responded. "As soon as you can, for the lands will be granted as tenants arrive just until it is gone."

Melissande could not let the matter rest so easily. "And what shall these tenants eat before next autumn's harvest?" she asked imperiously.

The hall fell silent, all eyes flicking between Michel and Melissande. The boy shuffled his feet.

"I just came from Sayerne," Melissande said. "As did you, Michel. Isn't the larder empty? And the storehouses? Is there a single morsel of food in all of Sayerne?"

Michel looked away. "No, my lady. There is nothing but what one brings."

Melissande looked to her knights. They all nodded agreement, although she noticed their reluctance to do so. Curse Quinn for so charming all who met him! His dream of rebuilding Sayerne was a fool's wager, but everyone who heard him talk about it was swayed into believing.

Melissande had to drive the point home. She had a responsibility to her tenants and she could not let any of them run to Sayerne without understanding the implication of what they did.

And that was only fair after Quinn had sent this scandalous offer into the midst of her own estate.

"Surely the heir of Sayerne does not expect his tenants to live on the promise of their freedom for the better part of that year?" she asked mildly.

Outrage rippled through the assembly at that and the murmurs erupted into muttering.

"My lord Quinn assures me that he will buy supplies for his tenants," Michel replied. "He made his own guarantee."

To Melissande's surprise, Roger addressed the boy. "A buyer has need of a seller in order to fulfill any transaction," he said stiffly. "People hereabouts cultivate what they need and little more. Your lord may have a difficult time fulfilling his pledge, however well-intentioned it might be."

Michel flushed. "I have brought the missive to you. That was all I was instructed to do. Maybe you should take your questions to my lord Quinn yourself, for I have no more answers." He met Melissande's gaze across the crowded hall.

"I can say no more, except that this Quinn de Sayerne is a most honorable man. I have been pledged to his hand for only a year, but he has already shown himself a man of his word, both noble and kind. I have trusted him with my own life and do not regret it."

Silence fell and Melissande suddenly dreaded what the boy might say.

"You might ask your own lady about Quinn de Sayerne, for she married him at the estates of the Lord de Tulley."

The hall erupted into an unholy din at that. Melissande felt the gaze of all swivel toward her and, unwilling to face the questions that would surely come, she fled to the sanctuary of the solar.

A fortnight had passed before Michel showed himself at Sayerne again. Quinn had been growing nervous about the boy's absence. A winter storm had ravaged the countryside a week after Melissande's departure and he worried about his little southern squire in the snow.

Quinn wondered throughout each night whether he had made a mistake in not following Melissande. He worried that he should have at least made certain that she had arrived within the walls of Annossy safely. He wondered if he had judged her too hastily and too harshly.

Silence only made him dread the arrival of news yet more.

"Ho! My lord Quinn! I am back!" Michel was full of smiles when he galloped into the bailey of Sayerne.

Although the snow was deep again, Quinn and Bayard worked outside, their breath making cold white puffs in the air. They were lengthening the rope for the well bucket, although they had yet to find any water. Quinn was afraid the well had gone dry.

"Michel! Greetings, boy!" Bayard lifted the squire from the saddle and set him on his feet. A pair of Annossy's knights lingered behind the boy and Quinn nodded to them. He caught his breath at the evidence that Michel had made it to Annossy and was glad Melissande had seen fit to send the boy back with company.

Michel immediately ran to Quinn, his face alight. "I have wondrous news, my lord, for many were excited about your offer."

"That is good to hear, but I am more interested in how you fared." Quinn tousled the boy's hair affectionately, relieved to have him home and apparently healthy.

Michel's eyes widened. "Oh, my lord. I have seen such sights! A great hall as high as the eye could see. Hundreds of people at the board and fine steeds in the stable." His voice dropped to a hush. "And tapestries to cover the entire walls of a hall. They had scenes on them of unicorns and lions at the hunt."

"Really?" Quinn urged him toward the hall. The knights dismounted and trailed behind and their squires tended their horses. "And what of the storm? Did you see that?"

"Yes, I was at Annossy when it broke and your lady insisted that I stay."

She was there. Relief broke over Quinn at the news and he barely restrained himself from smiling. "Come and warm yourself before the hearth. Berthe may well have some morsel for you to eat."

Michel frowned and leaned closer to Quinn as his voice dropped confidentially. "Have we the fare to spare, my lord?" he asked with concern.

Quinn smiled. "Yes, much has changed since you left. We have bought supplies and Berthe is busy. Though you may soon tire of salt meat and potatoes, there is plenty to eat."

"That is good news, for I am hungry!"

Quinn endeavored to keep his interest from echoing in his voice. "And everything was well at Annossy?" Bayard snorted behind him and Quinn's neck heated at the certainty that he had not been as circumspect as he might have hoped.

Michel however noticed nothing.

"Yes, my lord."

Quinn schooled himself to be patient, for the boy seemed to have no idea what he desired to hear. Bayard brushed past him en route to the kitchens and chuckled outright.

Quinn spared the man a dark look, but Bayard was oblivious. His gaze was fixed on Berthe as one of the knights from Annossy strolled to her side. Bayard's expression was sullen, but he did nothing to intervene.

The other knight winked wickedly at Berthe, who expertly snapped a length of linen at his roving hand.

"Yow!" he yelped. Berthe smothered a smile before she opened her arms to Michel, something about her expression making Quinn wonder if she teased Bayard on purpose.

Bayard folded his arms across his chest and glared at the floor in sour temper.

"You are the first one home!" she declared. "And I have a fine fresh bun with raisins for you as a reward."

"Really?" Michel asked with evident delight.

"Really. It's still hot, so you must take care that you do not burn your fingers or tongue. And we have no butter." Berthe spared a significant glance to Quinn at that, but he was more interested in gaining a response for his own query. "So one must make do."

"Have you not some warm buns for me?" the knight asked mischievously. Bayard's lips thinned disapprovingly.

Berthe granted him a scathing glance. "I see nothing that you have done to merit such a gift," she retorted, and Bayard's manner eased slightly.

Quinn cleared his throat pointedly. These two had been easier to live with when they had been at battle over every little matter. Bayard's brooding silences were particularly vexing as they were so uncharacteristic.

Not to mention how vexing Michel could be when he was distracted by food from a very important question.

"I asked a question of you, Michel," Quinn said. The boy blinked, his blank expression evidence enough that he did not recall. Quinn ground his teeth. "Did the Lady Melissande greet you at Annossy?"

"Yes, she did." He nodded to Berthe. "She sends these knights to bring you to Annossy."

Berthe pursed her lips but said nothing. Her gaze flicked to Bayard, who stubbornly stared at the floor.

Quinn's annoyance rose that Michel had not yet answered his question. He turned his gaze upon the boy and dropped his voice. "I would have news from you of my wife."

"She seemed well enough," Michel responded with a shrug. He bit into his bun with an enthusiasm Quinn thought unwarranted.

"And she greeted you?"

"Yes. She gave me hot soup and a warm pallet before the hearth. And she insisted that I remain after the storm until the roads were clear." Michel chewed thoughtfully for a long moment. "Although she was not pleased by your missive."

Quinn's heart took an unruly leap at the faint promise of her attention. He felt like a besotted fool, but it seemed he could not help his response.

At least he could hope the others did not notice. "No?" he asked as mildly as he could.

"No, not in the least," Michel said. "It looked as though some of her villeins might take advantage of your generosity until she commented that there was nothing to eat here."

Bayard caught his breath as Quinn felt his lips thin. So the lady would obstruct his efforts. He should have expected no less. Michel, blissfully unaware, smiled through a mouthful of bun at Berthe.

"She did not know about these," he enthused.

"That is not all that has changed since my lady departed," Berthe began. She began to count off on her fingers. "The stables have been repaired as have some of the homes in the village, though the mill has yet to be set to rights. The kitchens have been cleaned, though Bayard has not yet fulfilled his promise to see the kitchen garden weeded. . . ."

Quinn stifled a growl of frustration. This was like pulling teeth. But he would know the truth. Quinn braced himself against Bayard's ridicule and forced out the question, interrupting Berthe's litany.

"Did my lady ask after me?"

The boy shook his head. "No."

No.

There was his response. Quinn looked to his toes as he realized how much he had anticipated hearing the opposite. How could he continue to cling to hope? Clearly the lady had no regard for him.

"Of course, she was busy with the raid on Annossy," Michel continued conversationally.

"What?" Quinn's head shot up. "There was a raid on Annossy?"

"Annossy has been attacked?" Berthe demanded.

"Had anyone been injured?" Bayard chimed in.

Michel looked between them, evidently surprised at the response his news had brought. "No, no one was hurt. The mill had burned to the ground, and several houses in the village were damaged. The lady was busy hiring more knights to guard the walls."

"But she sent you two here," Quinn said.

The knights shrugged before one responded. "She said she had given her word to the maid."

Yes, that would be Melissande. She took great pride in the value of her word. Quinn found an unexpected lump had risen in his throat. "It must have been the brigands that Tulley feared."

"Yes," Michel agreed cheerfully. He gestured to Quinn with the remainder of his bun. "That was what the chatelain Roger said."

His marriage had been designed to eliminate the attacks on Annossy. Quinn saw now that his squabbling with Melissande had endangered not only her personal safety, but the security of Annossy and all of Tulley's estates.

He could easily guess what Tulley would have to say when he heard the news. Quinn had failed at his task, because he had been so preoccupied with the concerns of Sayerne. Regardless of their personal feelings, he and Melissande had a duty to their liege lord, and he, for one, did not intend to forget his obligation again.

Quinn told himself that it was because Tulley alone could invest him with Sayerne that he made his decision, but his breath caught at the promise of seeing his bride again.

"Muster the weaponry," he told Bayard curtly. "I ride to aid Annossy. You shall remain in charge of Sayerne."

"We shall ride back with you, my lord," one of the knights from Annossy said after exchanging a glance with his companion.

Quinn nodded, Bayard interrupting before he could agree.

"And I suppose you will depart, as well?" Bayard asked Berthe with unconcealed bitterness.

The maid eyed the knight for a long moment, then her lips thinned. Quinn thought he saw the glimmer of tears in her eyes before she averted her gaze.

"Yes," she agreed quietly. "Yes, I see now that there was no reason to remain at Sayerne."

At that, Bayard snorted and stalked out of the kitchen. Berthe turned hastily back to her work and the men exchanged glances of discomfort.

"There is work to be done," Quinn said, noting the relief on the other knights' faces. The one who had bantered with Berthe lingered for an instant, as though he might try to console her, but then he looked after Bayard, shook his head and left.

"We ride as soon as we may be ready," Quinn added quietly.

Berthe nodded and wiped a hand across her face before turning back to face him. Tears stained her cheeks. "I am ready whenever you are, my lord. Annossy is clearly where I belong."

Chapter Ten

It was mildly terrifying to Melissande that she was glad to see Quinn.

It had been only a week since Michel had left, but she had run the gamut of emotions in that time. First she had been infuriated that Quinn had not followed her, then despondent that he had cared so little. She was angry that Quinn dared to tempt her tenants, yet she was obliged to admire both his audacity and his insight into their desires.

And in the night, when every chance sound brought her heart to her throat in anticipation of attack, she wished she had not left Quinn behind. In those moments, she cursed Tulley for seeing the truth and herself for failing to take his advice.

But it was out of the question to return to Sayerne. Melissande could not admit that she was wrong, although she told herself that she remained because her villeins needed her.

And now Quinn had come! The word of his arrival at dusk was enough to have her call for a glass, to check her hair, to smooth her kirtle. She looked tired and Quinn would know she had not slept well without him, but there was nothing for it now.

Melissande raced down the stairs. The sight of Quinn before the hearth, his back turned to her and his arms folded across his chest, was enough to set her heart racing. There were others in the hall, but Melissande had eyes for none of them.

When she descended the last stair, Quinn must have heard her, for he turned away from the fireplace to glare openly at her. Melissande's footsteps faltered at his fierce expression.

"Why did you not summon me?" he demanded.

She had no answer. Her spouse was clearly less enchanted to see her than she was to see him. Melissande straightened and forced herself to walk slowly across the hall, as though she were supremely unconcerned.

"I beg your pardon?" she asked in as arch a manner as she could manage. If Quinn had touched her, he would have felt her trembling, but Melissande knew he would not.

His eyes blazed like molten gold. "Why did you not summon me? Surely you don't believe Tulley is wrong? How can you sit back and calmly wait for another attack?"

Melissande lifted her chin. She had not sat back! She had made preparations, as any good administrator would! "The wall has been repaired and there are extra sentries at night."

Quinn snorted, less than impressed with her measures. "Have you sent a sortie into the surrounding area to seek out the marauders? Have you found any evidence of their passing? Have you attempted to identify any of them?"

Melissande felt defensive, all the more so because she had thought of none of Quinn's suggestions. "The attacked sentry was surprised and saw nothing."

"That does not mean that no one else saw nothing," he retorted. "And if these troublemakers are bent on attacking Annossy repeatedly, as it seems they are, their camp cannot be far off."

She hated that his comments were most logical and wished that she had thought of them herself and much sooner.

"I suppose there is sense in what you say," Melissande admitted, not pleased to concede any such thing. Suddenly she was aware of the others in the hall and the fact that all eyes were fixed upon them.

"My lady," Quinn purred, and Melissande braced herself as he leaned closer. His mood had changed, his expression confidential, and she did not trust his intent. "May I suggest that this is a matter beyond your experience?"

Ha! So that was why he was no longer angry. He thought he had found her failing. Well, Melissande would not concede that point so readily, even though the evidence was damning. She knew nothing of tracking bandits.

Melissande swallowed and made the only argument that came to mind. "I have been well trained in administering an estate."

Quinn arched a brow. He stepped closer and she caught a chance whiff of his scent that almost completely undermined her ability to argue with him.

"But warfare would be beyond your experience?" he persisted smoothly.

A plague upon him for his perceptiveness!

"I can manage a marshal and ensure that the armorer is thorough about his work."

Quinn shook his head slowly and Melissande knew he had her cornered. That was not enough, and she hated that he knew it. It pricked her pride to admit that this problem was beyond her capabilities to solve.

"The strategy of war is my concern, my lady," he said.

Melissande's heart stopped. Quinn was going to make a case to Tulley that he should be invested now with Annossy. She knew it. What else could his comment have meant?

Melissande closed her eyes and braced herself for the inevitable suggestion. How could she have lost Annossy?

"As warfare is my field of expertise, I would suggest to you that my services might be useful to Annossy at this time."

What? Melissande regarded her husband with surprise. That had not been what she had expected him to say. To her further astonishment, his lips quirked in a smile at her response. Little lines fanned out around his twinkling eyes and Melissande felt as though she were the only woman in the world.

Her knees melted right on cue. How could this man disarm her so readily? And at such inopportune moments?

"Word is that you are hiring knights, my lady. If that is true, I would offer my own services."

Melissande could not summon a word to her lips, so surprised was she by this turn of events. She watched in amazement as Quinn dropped gracefully to one knee and pulled his sword from its scabbard.

He offered the blade to her on his flattened palms. "I would offer to champion the Lady of Annossy."

There was silence in the hall.

Melissande eyed Quinn, uncertain what to make of his offer, until she suddenly recalled his own objectives.

Sayerne. He only wanted Sayerne. Somehow this offer had to be tied to that objective.

Melissande's mind worked furiously. Quinn's offer to villeins would cost him dearly. Maybe this was just a way to see his own pockets lined, all to the greater cause of Sayerne.

Quinn did not care whether Annossy burned to the ground. The conclusion stung, but she forced herself to maintain her composure. It was time that Melissande accepted that she was only a means to an end for this intriguing man.

Even if her own desire was to be remarkably more. Melissande heard the clear resonance of truth in that thought and stared at Quinn. She noted every detail, the slight smile curving his lips, now tinged with doubt, the chestnut locks that she longed to run her fingers through, the eyes that sparkled with intelligence and sincerity.

She thought how similar his passion for Sayerne was to her own passion for Annossy and felt a kinship with him.

She recalled his outrage at Tulley making her break her word to Arnaud. She remembered how tender and gentle he had been with her when they made love and how angry he became when she did not put her own welfare first. She heard him confiding his story of betrayal that night at Sayerne, protecting her from the grisly details.

A lump rose in her throat when she thought of his earnest appeal to make this a real marriage. Melissande looked at Quinn, kneeling before her, and faced the truth.

She loved him.

Melissande panicked at the realization. It couldn't be true. She couldn't have fallen in love with a man who was manipulating her for his own gain. Only showing herself that Quinn cared nothing for her might banish this ridiculous idea of love from her mind and her heart.

"I do not pay overly well, if it is the coin you desire," she said harshly.

Quinn shrugged. "You need not pay me."

Melissande's eyes narrowed with suspicion. "You would work for nothing? I thought that restoring Sayerne would bring great expense."

"I have enough. Willing hands are all I need now."

"So, you would pretend to work for Annossy while you charm my tenants away from under me."

"Never, my lady." Quinn's gaze locked with hers and Melissande had difficulty not believing him. "This is the least I can do for my lady wife."

"Ha! More likely this is the least you can do for Tulley! I am sure that you have already petitioned him for the seal of Annossy to claim this estate as your own!"

Quinn shook his head with maddening slowness. "No, my lady. I have done nothing of the kind. Annossy is your legacy and I understand the desire to hold one's own lands."

No? Quinn's voice was rich and low, making Melissande's fight against his charm all the more difficult.

"I would not take Annossy, even if Tulley offered me the seal on a silver platter. It is yours and rightly so."

She took a deep breath and averted her face to make her accusation. Her heart pounded and Melissande wished she could change the truth.

"Then where have you been these past weeks, if not to Tulley?"

"Sayerne has required my attention. There was much to be done."

Melissande folded her arms before herself, hating how readily she was becoming convinced by his words. "Then why do you come now? Surely there is still more to be done?"

Quinn nodded slowly. "Yes, there is that. But the need at Annossy is greater. It was Tulley's intent, after all, that my presence here should dissuade these attacks."

There. He had said it. He had no concern for her. Melissande blinked back her tears and turned away without touching Quinn's sword. Quinn must never know how she felt.

"Then offer your blade to Tulley instead of me. Clearly you serve him, not me, despite your pretty words."

She walked away with her heart aching, hoping she could hold back her tears until she reached the privacy of the solar.

"Melissande!" Quinn's whisper was urgent and she could not keep herself from glancing back. Once she did, her gaze was snared by the intensity of his own. "It is not for Tulley alone that I am here."

She longed to believe him but she could not risk it. There was too much at stake. Melissande had too much to lose by confessing her trust and hence her love for Quinn de Sayerne.

"Liar," she murmured with a precision he could not help but hear.

Quinn's eyes blazed and Melissande impulsively ran.

"You would test the patience of the very saints!" Quinn bellowed.

With this one accusation, Melissande knew that she had finally pushed Quinn too far. Now she would see what kind of man he was.

But still she ran.

Melissande stumbled on the stairs and dropped to all fours, and clambered on in haste. She had to reach the solar and bar the door against him.

"And I warned you that I am no saint!" Quinn roared.

She heard him then, his footsteps heavy on the flagstones as he pursued her. Her breath caught in her throat, her hands shook as she tried to race onward. The top of the steps was too far away when his boot sounded on the first wooden step far below. Melissande looked back and unintentionally made a little gasp at her spouse's proximity.

She would never make it.

But still she had to try. Her mouth went dry as she scampered onward. Quinn's steps echoed in her ears. Melissande had her hand on the top step and victory within her grasp when she felt his breath on the back of her nape.

She had failed.

Quinn scooped her up into his arms. In one thundering heartbeat, she was cradled against his warm strength. Melissande squeezed her eyes shut, not daring to even see his anger, afraid he would see her feelings reflected in her eyes. He turned but she did not dare look to the hall below.

"My lady wife and I have need of our privacy," he declared to those evidently still watching from below. Melissande's cheeks flamed with embarrassment.

Then, Quinn was stalking down the corridor, his boots pounding on the wooden floor at an impatient pace. Melissande could feel the tension in his arms, but she did not dare struggle. It was no relief that he strode directly to the solar. Nor that he immediately kicked the heavy wooden door shut behind them.

"If I were the son of my father, I would beat you black and blue," he muttered, frustration evident in his tone.

His words echoed her fears, but something about his manner made Melissande doubt her conclusions. She dared to peek through her lashes, squeezing her eyes closed again at the flame burning in Quinn's gaze.

"But I am not that man and on this day, I will prove it to you for once and for all," he added in a murmur.

Before Melissande could make sense of that, Quinn's lips were upon hers. The taste of him was irresistible, especially as it was unexpected, and she found herself twining her arms around his neck.

Quinn tore his lips from hers and nuzzled her neck in a way that eliminated her resistance. Melissande was overwhelmed by his touch and she did not care.

"We have a bargain," he whispered into her ear. "And it is sixteen days overdue."

"Yes," Melissande answered simply.

That one word was apparently all the encouragement Quinn needed, for she found herself on the bed an instant later. His hands roved over her, fervently, admiringly, loosening the laces of her kirtle with impatience, then lingering on the curve of her breast.

Melissande reveled in the surety of his touch. As they loved silently, the love in her heart blossomed. It was unbearably sweet to be with him with her heart so full of love.

Even if she did not dare confess her feelings. Melissande knew her love could not be returned, but as Quinn touched her with gentle reverence, she began to hope. Maybe, in time, he would come to feel more for her than desire.

Maybe.

For now, the possibility would have to do.

Quinn dozed as he cradled his wife's weight on his chest. He could hear the gentle rhythm of her breathing as he cupped her buttocks in his hands and he savored the silken net of her hair cast across his face.

He felt replete as he had not these past weeks. He sighed with satisfaction that he had been brave enough to grant her one more chance. She needed him and his expertise in one matter at least, for the keep was poorly defended against attack.

He let his hands rove over her smooth skin and smiled into her hair. And the lady seemed to crave his touch, as well. There could be room in her life for Quinn. He only had to convince her to admit the truth.

He admired her strength and independence, although Quinn could imagine that the concession to needing another would be a difficult one for her to make.

That had to be why she had fled from Sayerne.

Quinn could understand that. But one glimpse of Annossy's organization and maintenance had shown him the inadequacy of his own skills at estate management.

He would not know where to begin to run such a manor. And this was the kind of manor he desired Sayerne to be. It was not easy to face his own inadequacy.

Quinn needed his wife's talents, just as she had need of his. They could be partners, each to learn from the other. There would be no shame in admitting that one did not know something the other did.

He would make this marriage work.

Quinn was beginning to think that this match might have been ordained to be, with or without Tulley's intervention. Certainly the woman who slumbered in his arms would have piqued Quinn's interest wherever and whenever he had met her.

He listened to the sounds of the others in the keep settling for the night. Voices rose and fell, implements clattered to rest, trestle tables scraped the floor below as they were folded down for the night.

But Quinn was where he belonged, in his lady's bed, and he was at peace as he had not been while he worked alone at Sayerne.

Melissande stirred before he could ponder the importance of that. The light was faint but he could still see the perfection of her smooth skin and the grace of her languid movements. Desire roused itself deep within him.

She propped her elbow on his chest and pushed her hair sleepily from her face. Those emerald eyes widened slightly when she found Quinn directly beneath her.

Quinn smiled. "Were you pleased?"

Melissande flushed scarlet and her gaze danced away from his. "Yes," she whispered. She flicked a look to him and away again before she continued, her voice husky in confidence. "And you?"

"Yes." Quinn spread his hands and urged her closer, grinning wickedly. "We have only fifteen more couplings to bring our bargain up-to-date."

"Quinn!" Melissande choked back a laugh, her expression revealing that she did not know whether he teased her or not.

Quinn laughed, enjoying her slight weight as his laughter rumbled through his chest. "Do you have objections, wife of mine?" he asked as he gave her a playful pinch. "I thought you were a woman of your word."

"Quinn." She endeavored to look disapproving and failed in a most enchanting manner. "It is of no benefit to couple more than once a day."

Melissande squealed as Quinn rolled her beneath him and covered her neck with slow kisses. She shivered, even before he whispered in her ear. "I would argue that."

She giggled. "You know what I mean."

"No." He slid his hand over her hip to capture the delightful curve of her breast. The nipple tightened in a most fascinating manner and Quinn ducked to taste it. "Explain these benefits to me," he murmured against her sweetly scented flesh.

"No, not *benefits*," Melissande argued, her tone unconvincing. "I meant that it is of no additional benefit to conceiving a child."

He glanced up as though surprised, letting his thumb slide across the tightened nipple as he held her gaze. Melissande gasped then bit her lip, but she did not look away. "And there are no other benefits to lovemaking than that?" he asked innocently.

Something flashed in her eyes before she abruptly rolled away from him to face the room beyond. "We do not make love." Her voice was tight, not playful as it had been just moments past.

Quinn eyed her back with uncertainty. What had he said to prompt this change? He laid a hand tentatively on the neat indent of Melissande's waist, but she shoved away its weight and stood.

"You will get cold," he protested.

Melissande drew a robe over her shoulders and did not look back. "No, I will light the fire."

Quinn frowned and sat up himself, not in the least pleased with this change of mood. "What is the matter?" he asked in confusion. "You said you were pleased."

"Yes."

She would not look at him. Quinn sensed that she would not appreciate him following her, although she looked young and fragile with her hair loose and her arms folded protectively about herself.

"Then?" he asked.

She spared him a tear-filled glance that sent a spear through his heart. "We are no better than rutting animals."

"Melissande!" Quinn rose to his feet then and crossed the space between them with rapid steps. He stopped short of placing his hands on her shoulders when she did not look up at him. "There is no shame in enjoying the pleasures of the marital bed."

"Yes! Yes, there is!" she declared. She spun to face him and Quinn's stomach twisted at the sight of her tears flowing over her cheeks. "There is shame in mating without tender feelings between us."

Quinn's heart sank. This was about that Arnaud. He had been too hasty to dismiss the other man's memory. Melissande wanted her betrothed. Any progress Quinn had thought made in earning the lady's heart had been just an illusion.

Quinn was surprised to discover how disappointed he was.

"There is feeling between us," he objected, because he felt he had to do so. He wished she would offer him some encouragement, but Melissande clearly did not intend to do so.

"No," she said vehemently. "Nothing holds us together but the possibility of conceiving the heir you need for Sayerne."

"No, Melissande, that is not so."

Her chin lifted with defiance though unshed tears sparkled in her eyes. "Yes, Quinn, it is."

Quinn shook his head as he lifted his hand to cup Melissande's face. An errant tear splashed over his hand, but he could not let her turn away. He could not let her believe he did not care for her.

If she cared nothing for him, that was another matter.

"No, my lady. You stir my blood as no one else could."

"Sweet words alone mean nothing," she said with a sniff.

"Then this should mean something." Quinn heard his voice become resolute. "I have never wanted a match made without love and mutual regard. I always have wanted a wife to hold my heart captive and hoped that I would similarly hold hers."

Melissande lifted her gaze to Quinn's and he thought he saw a glimmer of hope in those emerald depths. The sight fed his determination to continue and convince her of his sincerity.

"Nothing of my sire's character dwells within me, Melissande, except the certainty that he saw the world wrongly. Though we were not married in a way that I might have chosen myself, still I see the chance of the match of my dreams between us."

Melissande remained silent, her eyes wary. Quinn slipped his other hand into her hair and urged her closer. "We could have a match of love, my lady. We have only to reach out and take the opportunity. We just need to trust each other."

She shrugged suddenly and pulled back a bit. "We are too different."

"No." Quinn tipped up her chin so that she was compelled to look into his eyes. To his relief, he saw that her tears had halted their flow and he eased the marks of their passing from her cheeks. "No, it is our differences that give us strength and I shall prove it to you."

"How?"

"Let me pledge to your hand. Let me share what I know of warfare to rout these marauders from Annossy, once and for all."

Melissande turned sharply away and pulled out of Quinn's embrace. "I cannot allow that," she said and paced the length of the room. She turned only when there was a sizable expanse of floor between them.

If nothing else, her move showed that his touch affected her. Quinn dared to be encouraged.

"Why not?"

She made an impatient motion with her hand. "It would be improper. People would talk. You are my husband and they will say that you should be recognized as Lord of Annossy." Her voice faltered and he recognized how difficult the concession was for her to make. "The law says as much."

"But the law does not acknowledge the importance of holding one's own legacy," Quinn said softly. Melissande flicked a glance to him but said nothing. He saw that she was not yet convinced. "I have no interest in taking Annossy from you, regardless of your fears."

"So you say now."

"And so I will say always." Quinn ran his hand through his hair in frustration and strode across the room to grip her shoulders in his hands.

Melissande stared steadfastly at her toe.

"Listen to me," he urged. "I mean it when I tell you that our skills complement the other. We would make a fine team, my lady, if you would only give us the chance."

She slanted a suspicious glance in his direction. "What do you mean?"

"You have noticed that I know nothing of running an estate...."

"That did not keep you from concocting a clever plan to tempt tenants to Sayerne," she muttered. Before Quinn could protest that he had meant no harm, Melissande looked him directly in the eye. "It was brilliantly conceived," she said, and he saw a grudging admiration in her eyes.

Quinn grinned at even such scant praise. "But I do not know what to do with them when they arrive," he confessed. "Melissande, it will be a nightmare of the worst order if there is not someone better organized and more knowledgeable of the issues involved than I there to greet them." He gave her shoulders a minute shake.

"One glimpse of Annossy has shown me that you possess those skills which I lack. I could use your assistance at Sayerne, just as you could use mine here."

She frowned. "I do not need any assistance here. Annossy is run with fine efficiency."

Quinn snorted. "No? Then who will turn the marauders from your gates?"

"I have hired knights," Melissande said, though no conviction rang in her voice.

"Yes, and you know as well as I, that one fights harder for something when one's heart is engaged. Unlike me, these men have nothing to gain or lose with the fall of Annossy."

Melissande looked to him with consideration in her eye. "And what have you to gain?"

"The respect of my lady wife and a marriage in truth," Quinn said firmly. His vision blurred slightly as he forced himself to continue. "And that would be the fairest prize of all."

To Quinn's relief, Melissande did not immediately call him a liar. She stood silently before him and her hand landed upon his.

"You only have to admit that you have need of my skill," he prompted quietly. He captured her hands within his grip, relieved that she did not pull away. She remained silent. "Just as I have admitted my need of yours."

Melissande's lips worked with indecision and Quinn wished fervently that she would confess the truth. If she turned away from him now, he did not know what he would do.

Melissande parted her lips and flicked a glance to Quinn's face. He dared to hope.

But then a cry rang through the keep.

"Attackers at the gate! We are under siege!"

"Awaken all! Awaken while you may!"

"To arms! To arms!"

Quinn's gaze collided with Melissande's in time to see determination replace her fleeting fear. "The marauders," she whispered.

He nodded but did not release her hands. "It is time to decide, my lady. Will you accept me as your champion, or not?"

When her jaw set and she pulled her hands hastily from his, Quinn feared the worst. Melissande strode to the portal and tore it open, walking with purposeful grace to the head of the stairs. He trailed behind her, uncertain what to think as she paused to look out over the hall.

"Listen all and listen well," she called out, and the chaos below stilled immediately. "Things have changed within Annossy. From this night onward, all will follow the bidding of my lord and champion, Quinn de Sayerne. He is experienced in battle beyond anyone here. Do me proud and follow his bidding."

A chorus of "yes, my lady" rose from the hall below as Melissande turned to face Quinn. She was regal, this wife of his, her unbound hair catching the light cast by the fireplace below and forming a cloud of radiance about her.

Quinn's heart swelled with pride and something tender but unnamed when Melissande's eyes met his. He marveled at the resolve he found there.

This woman would stand by his side and battle with him, if he permitted her to do so. He had no fainting lady, but a warrior bound to defend her own. Quinn was proud to have her as his wife and, in that moment, his determination to win her heart redoubled.

To his astonishment, Quinn saw that Tulley had chosen for him precisely the kind of woman—no, the very woman—whom Quinn would have chosen himself.

He only had to convince Melissande of that fact.

"I accept your bargain, Quinn," she said formally.

Quinn smiled victoriously and strode forward to shake her hand. Though her flesh was soft, her grip was firm.

"Another bargain between us can only be good. We shall win this battle in the end, my lady. You will see."

"I should hope so."

Quinn could have drowned in the emerald pools of her eyes.

Cries rang from the bailey and Quinn pivoted at the reminder, dragging Melissande back to the solar. He had a battle to win before he could savor this personal victory.

His mind began to work. "You must be dressed by the time I am ready," he said tersely. He shrugged into his hauberk, talking all the while.

"We will need water heated and linens torn for bandages, for there will be wounds. And have the women and children ready to haul water in case of flames. The vast majority—including you—I would have stay safely within the hall here. I will post a sentry outside to warn you of attack."

"But..." the lady protested.

Quinn was dressed, though, and out of time for niceties. He grasped her around the waist and kissed her full on the lips. "Downstairs," he whispered. "Now. And do not argue with me."

Melissande smothered a smile and he noted her concession with relief. "Yes, my lord. But I would learn of this warfare from you. Promise me that you will explain it all later."

"I will."

Melissande's fingertips trailed over his face and their gazes clung for a moment. He saw her fear for him and the very sight buoyed his hope for their future.

"May Dame Fortune stay at your side this night," she whispered.

Quinn touched her cheek with his fingertip. "Do not worry," he murmured. "I have too much to live for these days." Quinn grinned wickedly at her evident surprise, then hurried her toward the stairs.

Quinn was born to lead.

Melissande saw it the very instant he turned from her side in the hall. He summoned men to him with an ease born of experience and they listened to him avidly. Quinn had a manner that commanded respect.

"How many are they?" Quinn demanded.

"We think two dozen, my lord."

"And where do they attack?" All the while, Quinn was donning his armor in haste.

"On the east wall."

"What is the weakest point in our defense there?"

"Between the towers, there is a low point in the wall."

"Take me there."

The men headed purposefully from the hall as another cry rose from outside. Quinn paused on the threshold and looked back, although Melissande could see only his silhouette against the night. She knew he looked to her and her heart leapt with the certainty that he meant to reassure her.

She would show him that she was no weak woman who would not support him in this.

She snapped her fingers purposefully. "Bring every bucket you can find," she said, knowing that Quinn would hear. "We must do our lord's bidding and be prepared."

Melissande knew when he turned away, but her heart still glowed with hope. A new moment was dawning between them, a moment that might promise the opportunity for Melissande to someday confess her new feelings.

As the women hastened away and the men left, Melissande noticed Berthe.

"Greetings, my lady," Berthe said softly. She looked sad and Melissande lifted a hand to gently touch her cheek. She was certain she knew the reason for both Berthe's sadness and her return.

"Bayard had his way and turned you aside, did he not?" she asked quietly.

To Melissande's surprise, Berthe shook her head, scattering tears as she did so.

"No, my lady, I did him the disservice. Our deceit was too much for him to forgive." She took a shuddering breath. "He has not spoken to me kindly since that night you left."

Melissande was astonished. "But you remained behind because of your concern for him."

Berthe's eyes remained downcast. "He did not care."

"But surely his anger has cooled? Surely he forgave you?"

"No, my lady. Bayard has closed his heart to me forever." Berthe lifted a gaze welling with tears to meet Melissande's concerned gaze. "I have done something unforgivable in his eyes," she whispered hoarsely, "and lost everything I hoped to gain."

This was Melissande's fault and she felt guilty that Berthe's assistance had cost her so dear.

"It will all work out," Melissande murmured, and gathered Berthe in a tight hug. As soon as her arms were about the other woman, Berthe began to sob.

"Oh, my lady! It will never work out! Bayard despises me!" And she wept, each heartfelt sob making Melissande feel worse about her role in this.

Maybe Quinn could help. Melissande was encouraged by the thought, but she would not build Berthe's hopes falsely. The maid had lost her heart and if Bayard was not feeling the same way, it might be better that they were apart.

Melissande could not help but hope, as she rocked Berthe in her arms, that the regard between the pair was mutual.

Quinn would know what to do.

Steel rang on steel as the guards strove to defend Annossy from the attackers. Men danced back and forth across the ramparts, the heaviest activity on the east wall. Burning rags were lobbed over the walls with a relentless efficiency that made Quinn question the renegade nature of the attackers.

It seemed that there might be a military man among them.

Some of the rags hissed in patches of snow, some burned fitfully along the ground, still others landed in bales of straw and blazed into towers of flame and smoke. There were enough of them coming over the walls to guarantee that they were a menace.

"Buckets!" Quinn bellowed as he raced to the east wall. "See these fires put out before they spread!"

He counted eight men on the wall in ragged garb, fighting hand to hand with the men pledged to Annossy. More renegades were coming over the walls from outside. There were only ten more knights with him.

In haste, Quinn climbed a ladder leaning against the inside of the wall. As he neared the top, the renegade above dispatched an Annossy guard with a fatal blow. He glanced down and saw Quinn.

"Annossy shall burn!" he whispered. "And you with it, trapped inside its walls."

The renegade's confidence infuriated Quinn. That some stranger should try to destroy Annossy after the many years of labor required to build so fine an estate was wrong beyond belief.

As Quinn stepped onto the wall, another renegade leapt out of the darkness. Quinn bellowed as he unsheathed his blade and his followers spilled onto the wall behind him. A knight of Annossy already on the wall spun at Quinn's cry and they dispatched the two invaders simultaneously.

Quinn strode across the wide wall and kicked away a ramshackle ladder that had been propped against its outer side. Someone yelled far below but he had little interest in their plight. He scanned the wall critically as his men fanned out and acknowledged that this was its most vulnerable point.

"You and you—" he pointed to two knights behind him, then to a ladder being propped against the outside of the wall by renegades "—see that ladder destroyed. And you two, make sure that this one is not used again.

"That knight needs your aid," he said, and dispatched another soldier, then turned back to face the knight who had already been on the wall.

"I am Quinn de Sayerne, spouse of the Lady Melissande and entrusted to regain the security of this keep," Quinn said briskly. "And your name?"

"Philippe d'Epergne, my lord."

Quinn scanned the ground below. He quickly located the parties below responsible for the hail of burning rags.

"Is there a clear vantage of that place from the tower, Philippe?" he asked. The man stretched to look, then nodded quickly.

"Yes. I know I can see this place from my usual station."

"Good. I will need archers," Quinn whispered.

"Yes, my lord. We have a fine one."

One? They had only *one?* Something had to be done about Annossy's meager defenses. Quinn would see to the matter as soon as this fight was won. His gaze flicked along the length of the wall and lighted on the one tower with narrow windows. "Then bring him to that tower. And be sure he is not seen."

Chapter Eleven

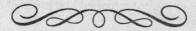

Quinn dodged the battles on the wall, ducking the incoming volleys of burning rags as he made his way to the tower. He heard grunts and curses as he drew closer to the squat tower and he knew its possession was in contest. He quickened his pace, but just as Quinn reached the darkened doorway, someone lunged out of the darkness.

Quinn jumped back as a knight of Annossy fell dead at his feet. The tower was silent, and Quinn knew this man's opponent must still lurk inside. He could barely see the stairs curving upward to the sentry room and downward to a storage cellar. Quinn glanced back, but the men behind him were all occupied. He gripped his blade and stepped into the darkness.

The walls of the tower closed around him and sheltered him from the noise of battle. He was in a separate world of shadows and silence. Quinn took another step, straining his ears for some hint of his opponent's location.

There was none. His pulse thundered in his ears. He took another cautious step and another, carefully rounding the tower, his back against the outside wall as he climbed upward.

Silence. Quinn wondered if the man had taken refuge in the cellar below.

Suddenly he saw the glint of steel. Quinn barely had time to duck before the blade whistled over his head. He lunged forward and jabbed where he guessed his attacker would be. A grunt greeted his efforts and Quinn knew his blade had found a mark.

But the other sword swung again. He winced as it caught his forearm and he felt the warm trickle of blood. Quinn sensed that his opponent retreated and pursued him toward the room above.

He swung at the gleaming point of steel as soon as he saw it. Some light crept through the arrow slits into the small room and Quinn could see his opponent now. He was short of stature, but wiry and moved quickly. Quinn knew the other man had been wounded somewhere, but could not tell by his movements where the blow had been struck.

The man acted as though the blade had not found a mark, although Quinn could see the dark shadow of blood on his own sword.

They circled silently. Suddenly the marauder moved to the right. Quinn moved to parry, only to see too late that it was a feint. He twisted but felt the steel bite deeply into his thigh. Quinn bellowed and spun, lurching after the other man, who dove for the stairs before Quinn fell to his knees in pain.

The marauder's boots echoed on the stone stairs below, then the tower was silent again. Quinn sat down heavily and leaned his back against the wall. He took a deep breath and told himself to forget the pain. He looked at the blood running on his forearm and told himself that the wound was only a scratch.

Hasty footfalls on the stairs brought him laboriously to his knees again, his blade at the ready. Did the renegade return to finish him?

"My lord?"

Quinn breathed a sigh of relief.

He sank back to the floor as the sentry burst into the sentry room. That man's face lit immediately with concern.

"My lord, there is blood on the floor."

"And some of it flows out of me," Quinn confirmed grimly. "We have something to do before it can be tended." He looked expectantly behind the messenger but there was no one there. Where was the archer? Then Quinn noticed the bow and arrow gripped in the man's hands and his heart sank. "Where is the archer?"

"He was wounded, my lord. In the arm. He lies in the hall now, and the lady has forbidden him to move any further."

Quinn grimaced, wryly thanking his lovely wife for unwittingly adding to his difficulties yet again. She was right, but that didn't make his task any easier.

"Give it here," he said tersely. "And we shall see how good a shot I am these days." Quinn eyed his companion's sturdy garb and guessed this man was usually posted to outdoor duty. "Do you know where we might find some eau-de-vie?"

The man sheepishly revealed a flask concealed in his clothing. Quinn grinned, relieved that something went his way.

"Then maybe we shall manage after all."

The man grinned in turn, willingly following Quinn's hasty direction. He tore a length of cloth from his tabard and tied it around the end of one of the archer's arrows. Quinn spilled all of the eau-de-vie on the cloth, then rummaged for his flint.

He looked the sentry in the eye. "We will have only one opportunity."

The sentry nodded. "They will turn their missiles of burning rags upon us once they see that we are here."

"Yes." Quinn loaded the arrow into the bow and eyed the distance to their point of attack carefully, knowing that he would not be able to get far with his injury. "Strike the flint," he ordered.

The sentry did as he was told and the chamber was flooded with golden light as the liquor burned. Quinn spun and shoved the arrow through the slit, took his sight and drew back the bowstring.

The arrow whistled as it burned an arc through the night sky. The men below looked up, their astonished expressions illuminated for only an instant before the arrow was buried directly in their own stock of treated rags.

The rags caught and the flames immediately raged high. A number of the attackers had stood close to the supplies and their clothing quickly caught fire, too. Panic broke out in the rebel base outside the walls as men ran in fear.

Quinn grinned and the sentry let out a hoot of delight. The marauders on the ground outside the walls shouted to each other in frenzy, then turned and ran into the woods. Their companions on the walls leapt down to the ground, risking life and limb to flee in pursuit. Horses snorted in the woods and hoofbeats rang upon the ground as the attackers fled.

One lingered on the walls, apparently reluctant to jump. "Seize him!" Quinn roared. "He shall taste our hospitality!"

The man looked upward in fright, apparently hearing Quinn's command, just before the knights of Annossy grasped both his arms and restrained him.

Quinn shook the sentry's hand with satisfaction, knowing they would soon know the whole story of who was behind these attacks.

Quinn's arm was bleeding.

Melissande leapt to her feet as soon as she saw him return to the hall. He was limping in the middle of a group of knights, but she did not see anything except the growing crimson stain on his sleeve.

Quinn was hurt! Her hands rose to her lips in fear before she ran to his side.

"Quinn! What has happened to you?" Melissande shooed one of the men away and took Quinn's bleeding arm into her hands. "And why did you not come sooner? Surely nothing could be so important to keep you from guarding your own health."

"Surely, my lady, you have not forgotten the brigands on the walls?" Quinn's attempt at humor reassured Melissande slightly.

"No, I have not forgotten," she responded. "But you can do little good wounded."

"It is not even my sword hand," he protested, though there was little fight in his tone.

To her relief, there was only a small gash visible through the torn tunic. Melissande took a steadying breath and summoned an efficient smile.

Quinn would be all right. She knew how to treat a wound of this size. "Come over by the fire," she urged him. "Let me look at this. I suspect it will take just a few stitches."

Quinn stubbornly held his ground. "It is nothing, Melissande, and I have work to do. It will have to wait."

"Nonsense!" she said as sternly as she could. She could not risk him guessing how much the sight of him wounded had affected her.

And it could have been worse. She realized now that Quinn might have easily been among those few men who had been killed in the attack. It would have been too cruel to lose him at the very moment their future held such promise! "Any wound must be tended and the sooner the better."

"Later will have to suffice for this one," Quinn insisted. "We have taken a prisoner and he has to be questioned."

"Surely that can wait a few moments," she argued. "If the man is arrested, then he goes nowhere."

"We must discover the brigands' plans as soon as possible," Quinn said, a note of dogged determination in his tone. He flicked her a significant glance. "I granted you my word that I would see this matter resolved and I will not permit the opportunity to do so to slip through my fingers.''

Melissande looked up to her husband and noted suddenly the tension in his features. Could this small wound hurt as much as that? She eyed him carefully and guessed that he deliberately kept his expression bland.

Then Melissande glanced down and saw the blood.

So much blood. She gasped and the room swirled about her for a moment before Quinn's hands landed heavily on her shoulders.

''Easy, my lady!'' he murmured.

''Quinn,'' she said weakly, her gaze straying unwillingly back to the blood pooling about his right foot. He was wounded much worse than she had guessed, although the sight of blood had never affected her so adversely. ''You must have this tended.''

''It is nothing,'' he said.

His words slowly sank in and Melissande regarded him in shock. ''Nothing?'' she repeated, dumbfounded that he could even think thus. ''You have been sorely injured! Look at the blood! The wound must be deep!''

''Yes,'' he said grimly. ''But as I say, there is work to do. Melissande, I will keep my word to you, then come to be tended.''

That was quite enough. This was serious and Melissande was not about to let her husband dismiss her fears.

What if she should lose him now? Melissande could barely stomach the thought. The idea alone of being without Quinn was enough to make her dizzy. She could not lose him, not over such a foolish matter.

Once she began to explain her stance, it seemed her fear took possession of her tongue.

''Quinn de Sayerne! Have you lost your wits? This is no small scratch and if you do not have it tended immediately, you will find yourself without that leg! I think that preserv-

ing your leg is well worth leaving some petty prisoner to
languish in the dungeon for a few moments. Have you gone
mad out on the walls?''

''No, but the prisoner must be questioned immediately.''

The strain evident in his features redoubled her conviction. Melissande propped her hands on her hips and tapped
her toe impatiently on the flagstones. ''Every moment
counts with regard to your leg, sir, not your prisoner. Do
you not understand you could lose your leg, if not your life?
I will not permit you to leave this hall without seeing it
treated.''

''Time is of the essence,'' he said through gritted teeth.
''And if you permit me to proceed, then I will be back
sooner to be tended.''

''If time was of such import, you should have come here
sooner.'' Melissande swiveled and glared at one of the
knights supporting Quinn. ''You, sir. Why did you not bring
your lord to the hall earlier? Why did you not compel him
to come here the very moment he was wounded?''

''We knew nothing about it, my lady, for he was in the
tower. It was by his hand alone that the brigands were dismissed. Only then did we see his injury.''

''That is a feeble excuse. Didn't any of you stay with your
lord to make certain of his safety?'' Melissande folded her
arms across her chest and steadfastly met the gaze of each
knight in turn. ''Did I not tell you that my husband would
be your lord and leader in this matter? How were any of you
trained that you did not keep him within your sight and
protection? What manner of men are you to not see to your
own lord's safety?''

The knights shuffled their feet and exchanged sidelong
glances with one another, though none spoke up.

''None of you has an answer while your lord stands
bleeding,'' she snapped before looking to Quinn again.

Quinn's amber gaze met hers, but the twinkle lurking in
the depths of his eyes disarmed her.

"Do you defend me, my lady?" he asked, a thread of amusement in his tone. Melissande knew by his expression that he referred to her protectiveness toward Annossy and Berthe that he had remarked upon before.

She flushed scarlet. It was too much that he mocked her in this moment when she felt so vulnerable. Especially when she was still too uncertain of Quinn's own feelings. To her own astonishment, Melissande felt tears rise to her eyes and was powerless to stop them from cascading over her cheeks.

"You could have been killed!" she burst out.

Quinn immediately stepped closer and enfolded her in his embrace. Melissande inhaled deeply of his scent and silently cursed her own weakness. What should she have done without him? The warmth of his hand was on the nape of her neck and she felt his cheek against her hair.

"Fear not, my lady," he whispered. "Did I not vow to you that I would return to your side?"

"But Quinn, your leg must be tended."

"I would know the plans of these brigands first," he insisted. The weight of his hand passed over her hair. "Then, you may rest assured, I will come to bed and you may tend me for as long as you desire."

The surrounding knights chuckled discreetly.

"Quinn!" Melissande's cheeks stained pink. "You need another kind of care."

It was only when she looked up into his eyes again that she saw that he teased her. He touched her chin and smiled down at her.

"It will be all right. I shall be only a few moments. Do not worry, for I am a tough old knight. Make your preparations and I shall be in the solar before you are even ready for me."

"I do not believe you," she murmured unhappily. "You will spend too much time with the prisoner and endanger your leg. We have already wasted too long in discussion."

"Imagine the horror of being confined to bed for the remainder of my days," Quinn jested. Melissande thought sourly that her tears seemed to have improved his mood. The realization made Melissande even more self-conscious.

"Quinn! This is most serious!"

He sobered and ran one fingertip across her lips. "And I know it. I do not intend to lose my leg, Melissande." His eyes were dark, his gaze steady. "Now, go that I might be there sooner."

Their gazes clung for a long moment, then Melissande backed away with a nod. "Yes, my lord," she whispered, hoping against hope that Quinn did as he vowed.

He granted her a smile and limped away with the aid of his men. As Melissande watched him go, her frustration with him rose yet again. If that stubborn man put his leg in jeopardy, she would throttle him for his foolishness!

"Hot water to the solar," she demanded, dispatching servants with her usual efficiency. "See that the fire is lit and place some hot stones in the bed that the lord is not chilled. Hasten yourselves, if you please!"

The captured bandit was small and his expression was surly. He slouched on the bench between two knights, periodically glancing balefully at one or the other. The knights stared straight ahead, their hands resting on the hilts of their blades, their features impassive.

The little man's expression brightened when he saw the blood on Quinn's chausses. He noted Quinn's limp with unexpected malice and grinned with delight.

"So, we did strike at least one blow this day," he said by way of greeting.

Quinn did not appreciate the comment. "And you will pay dearly for it."

"Oh, yes," the little man sneered. "A lame man is a dangerous opponent."

One of the knights accompanying Quinn dragged over another bench and Quinn sank onto it gratefully. His leg throbbed painfully, though he would never have admitted as much to Melissande. The memory of her concern almost made him smile, then he met the cold gaze of his prisoner.

He thought of responding to the little man's comment, but decided instead to let his smile widen with confidence. The prisoner's assurance eroded as he eyed Quinn warily.

"What kind of man are you to smile when your own blood pools about your feet?" he demanded.

Quinn settled back into his seat and regarded the other man carefully, his smile unwavering. "I believe it is my place to ask the questions," he said pleasantly.

Five knights of Annossy were in the chamber, and the prisoner flicked glances from one to the other before looking back to Quinn. "You are their leader?" he asked insolently.

"I am lord of this keep." It wasn't precisely true, but Quinn knew no one would argue the point with him now.

The prisoner sneered. "Annossy has no lord."

Quinn permitted his smile to broaden. "Evidently you have not corresponded with the Lord de Tulley of late." The prisoner's eyes narrowed, but Quinn saw that he had the man's attention. He began to toy with the idea of releasing this one, once he was done with him, to let him take the word back to his leader.

Of course, it would all depend on how much this man cooperated in sharing what he knew with Quinn.

"What has Tulley to do with this?"

"Surely you know that Tulley is the liege lord of Annossy?" Quinn continued in an amiable tone, enjoying how his manner troubled the little man opposite.

The man scanned Quinn skeptically. "Do not tell me that Tulley has acknowledged one of his bastards—" his expression planted Quinn firmly amidst that august company

"—and granted Annossy to you. I shall not believe a word of it."

"I am only one of Tulley's vassals." Quinn decided to stretch the truth slightly in the interest of simplicity. "Quinn de Sayerne am I, Lord of Sayerne, and now, with my marriage to the lady Melissande, Lord of Annossy."

The man's eyes nearly popped out of his head. "Jerome de Sayerne's son?"

"Yes, in point of fact, I am."

"One of his bastards?"

"No, his legitimate son."

"But, but, Sayerne only had one. Who rode to the East years past and was never heard from again." The man's expression was skeptical.

Quinn permitted himself another slow smile.

"I returned."

Quinn held the man's gaze while that one came to terms with his tale. Quinn had no doubt that the man believed him, though he gave him a moment.

"And who," Quinn asked deliberately, "might you be?"

The little man drew himself up proudly. "That is no business of yours."

"I should think it is every business of mine to know whom the rats in my dungeon gnaw upon."

The man glanced over his shoulder to the dark shadows behind. He shook himself visibly and looked Quinn squarely in the eye. "I am not afraid of rats."

"Good. They have been without guests so long that I suspect they may be quite, shall we say, *interested* in your company. I am glad that will not trouble you overmuch."

The man shivered visibly. "I have nothing to tell you."

"Hmm." Quinn frowned at the floor, apparently lost in thought.

When the man remained silent, Quinn shot a glance to the knight beside him and grimaced. "Amalryc, are they truly as large and numerous as you confided in me?"

The knight did not miss a beat. "Yes, my lord. As big as dogs. In fact, the dogs will not venture down here any longer. The rats ate the stores away three months past—and the lady was sorely vexed—so I expect they are hungry by now."

Quinn shook his head and glanced up to the prisoner with a philosophical shrug. "Too bad. It is unlikely that you will be able to tell me anything in the morning." He leaned forward confidentially. "I always think it fitting to grant a guest a night or two of hospitality to consider his options, but you, it seems, will have no such opportunity."

Quinn pushed to his feet and limped to the door with his knights. He paused on the threshold to watch the last two knights lock manacles around the prisoner's wrists and ankles.

"I wish you a good night's rest," he said in the same conversational tone before he turned away.

The other knights followed and the door to the cellar chamber was closed. The sound of the lock's heavy tumblers rolling echoed in the damp cellar. Quinn made a few hand signals to his accompanying knights and they all grinned in understanding before the lantern was extinguished.

Two knights stamped up the stairs noisily while the others remained at the foot of the stairs. Above, the trapdoor was dropped closed and the bolt shot home.

The cellar was as black as pitch.

Quinn leaned over and scratched the stone step with his nail. The sound carried through the darkness much louder than one might have expected. The other knights followed suit and the cellar was filled with a sound not unlike small scratching feet.

The prisoner lasted less than a dozen heartbeats with that sound in his ears.

"Quinn de Sayerne!" called the prisoner in a distraught voice. "Quinn de Sayerne! Do not leave me to be eaten by rats! I will confess to you all that I know, I swear it!"

Quinn continued to scratch, so that the man might become more agitated, before he responded. He would not risk him changing his mind—or worse, suspecting the trick—when the light was quickly restored.

The prisoner's voice rose to a screech and his manacles rattled in agitation. "Quinn de Sayerne! I beg of you—help me now! I have reconsidered! I will tell!"

At Quinn's touch on his sleeve, one of the knights crept silently up the stairs and tapped on the trapdoor. It squealed open a moment later and the prisoner's exhalation of relief was audible. The knights exchanged a grin with Quinn.

"You! In the cellar!" Quinn roared as though irritated. "Keep quiet that I might enjoy my dinner!"

He flicked a finger to the knights above and the trapdoor was dropped resoundingly back into place. Quinn scratched the stairs again, the others following suit. The knights struggled to contain their chuckles as the prisoner wailed in anguish.

"Quinn de Sayerne, have mercy upon me! I beg of you, sir, grant me the opportunity to share my tale!"

The trapdoor opened again. Quinn beckoned and the knights stomped down the stairs with vigor.

"What ails you?" one demanded at the prisoner's door. "Can you not leave the lord to consume his meal in peace?"

"Please, please, tell him I have reconsidered. Tell him that I will explain the identities of the attackers."

The knight snorted skeptically. "You are quick to reconsider your position. You were quite obstinate just moments ago."

"But the rats!" The prisoner swallowed audibly. "They are everywhere. Hundreds of them! No, thousands of them! I can hear them. I can feel them nibbling on my toes in the darkness."

The knight harrumphed. "The lord may not be interested in interrupting his meal."

"I do not care if I have to wait!" the little man wailed. "But please, I beg of you, leave the light in the cellar that the rats might be kept at bay."

"We shall see what the lord has to say about this," the knight said. They stomped again on the stairs, the knights no longer able to even look at each other without grinning. Quinn waited, wanting to be certain that the prisoner was truly willing to talk.

When the imprisoned man whimpered to himself, it was time.

A different man waited inside the chamber than the one they had left. The insolent sneer and the cocky assurance were both gone. His eyes were wide now and there was sweat upon his brow.

He nearly fainted at the sight of Quinn.

"Sir! You are most kind to come to my aid. I will tell you anything you might want to know, but please, I beg of you, do not leave me with the rats again."

Quinn settled himself on his bench. "What is your name?"

"Percival, sir, Percival de Provins."

"And what brought you to Annossy?"

Percival took a deep breath. "My liege lord, sir, he planned to attack Annossy and claim it for his own."

Quinn frowned. "This was an invasion by renegades."

"No, sir. My liege lord but wanted it to look that way. He did not want to attack outright, lest Tulley take retaliation against his own holdings before my lord claimed Annossy successfully."

Quinn's brows rose. "Your lord has holdings of his own?"

The man nodded. "Yes, sir. His wife's hereditary estate is one Perricault."

"Perricault is not far from here."

"No, it is not. It shares a boundary with Annossy."

"But Tulley would still march on Annossy if it were lost," Quinn observed.

The little man shrugged. "My lord declares that he has a plan that will silence Tulley's objections, once Annossy is in his possession."

Quinn folded his hands together thoughtfully. The estates of one heiress were not enough for Perricault's lord. He would now annex Annossy, weakening the estate with what looked like the looting of brigands, then riding to an easy victory. It was a clever ploy, if unethical.

"And who is this lord who wed the heiress of Perricault?"

"Arnaud de Privas," the prisoner supplied.

Arnaud de Privas. Quinn frowned. The name was too familiar. Melissande had been pledged to an Arnaud. Had she not said Arnaud de Privas? Quinn believed she had.

Yet this man attacked Annossy? Was this the vengeance that Quinn had feared for his taking the wife that should have been Arnaud's?

But then, why had Arnaud married the heiress of Perricault?

"Why does your lord attack Annossy?" he asked.

The prisoner shrugged. "Because it is a neighboring estate, I suppose, and well-known to be prosperous. Since he wed the lady of Perricault last summer, he has secretly been pledged to the task."

If that was true, then this could have nothing to do with Quinn. Arnaud had been married before Melissande, so he had broken their pledge first. Maybe this man had misspoken.

"He has been pledged to this since last summer?" Quinn asked dubiously. "And you still have not taken the keep? I confess that I would not want your lot of knights at my side."

As Quinn expected, the little man bristled. "It was by the lord's own dictate that we only harassed the estate. Setting fire to the mill was the boldest play to date, although now he decreed that the stakes should be raised."

On the very night that Quinn had returned. That was too much of a coincidence for Quinn's taste.

"Why now?"

The prisoner shrugged. "He grows impatient with the game. He says he would have the matter resolved. This very night he came to supervise the attack himself for the first time."

"Really?"

The prisoner nodded. "Yes. He was the one who you sent fleeing from the tower. That was why the others followed his lead and fled in his wake."

Quinn eyed the gash in his thigh and did not like that Melissande's betrothed had attacked just after he rode through the gates.

That he had been wounded so deeply reminded Quinn of his past experience in the East. And that his wound had been granted from the hand of Melissande's betrothed was not welcome news.

Could she have been in communication with Arnaud while Quinn was at Sayerne? Could Melissande have made some kind of arrangement to guarantee that Annossy became hers? Quinn supposed that the attackers could have waited in the wood for his return. Surely Melissande could not have betrayed him?

But she had before.

She *had* said on their wedding morn that she loved this Arnaud. And she had sworn to see Annossy hers alone.

Of course, Tulley would have tried to marry her to another unsuspecting spouse, but maybe Melissande had concocted another plan against that. If she barricaded Annossy against Tulley, he would have difficulties seeing his will done.

Quinn felt suddenly ill.

Now that he thought about it, it was suspicious that Melissande had fled Sayerne, but then greeted him here so willingly. It was too easy to find evidence for his fears in his wife's behavior, even though Quinn wanted to believe that she had been growing to trust him. The blood on his chausses dared Quinn to believe her sweet lies.

Quinn pushed to his feet, his heart twisted with the certainty that Melissande had deliberately feigned concern for his injury to gain his trust.

He had been betrayed again. And by a woman who had already shown herself untrustworthy. Bayard had been wrong. Quinn might usually be quick to trust and to turn away, but this time, it appeared he had been too quick to forgive and forget.

But everything within Quinn fought against his conclusion. He had to be wrong. Melissande could not have deceived him deliberately.

Quinn's stomach rolled restlessly. He had to talk to Melissande. He had to know the truth. He had to look her in the eye and see her expression when he asked her about this Arnaud. He would hear the truth fall from her own lips.

He wanted to do it now. Quinn pivoted in the doorway and fixed his prisoner with a stare. "I will release you, for there are enough vermin in this place without the taint of your scent. Get yourself back to your liege lord and tell him that I do not readily release that which is mine."

Quinn stalked stiffly up the stairs to the hall. He made his knights swear to keep silent about the prisoner's confession. Quinn wanted to talk to his wife first.

Melissande was waiting for him, exactly as he had bidden her. Her concession both undermined and fed his suspicion. Those green eyes were wide with concern and as soon as Quinn limped across the threshold, she was by his side.

Quinn steeled himself against her allure. Hadn't she insisted upon her independence? Surely it could only be an act that she bent to his will now?

"You have remained too long on your feet," she scolded him gently. "Come to bed and be tended."

With an aching heart, Quinn let himself be led. A maid bent to aid with his boots, but Melissande shooed the girl away.

"I shall tend him myself." Her tone was impatient and Quinn wished she could really be so protective of his welfare. Did it not appear that he had exactly what he desired?

"Just bring the water and then you may leave," she told the maid tersely.

"Yes, my lady."

In a twinkling, they were alone. Quinn could not look to his wife's face. If he was wrong about her intent, his thoughts were unfittingly disloyal. If he was right, the pain of her betrayal would tear him in half.

Quinn stared at his leg.

Evidently Melissande assumed he was tired by the pain. She peeled off his garments with efficient hands, hesitating for only a moment when the wound was revealed. He flicked a glance to her face to find her nibbling her lip with concern.

If the woman pretended, then she made a good show of it. Quinn leaned back and closed his eyes in exhaustion. The leg ached.

And Melissande set to work. The rhythm of her washing soothed him and Quinn savored the weight of her hands on his skin, fearing that this might be the last time. She did not falter after that first moment and he appreciated that she was a woman of purpose.

He was in love with her.

Quinn stared at the canopy over the bed with its woven pattern of twining vines and looked the truth squarely in the eye. Melissande was everything that he had always desired in a partner and more. Practical, possessed of a mind of her own, sensuous and loving, beautiful to look upon and keen of intellect.

And possibly deceitful.

She finished and he propped himself up on his elbows to watch her. Her hair glinted golden in the firelight and he noted the length of her lashes as she gave the dressing one last scrutiny. Her ruddy lips pursed in a most delightfully feminine manner as her gentle fingers danced over the bandage.

She glanced up and he was snared in her magnificent gaze. "There," she said, summoning a smile that was meant to be reassuring. "You will be hale again in no time at all."

Quinn said nothing and gradually Melissande's smile faded away. She eyed him and shook her head slowly, but before she could ask what was wrong—before she could show any concern that might undermine Quinn's determination—he blurted out his question.

"What was the name of your betrothed?"

Melissande blinked. She looked away, then back to Quinn, her fingers nervously pleating the coverlet. "He was not exactly my betrothed," she said carefully.

Quinn deliberately schooled his hopeful response. "I thought you said you had taken a pledge to him?"

"Yes," she conceded. "Yes, a pledge was exchanged between the two of us years ago, but it was not an official betrothal with contracts signed and all."

"What was his name?"

Melissande sighed. "Arnaud de Privas. But, Quinn, I would talk to you about..."

Arnaud de Privas! It *had* been her betrothed who buried his blade in Quinn's thigh! The very sound of that same name made Quinn's heart begin to pound.

"And you love him?" The question was difficult to even utter, the way Melissande looked away doing nothing to reassure Quinn's fears.

"Quinn, I . . ."

"Answer my question."

Her lips thinned stubbornly and she flicked a glance to him. "Yes, I thought . . ."

That was all the confirmation he needed. She loved Arnaud. Quinn did not want to hear anything more.

"Spare me the details," Quinn snapped. "Do you know where this Arnaud is now?"

Melissande shook her head. "No, but, Quinn, I do not care."

That could not be true. Quinn's heart lurched but he steeled himself against the appeal of the words he wanted to hear.

She said she loved Arnaud and that was that.

"Spare me your pretty lies!" he roared. "You have told me of your regard for him—do not suppose that I will believe anything has changed so hastily!" He gritted his teeth and leaned closer, wanting to do nothing but hurt her in return. "But tell me this, my lady, why did this Arnaud marry another woman?"

"*That* is a wicked lie!"

The lady's fury was the last shred of evidence Quinn needed to conclude her guilt.

"Tulley told you that and Tulley is wrong. Arnaud would *never . . .*"

"Spare me the tale of your lover so true," Quinn said bitterly. "A wounded man has need of his sleep."

"This wounded man has need of the truth before he sleeps!"

"I have the truth already, and it is not a fair sight."

Melissande drew herself up tall and her eyes flashed. "I would discuss this matter with you, if you would be so good as to give me the chance."

"There is nothing to discuss." Quinn rolled over and winced at the pain in his leg. He recalled in a sudden flash his opponent's determination and wondered if the plan had been for Quinn to not leave that tower alive. Had he been more of an opponent than Arnaud had expected?

Would Arnaud return to finish what he had begun? Quinn's heart went cold. He could not afford to remain at Annossy. He would sleep tonight in this treacherous den, but in the morning, he would return to the safety of Sayerne.

If this Arnaud decided to hunt Quinn's hide there, he would have fewer allies within the walls.

"There is everything to discuss for it is clear that you have come to false conclusions."

It was too much that she should continue to argue with him once he had unveiled her deception.

"I would only make more false conclusions, if I listen to the words that fall from your own lips." Quinn sat up and glared outright at his wife. "You said yourself that you love this Arnaud de Privas and I simply believed you. You said yourself that you did not want this match with me. You said yourself that you would fight me to the end to maintain your independence at Annossy. You tell me that I know nothing of running an estate and that I would drag down your precious Annossy with my blundering."

"Quinn, I did not mean . . ."

"Well, I have now seen Annossy for the prize that it is," Quinn thundered on, ignoring her attempt to interrupt. "And I have endeavored to make peace with you as many times as I am inclined to do so. I should never have agreed to follow Tulley's will, but I have and now will make my own peace with it. In the morning, I shall return to Sayerne alone and rebuild it with whatever aid might come to hand. I ask nothing of you and will never trouble you again."

"What of our bargain? What of conceiving a child to fulfill Tulley's requirement?"

Quinn waved off her concern and burrowed in the bed. "I do not care for Tulley's demands any longer. If he is ill disposed to grant Sayerne to my hand one year from now, then so it shall be. I have done all a man might do to fulfill his requests and can do no more. I have earned my way with my blade before and should I need to, I will do so again.''

"But, Quinn, you cannot leave Annossy now!'' Melissande declared. "What if we are attacked again?''

Quinn shot a glance in her direction. "I doubt that that will be a problem.''

"But why?'' Her face showed confusion perfectly. "What did you find out from the prisoner?''

"Nothing that you do not already know,'' Quinn said darkly. "I do not want to talk about it anymore.'' He rolled so that his back was turned to her, not wanting to see the hurt in her eyes. She had deceived him, he reminded himself forcefully.

"I will petition Tulley myself for you,'' Melissande argued with an earnestness that Quinn wished he could have believed. "It would be unfair if he did not invest you with your legacy.''

Quinn sighed, wishing he could take hope from her defense of him. He simply did not trust her any longer. "I ask you for nothing, my lady. Please leave me be this night.''

"But, Quinn,'' she protested, her voice as soft as that of a scolded child. Quinn squeezed his eyes closed against her appeal.

"But *nothing*,'' he said angrily. "Let me sleep in peace.''

She lingered for a moment and he felt her fingertips tapping gently on the coverlet as though she did not know what to do. Quinn remained stubbornly silent. Melissande sighed, a sound fit to wrench even the coldest heart, then her footsteps trailed away across the room.

Quinn called himself every manner of knave, even knowing that he was right.

* * *

That night, he dreamed of the East for the first time in months. Quinn relived every moment of that ill-fated attack and his new wound burned in recollection of the old. He tossed and turned, haunted by visions of infidel prisons.

The first finger of the dawn's light awakened him. He felt as though he had not slept at all. When he sat up, his gaze fell upon Melissande, curled like a cat before the hearth.

She looked so innocent for all the darkness of her heart. Quinn longed to bring her back to bed and awaken her with gentle kisses. He marveled that he could still desire her, even knowing what he did about her treachery.

He had to leave Annossy. The temptation was too great.

Although once he had dressed in the chill of the morning, Quinn could not abandon her to sleep like a servant. Carefully he lifted his wife into his arms and carried her to the bed. His gaze ran over her features, relaxed in sleep, as though he would memorize them.

This would be the last time he held her. The realization made the moment bittersweet, but before Quinn could change his mind, he laid Melissande on the feather-filled pallet and drew the covers over her.

She smiled and snuggled into the indentation left by him.

Quinn blinked back his tears, knowing he mourned something that had never truly existed, and turned away.

He was alone. And he would be better alone at Sayerne.

Quinn was startled to find an older man huddled in the stall beside his horse. The ostler shrugged as he led the stallion out of the stables.

"He has been here all night," the ostler commented.

"I could not risk missing the lord's departure." The man rose hastily and brushed the straw from his simple garb. He lifted his chin and looked Quinn squarely in the eye.

"I saw you last night, sir, and heard tell of your bravery in the battle. I would come to Sayerne if I knew the way," he said proudly.

Quinn glanced away for a moment, knowing that Melissande would not appreciate his taking a villein from Annossy.

But she had deceived him. And he had need of willing labor.

"Have you a mount?" he asked.

The man shook his head. "Just a donkey and a cart. My wife would bring our possessions along if we moved to Sayerne, but you need not fear. She is a hardworking woman and no burden, like our three sons."

It was clear the man thought Quinn would turn him aside.

Quinn smiled and stretched out his hand to the tenant. "I would welcome the assistance of you and your family at Sayerne," he said. The man smiled in nervous relief as he gripped Quinn's hand.

"It is not that we are unhappy at Annossy," he said quickly. "And I would not want your lady wife to think so. But three sons are both blessing and curse, for they labor hard but eat like men. Our share here is no longer enough. There is no more land to divide at Annossy and maybe our departure will help others in a similar bind."

"Are you a free man?" Quinn asked.

"Yes, my lord. Free except for the need of land to till. And should your word be as good as your sword hand, we shall be glad to travel with you."

"My word is my bond. Just bring a declaration of your

holding size at Annossy from the steward and I shall see your land increased by half again at Sayerne.''

The man exhaled in relief and bowed deeply. ''I thank you, my lord.''

''You have told the steward of your intent?''

''Yes.''

''Then, my squire Michel will travel with you and show you the way. Michel was the one who brought my missive here weeks past.''

''Yes, my lord. I remember him well.''

''Then we shall meet again at Sayerne.''

The man smiled. ''Yes, my lord. In time to sow.''

Chapter Twelve

Melissande lasted only a fortnight before she decided to follow Quinn to Sayerne. Clearly he had no intention of returning. The sting of awakening to find him gone had faded enough that she could consider seeking him out. They needed to talk about whatever he had decided was her crime.

The fact that she had missed a bleeding was no small factor in her decision. Melissande knew that she was pregnant with Quinn's seed.

He would be pleased with the news and she knew she owed it to him. How could he not be since it would guarantee his investiture with Sayerne? But still she worried that the conception would eliminate any need for Quinn to spend time with her. She knew she needed to go, but she dreaded giving Quinn an excuse to avoid her permanently.

Melissande walked down to the fields where the oxen hauled the plow, savoring the warm sweep of the spring wind. Spring had come with a vengeance. The mud was thick on the ground and the cry of the boys driving the team of oxen rang in her ears. Curiously Annossy had not been attacked again and Melissande wondered how Quinn could have known.

Her chatelain, Roger, bustled to her side, evidently well pleased with how matters were proceeding. He chatted about this and that as Melissande lent half an ear to his news.

"How much seed do we have?" she asked idly.

Roger winced as he calculated. "Enough and a bit to spare. It is hard to come by this year, so we are fortunate that we do not need to buy seed."

That assertion caught Melissande's interest. "My lord may have difficulties in buying seed for Sayerne then."

"Oh, I should think so," Roger confirmed. "Yields were not as good as usual last fall, yet just as much was needed for the winter months. I should think he would have to go far afield to find what he needed."

Melissande bit her lip as she glimpsed a viable excuse for visiting her husband. "Can we make do with less that the remainder might be sent to Sayerne?" She hoped suddenly that such an offering might convince him to listen to her side.

Roger frowned. "It would be close, too close that I would make that choice myself."

Melissande straightened and looked over the freshly tilled fields. She wanted to see Quinn. She wanted to show him that she cared for his goals, even if he did not care for hers.

Sayerne held his heart and the rebuilding of that estate occupied his mind. It was clear that if she wanted to be a part of his life, Melissande needed to show interest in that task.

"Then I shall ask the villeins for their support in this matter," she said. "They might voluntarily contribute seed since my lord did see our walls free of brigands."

"Yes, that he did, that he did," Roger admitted. "It has been quiet these past weeks. It is good for the spirit to be free of fear of attack." The older man cleared his throat. "I would personally contribute seeds from my vegetable garden that my lord's tenants might have something other than bread to eat."

"That is a fine idea, Roger." Melissande thought for just a moment before she decided. "I shall ask the cook to share seeds from the herb garden, as well. And we shall ask the tenants to contribute."

"It would be my pleasure to organize the matter, my lady," Roger offered.

Melissande smiled, knowing that every type of seed would be clearly labeled and separated with Roger at the task. "And I shall take our contribution to Sayerne."

"It will be arranged in short order, my lady."

Melissande nodded and Roger bowed before he darted purposefully away. She followed his path, her gaze caught by someone leaving the château gates. It was a dark-haired woman and Melissande recognized Berthe's figure.

Yes, she would go to Sayerne and take the lovesick Berthe along. There must be something she could do to heal the rift between her maid and Bayard, even if she and Quinn were doomed to live apart.

The fear of that eventuality would not keep Melissande from doing what she knew was right. She would share seed with Quinn and bring him the news of the child he desired.

And she would find out why he mistakenly thought she had betrayed him.

Arnaud de Privas watched the little procession leave Annossy's gates under bright blue spring skies. Although he stayed under the shadow of trees that he might not be spied, he could still identify Melissande's figure.

Arnaud frowned, uncertain where she might be going. A responsible landholder like Melissande would not travel abroad at this time of year. There was too much important labor to leave to the supervision of a chatelain. He watched the loaded cart leave the gates and wondered where the lady took supplies in this season.

This was most irregular.

As was the news and message his released warrior had carried back to his ears from the supposedly new Lord d'Annossy. Arnaud snorted. There would be no Lord d'Annossy before himself.

But Quinn de Sayerne had been a formidable adversary. Arnaud knew that it had only been good fortune that had seen him survive that surprise.

He was determined to have a plan that left nothing to chance when they next crossed swords.

Arnaud could easily dismiss Quinn de Sayerne as a small complication, like Arnaud's wife, Marie de Perricault. This was a slight detour along the path to making fair Annossy his own, and Arnaud fancied his plan—with slight revisions—could still be made to work.

He smiled in anticipation. Soon he would be lord of three estates, merging them all beneath his hand.

Arnaud ground his teeth once more in frustration. This would have been so much easier if his man released from Annossy had made better time in returning to Perricault. By the time Arnaud posted a watch outside Annossy, Quinn could easily have left. He had waited and watched himself, hoping for some sign.

Melissande's departure alone might be one. Surely she would not ride out alone if her husband was in residence? When Melissande's little party turned onto the road that led to Sayerne, Arnaud smiled, his question answered.

It might be good to have Quinn de Sayerne's fatal "accident" far from Annossy and Perricault. That way, there might be no suspicion of Arnaud's role. He waited until the party had traveled a good distance ahead, then trailed them discreetly under the cover of the woods alongside the road.

Quinn was moving fieldstones with the villeins when Bayard sought him out.

"The Lady Melissande approaches the gates," the knight said so casually that Quinn thought he had misunderstood the words. She could not have come to Sayerne. She would not have come to Sayerne.

His head snapped up from his task of lifting a particularly large and tenacious rock, but Bayard returned his stare levelly. Quinn did not doubt that his old companion had noticed every nuance of his response. But Bayard, mercifully, refrained from making any comment.

"Shall I give word that she may enter?" he asked mildly.

Melissande *was* here. Quinn exhaled and ran one hand through his hair, knowing he was a fool for being pleased at the prospect of seeing her again.

The lady had used him. The lady tempted him with her deceitful charms. The lady did not care for him.

And still he was haunted by dreams of her touch. Still his unruly heart skipped a beat at the mention of her name.

Quinn was a besotted fool. These weeks had gained him little, as he ached for Melissande as stridently as he had on the day he had left Annossy.

And now she had come to torment him.

He should have the gates barred before her. He should have the keeper tell her that she was not *invited* to Sayerne.

"Do not trouble yourself," Quinn found himself saying calmly instead. "I shall go to the gates and greet her myself."

He doffed his gloves and brushed the dirt from his chausses, not in the least interested in what Bayard would make of his answer. Quinn wiped his face on a cloth and strode toward the gates.

He was amazed at how casually he did so. As though it were no matter for his wife to arrive. As though his heart were not pounding fit to burst within his chest. As though it did not matter to him that she was here.

His mouth went dry when he first spotted her, though. His pulse echoed in his ears, even as his gaze took in every detail of her appearance.

Melissande rode her horse, her slight figure tall and straight. She held her chin high, her golden hair coiled out of sight. She smiled politely to the gatekeeper as she passed under the shadow of Sayerne's arched gate and Quinn ached with the knowledge that she would have no such smile for him.

She looked radiant and something writhed within Quinn that she had not apparently missed him as he had missed her. A party of knights accompanied her, he noted with satisfaction. At least she traveled in safety. And with a cart, curiously enough. She spotted him then and he thought his heart would stop at the weight of her gaze upon him.

But then, she glanced away, as though it were of no import at all to see him again after this time. A vestige of hope that Quinn had not known he sheltered within his heart died then in the sunlight of Sayerne's bailey.

And anger replaced it. He was angry with Melissande for seeking him out—the cart could only mean that she had come to live at Sayerne. He was suddenly furious—as only Melissande could make him—that she would so invade his sanctuary without even requesting his agreement.

But the root of his anger, Quinn knew, was her refusal to love him.

Then she smiled. It was an uncertain smile, as though she did not know what to expect of him, and Quinn's heart wrenched despite himself.

He would cast her out, he vowed silently. She deserved no less.

"Good day," Quinn said formally. He did not step closer and she halted her horse a dozen feet away. The ostler stepped forward to take the reins, but Melissande eyed Quinn with doubt clouding her eyes. Clearly the lady had hoped for a different greeting.

"Good day," she returned with less enthusiasm than she had smiled.

What did she expect after deceiving him?

Quinn folded his hands before himself. "I did not expect your arrival. You must excuse my lack of preparation."

Melissande blinked. She looked to the ground and her lips worked silently for a moment before she looked back to Quinn. "Have you no kinder greeting for your wife than that?" she asked softly.

Her voice nearly undid him, but Quinn gritted his teeth. "I have work to do," he said, "if you would excuse me?"

And Quinn turned to walk away. He heard Melissande gasp behind him but steeled himself to continue onward.

She pursued him, her light footsteps filling his ears, and Quinn wondered what he had expected from her. The woman was determined, if nothing else. He stomped into the hall, pivoting on his heel before the hearth.

It was here they had mated so splendidly that night, he recalled too late to move elsewhere. The recollection of his easy trust that night taunted him, but Quinn forced himself to meet the false innocence in her eyes.

"This is not the greeting I expected, husband," she said, again in that achingly soft voice.

Quinn snorted. "I do not know what else you might expect from me."

"I?" Her eyes flashed like emeralds in the sun and she closed the distance between them with angry steps. "It was you who left in the night like a coward creeping away in the dark!"

"That was only justified after all that had passed between us."

"After all that has passed between us? How dare you leave me in the middle of the night with no word of where you were going?"

"I could not imagine that you cared."

"Could not...! What kind of fool are you, Quinn de Sayerne? Was it not you who swept me off to bed to make love immediately upon your arrival? Was it not you who was wounded at Annossy? Was it not you I worried over and tended with tears in my eyes? Maybe it was another Quinn de Sayerne who was there since you do not seem to recall the event as clearly as do I.''

Quinn folded his arms across his chest, hating how Melissande's outrage so easily undermined his anger with her. ''Maybe it was another Quinn who foolishly trusted you before he knew the truth.''

Melissande's eyes narrowed speculatively. ''What truth?''

''The truth you hid from me.''

Quinn's wife flushed, granting him all the confirmation he needed. ''How did you know I hid anything from you?'' she asked, her voice uncharacteristically tremulous.

Quinn snorted. ''I had no idea until the prisoner we captured on the walls spilled his tale.''

Melissande frowned. ''What has the prisoner to do with this?''

''Everything!'' Quinn's frustration increased when she returned his gaze uncomprehendingly. ''Do not play your games with me any longer, my lady! I *know* the truth of it. I may not be an administrator trained as aptly as you, but I still have some wits about me!''

''What *are* you talking about?''

Quinn flung out his hands, unconvinced by her fine display of confusion. ''I am talking about you and Arnaud de Privas. I am talking about your desire to wed your betrothed. I am talking about the scheme you devised with Arnaud once you fled to Annossy!''

To say Melissande's expression was incredulous would have been an understatement, but Quinn did not underestimate her ability to feign a response.

''You are mad,'' she murmured. ''How did you manage to concoct this ridiculous idea?''

''Ridiculous!'' Quinn bellowed. ''*Ridiculous!* I shall tell you what is ridiculous, my lady. What is beyond absurd is that even knowing all of this about you, even knowing how you deliberately deceive and manipulate me, that you probably plan my death, still I cannot erase you from my mind. Still the memory of you plagues my nights and haunts my days. Still I cannot cease to think of your smile, your touch, your laugh, your complete inability to care about anything other than your precious Annossy!''

He stalked away from his unusually silent wife and jabbed a finger through the air toward her. ''That, my lady, is beyond ridiculous.''

Melissande stared at him and Quinn wondered suddenly why she had remained so silent throughout his tirade. It was most unlike Melissande and he could not imagine what ailed her.

''You addlepated idiot,'' she murmured finally. Quinn bristled, but apparently his wife was ready to have her say. ''What kind of mind do you have that you can twist the facts into something they are not?''

''I? I have done no twisting, my lady. It was you who told me that you loved Arnaud. Maybe you recall our wedding morning. Maybe you recall how you cried so sweetly for the love you had lost and made me feel the knave, when in truth it was you who had not been honest with me.''

''Quinn, I never did love him.''

Her short statement took the wind from Quinn's sails. He fell silent and glared at her. ''You told me that you did,'' he said with great precision.

Melissande shook her head. ''That was only a ploy to keep you from touching me again.'' She coughed and stared at her toe for a moment. ''I did not want to care for you.''

''Aha! So you admit to deceiving me!''

Melissande shrugged, her gaze disconcertingly warm upon him. ''I stretched the truth slightly that one time alone.''

He wanted to believe her but Quinn knew she lied.

''No!'' he countered. ''No, that was just the first time. What of that night right here, when you curled so close to me and tempted me over and over again throughout the night? Was that not a ploy to see me soundly asleep while you fled to Annossy?"

Melissande flushed and shuffled her feet. "Well." She glanced away and back to him, as nervous as a young girl. "I did plan as much, but I forgot any such plan once you turned your charm upon me. It was difficult to leave afterward."

"Pretty words will gain you nothing."

She fixed him with a steady stare that he could not turn away from. "Our bargain was entered in good faith, Quinn. There was never insincerity in my touch. You showed me a new world and I have missed your touch these past weeks."

"Ha! I am not such a fool as to believe your lies again. You have already admitted that you held the secret of your plans with Arnaud from me."

Melissande grimaced. "I do not know where you concocted that nonsense. Quinn, you make me wonder if it was your head that saw injury at Annossy."

"You held a secret from me and I know it."

Melissande flushed prettily once more but she did not back down. "Yes, I had a secret from you, but if you think it involved Arnaud, you are seriously mistaken."

"Then what? What else could you possibly have withheld from me? I challenge you, my lady, to convince me that you do not lie in this."

Melissande smiled and shook her head in a most disconcerting manner as she regarded him. "Just one thing I hid from you, Quinn, and that was the realization that I loved you and you alone."

Quinn's heart took a dizzying leap before he sternly checked his response. She toyed with him. She tried to trick him anew by telling him what he wanted most to hear.

But it was a lie. A lie of the worst kind.

"Is he your lover?" Quinn bit out the question between gritted teeth.

"What? Quinn de Sayerne! You go too far!" Melissande stalked him across the hall, grabbing his tunic and giving him a hearty shake before she shoved him into the wall. Quinn was so surprised by her anger that he did not fight her.

"You cretinous fool! Do you imagine that I rode all this way to lie to you? I have been worried since you walked out without a word of explanation! I have tried to be patient, but you test me too much with this nonsense about Arnaud. I have not seen that man in a decade." She looked him squarely in the eye. "I swear it to you."

He was almost tempted to believe her.

"But you have heard from him," Quinn insisted stubbornly.

"I have not. I do not even know where he is."

Ha! Melissande had revealed herself with that obvious fallacy! That she should stand toe-to-toe with him and lie about this was beyond Quinn's belief. He snorted his skepticism and glared down at her.

"Spare me your nonsense. You knew it was Arnaud attacking Annossy that night after I arrived and I know that you knew."

"Arnaud?" Again she feigned astonishment so perfectly that Quinn doubted his own certainty. He clung to his conclusions, though, hurt fueling his accusations.

"Yes, Arnaud and his merry men. It was Arnaud who saw his blade planted in my leg, although I am sure that you knew about that, as well." Quinn shrugged off the weight of Melissande's hand and eyed her warily.

"Did you have him await my arrival in the woods? It must have been a shock for you to have me return to the hall alive, but do not blame your betrothed. I showed him a healthy fight."

"Quinn. No, this cannot be," Melissande breathed. The color had drained from her face, but Quinn continued on.

"It was precisely that way and you knew it. I have no doubt that the two of you planned the entire event. Do not tell me that you missed me and spare me your tales of your lover true."

"You are wrong."

"I am right."

"I knew nothing of Arnaud's involvement."

"You had to know."

"I did not!" Melissande stamped her foot impatiently. "Listen to me, you bullheaded fool! I knew nothing of Arnaud being behind the attacks on Annossy. It makes no sense to me that he would be and I cannot imagine how you contrived this ridiculous idea."

"So, you still defend him over me." Quinn folded his arms across his chest. "It seems that you have made your choice."

Melissande looked ready to spit sparks. She glared at him for a long moment and Quinn unflinchingly watched her temper rise.

"Yes, I have made my choice, but as I stand here, I must wonder what kind of fool I am. You left me, so I followed to seek you out."

"And a trip of days took weeks, because you were so intent on arriving," Quinn scoffed.

"Quinn! You are the most frustrating man I have ever met! When you disappeared without word, I thought you intended to return shortly. I waited for you. Then I was afraid that you did not wish to see me, so I stayed away."

"Then why do you come now?" he asked belligerently. "Why did you not just stay at Annossy?"

Tears pooled in her lovely green eyes and Quinn felt cruel for being so harsh with her. To see her defiance fade so suddenly made him long to gather her close and make her smile anew.

He was confused. Quinn no longer knew what to believe.

"Because I was afraid you would have no seed for your fields," she whispered. "That is what is in the cart."

Quinn was not in the least pleased to learn that his wife had solved his most pressing problem. Seed had been impossible to buy in quantity this spring and he hated that she had guessed his predicament.

And worse, she had solved it.

Curse her! Melissande was the last person in all of Christendom to whom Quinn wished to owe a debt. It did not help to know that she did not need him, while evidently he did need the aid of her Annossy.

Somehow he managed to force out an answer. "I shall see you paid."

"Quinn, it is a gift from those of Annossy to those of Sayerne. We are neighbors and we...I would see your holdings prosper."

"I do not need your charity."

She took a deliberate breath and her voice was low when she spoke. "Please take the gift, Quinn. Even if you turn away from me."

She sounded as though he had wronged her with his doubts. And to hear Melissande tell it, he had. Quinn felt his ears burn that he might be treating her unjustly. But all the facts and hints fit together perfectly.

At least they had until Melissande had come today and begun to confuse his thinking.

It was clear that Quinn could permit her to stay no longer. His feelings for her had not diminished as much as Quinn might have hoped and he could not risk remaining in her presence. Melissande might cast her spell of deception about him again.

"If that is your mission, consider it done. I thank you for your generosity and wish you Godspeed."

Melissande's mouth dropped open at his rudeness before she composed herself. "That is not all," she finally said firmly. Quinn glanced back at her to find defiance in her eyes as it had been when first he had met her. "I came here today to grant you news, as well, husband of mine."

Quinn forced his expression to remain impassive. "And what might that be?"

Those tears returned to her eyes, but still Melissande held her chin high. "That your child will arrive before the Yule," she said in a choked voice. Quinn said nothing, disbelieving her claim. She stared back at him, then shook her head. "Clearly I overestimated your interest in the news that soon you will have all you needed of me."

Still Quinn held his tongue. He would not trust her word. He did not dare, so afraid was he that she would steal this sweet promise away from him if he made any response.

Melissande watched him silently, then tears spilled over her cheeks in a torrent. She made a muffled gasp, turned abruptly away and fled to the portal.

Melissande glanced back to her astonished husband once more from the threshold and their gazes clung across the shadowed hall. "I love you," she admitted in an uneven voice. "Although at this moment, I cannot imagine why."

Quinn did not know what to say. He watched dumbfounded as his lady fled into the bailey. He heard her argue with the ostler, then heard the horse gallop away.

They were having a child! Quinn stared down at the floor as he struggled to come to terms with Melissande's claim. A child. The child Tulley required to grant to him Sayerne.

All of this would be his.

Quinn turned and looked about the château he had long loved. He wandered to the portal in his wife's wake, his gaze falling finally on the cloud of dust lingering before the gate house.

Melissande was gone.

The despondency that had filled his heart since he had left Annossy lodged firmly once again in his chest. Without Melissande, even Sayerne meant nothing to him. It had been only a task since he returned this last time. Quinn realized too late that the pride he had felt in restoring this place had abandoned him in the solar of Annossy.

He did not care about any of this without Melissande. Without her by his side, it was all ashes in his hands.

But she had said she loved him. Hope dawned within Quinn. Was it even possible that Melissande might care for him? Had he dismissed her tender feelings with his accusations?

Or was there a chance he could have her by his side again? Could he have been wrong about Arnaud?

Quinn spared a glance to the darkening sky and his lips thinned. Fool woman! She took no care for her own safety, riding out alone at such an hour. He would ride in pursuit. He would find Melissande and bring her home to Sayerne.

And he would find out the truth, once and for all. Quinn dared to imagine the two of them and the child Melissande bore making their home together. It did not matter whether it was here or at Annossy.

What mattered beyond all else was having his wife by his side. Quinn barely noticed that the spring had returned to his step as he hastened toward the stables.

"So, you have come back."

Berthe spun at the achingly familiar sound of Bayard's voice. She stepped away from the cart of seeds and dropped the bag of carrot seed she had been holding, aware of nothing but Bayard's dark gaze.

This was the moment she had both anticipated and dreaded. He watched her, wariness lurking in his eyes, and her heart took off at a gallop.

At least he spoke to her.

Berthe bent and carefully picked up the seed bag. She replaced it in the cart, taking more care with the matter than it certainly required. "My lady requested that I accompany her."

"Hmm." Bayard lifted a brow, then slid farther into the stables. They were alone, despite the odds. Berthe felt her palms go damp, but she held her ground.

Bayard flicked a glance to her, then looked to his toes again. "And there is no other reason you came?"

Berthe cleared her throat. His tone was so casual that she dared to hope he tried to hide his interest. He had come to talk to her. That must be of some importance.

She would still be cautious. "I understood that I was foolish to expect anything else here."

Bayard's chin shot up and his eyes narrowed. "From who?"

Berthe sighed with impatience. "From you, of course," she snapped.

"Me?" Bayard made a disgruntled noise in the back of his throat. "I cannot imagine that you even noticed *me*, what with all the other knights sniffing around your skirts when you were last here."

"And why should they not?" Berthe propped her hands on her hips. "I thought that I was a woman with some charms, but suddenly, I ceased to exist."

"There was nothing sudden about it! You saw me hit on the head!"

"That was an accident and you know it."

"You lied to me about riding out to talk that night."

"Well..." Berthe pursed her lips thoughtfully as she considered how much to confide in this knight, then decided she had nothing to lose. She had already lost him, it seemed. "Maybe I lied about doing so that particular night, because of my lady's own plans, but I never misled you about my interest in doing so."

There. She had said it.

Bayard's gaze brightened and he met her eyes. "Really?"

Berthe rolled her eyes. "Of course, *really*. Why would I lie to you about such a thing? You knew all along that I was interested and if you had granted me a moment of consideration, you might well have—"

Berthe got no further before Bayard kissed her firmly and directly on the lips. She gasped but he swallowed the sound, his arms winding around her in a most seductive manner.

"I told you that I was no promiscuous miss," she protested when he granted her room to breathe.

Bayard smiled a slow, sensuous smile as he stared down into her eyes. "I like that in a wife," he murmured.

Wife? Berthe's eyes widened, but she had no time to protest before he was kissing her again.

Wife. He intended to see them wed. Berthe's heart sang and she slipped her arms around his neck. This time, she kissed her knight back.

It was only fitting, since they were betrothed, after all.

Cursed man! The tears streamed down Melissande's cheeks as she rode, uncaring how the horse took the path. She had confessed all to him, she had poured out her heart and still he stood before her like a man wrought of stone.

He did not care for her. He had no heart. He did not even care for the child growing within her that was a precious gift of their love.

All Quinn cared about was Sayerne. She had expected that he might at least be pleased at the news of the child that would guarantee his inheritance, but apparently even that did not gain his attention. Melissande had been a fool to think that she could matter to him even for that.

Clearly Quinn had resolved the matter with Tulley another way. He did not need her at all to obtain his precious Sayerne. His accusations about her and Arnaud were just made to hurt her and distract her from his new arrangement.

To hell with Sayerne! And to hell with Quinn! Melissande would return to Annossy. She would raise her child alone, since its sire cared so little. She had been independent before and she would be independent again.

Even if the prospect was empty without Quinn.

Melissande brushed her tears away with an impatient hand and hoped against hope that the babe did not have the amber eyes of its father. She hoped the babe did not resemble him at all, for then the memories of their short time together would torment her. It would be almost impossible to continue without Quinn should she have a small reminder of him directly at her hand.

But Melissande would manage somehow. She always had. She lifted her chin and took a deep breath, knowing she would be back at Annossy before long.

It was then that Melissande saw the cloaked figure on the road ahead.

He was silhouetted against the sunset, his black cape blowing nonchalantly in the wind. He sat silently, his attention fixed upon her, and a chill tripped down her spine.

A brigand!

Melissande drew her steed to a halt and glanced back over her shoulder. The road was empty behind her. She could not even see the gates of Sayerne any longer.

She was alone. On the road at night. Under her breath, Melissande called herself seven kinds of fool.

Though she saw little joy in the days that stretched endlessly before her without Quinn, her babe deserved better. Melissande would not see harm come to her child and she gritted her teeth with determination.

She eyed the road ahead, but the rider held his ground. Melissande swallowed with the certainty that he waited for her. And there was no one to aid her or her babe.

As always, she had only herself to rely upon.

Quickly Melissande examined her options and found only one. She could run. His steed was large and sleek, she saw, and Melissande gripped her reins, knowing that her small palfrey would be no match for its speed. This would be a losing proposition.

Still she had to try, for she could not so readily admit defeat. And the woods were her best chance, for the palfrey was smaller and would be more certain of foot there.

The brigand urged his horse forward and Melissande panicked. She turned the horse hard to the left and dug her heels into its sides. The beast leapt into the woods and charged through the undergrowth.

"Halt!" the man behind her cried and Melissande's heart skipped a beat. "Melissande d'Annossy! Cease your flight!"

That he should know her name was terrifying, for Melissande did not recognize his voice. Had he been waiting for her? She crouched low and urged her horse faster and yet faster.

When she did not answer, she heard the man curse.

Then she heard pursuing hoofbeats in the brush. The dry bracken from the winter past crackled and snapped beneath the horses' feet. The palfrey ran at breakneck speed, evidently sensing Melissande's fear.

But still the larger horse closed the distance between them. Melissande heard branches snap behind. She glanced back to find the shadow of her pursuer too close for comfort. When she looked back, she was slapped across the face with a young green frond and ducked low over the saddle.

Too late she wondered where she would go.

Too late she wished she had fled toward Sayerne. Quinn would have helped her, no matter what his feelings for her. Quinn was a man who could be trusted to take the noble path.

But Quinn would never know what fate met his wife in this woods so close to his own walls.

She could hear the horse behind thundering closer over her pulse pounding in her ears. What would she do? She had only a small knife on her person. What did he want from her?

"Melissande d'Annossy!"

The man's call served only to increase Melissande's fear. A stream glinted ahead in the moonlight before her horse plunged abruptly into its course. The water splashed about the beast's knees and splattered on Melissande's feet.

The water crossed the path, running parallel to the road as near as Melissande could guess. She wondered suddenly if this might be the stream that ran through Sayerne's village. It ran in the right direction.

It was worth a try. She had little to lose at this point. Melissande tugged on the reins to have the beast turn and follow the stream back toward Sayerne.

The streambed was covered with smooth stones. As the horse turned, its hooves slipped on the slick stones. Melissande screamed as she felt the palfrey's weight shift and she knew the creature had lost its balance. The horse's cry of terror rang in her ears as she fell toward the glittering water.

Melissande landed on her hip with a painful splash. She immediately pulled her feet toward herself as the horse fell beside her.

Water splashed over her in a torrent as the horse fell. She gasped with relief when the horse's weight just missed her ankle. The cold stream flowed beneath Melissande's kirtle and she was immediately chilled in the spring air. She struggled to stand despite the wet weight of her garments, even as her horse did the same.

Melissande managed to get to her feet. The horse was less successful, and she watched with concern but it finally managed to rise. It deliberately kept the weight off one foot and Melissande's stomach twisted with the suspicion that the ankle was broken.

They would go no farther this night. She stroked the beast's brow to calm it, and the palfrey nuzzled her neck nervously. Melissande glanced fearfully over her shoulder and her heart plummeted to her toes.

The rider waited silently on the riverbank.

Chapter Thirteen

Melissande swallowed, knowing she had no way to flee any further. She stood proudly in the shallow water and faced her opponent as though she were in her own hall.

"Who are you and what do you want?" she demanded. "I have no coin."

"Melissande," he scolded softly. There was an unacceptable undercurrent of intimacy in his tone and Melissande stiffened. "Is that any way to greet your long-lost betrothed?"

"I have no..." Melissande began, only to stop as the man dismounted. He was small of stature and wiry of build, not unlike a man she vaguely recalled.

He pushed back his hood and doffed his helmet. Melissande frowned, her memory uncertain. It had been so long since that hasty promise in the garden. Could this really be him?

"Arnaud de Privas, at your service," he said smoothly. He bowed and the way he held his left leg removed all doubt from Melissande's mind.

Arnaud had told her once he had a hunting injury there, she recalled, and that the joint was stiff. The way he bowed was distinctive and she fidgeted uneasily at her new certainty.

"Arnaud, this is rather a surprise." Melissande held herself tall, her mind flooded with questions. Had Quinn been right about Arnaud? And what would Arnaud say about her taking a spouse despite their vow? Guilt coiled within Melissande and she dreaded Arnaud's response to the news. "A visit at Annossy might have been more appropriate."

Arnaud chuckled to himself. "You were unavailable when last I was at Annossy." He offered her his hand, but Melissande was surprisingly loath to accept his assistance.

She chose to stay with her horse, shin deep in water. She frowned at his assertion, not understanding what he meant.

"Do not be ridiculous, Arnaud. You have not been to Annossy in years." Melissande eyed the cocksure man on the shore as doubt dawned in her mind. Both Tulley and Quinn had asserted that Arnaud had wed another. Could it be true? "In fact, I would be interested to know where you *have* been all these years. I expected you to return to Annossy long ago to make good on your pledge."

"Well, I had a few matters to resolve. But you may rest assured that I had our ultimate well-being in mind."

"What are you talking about?"

"But what tales have you to share?" Arnaud asked, deflecting her question. "I hear that you have taken a spouse."

Melissande felt herself flush, knowing that this was the confrontation she had most dreaded. What would Arnaud think when he discovered that she loved that new spouse?

When she spoke, her tone was more defensive than she had intended. "It was Tulley's doing, if you must know the truth. If you had returned as you had promised, it would not have happened."

"Tulley never did care for me."

His indifference was a far cry from the response Melissande had expected. Had Tulley and Quinn been right about Arnaud breaking their vow?

The question left her lips before she could stop it. "Tulley said you were wed. Is it true?"

Arnaud folded his hands behind his back and stared up at the twilit sky. "That is no longer a matter for concern."

Melissande frowned. "What do you mean? Are you wed or not?"

Arnaud smiled. "My wife, it seems, passed away this day."

"Oh, Arnaud, I am sorry." Directly on the heels of Melissande's sympathy came the question of what Arnaud was doing abroad when his wife had only just died.

She dismissed the suspicion as unkind.

"Are you?" He arched a brow and his smile broadened. "How odd, for I am not in the least sorry."

Melissande was shocked that he could be so callous. "Arnaud! How could you say such a thing?"

"It was not a love match, Melissande. In fact, Marie was a shrew, to put the matter kindly." He laughed then and the sound was chilling. "But she will torment me no longer."

"Arnaud! That is a shocking thing to say of the dead!"

"It is not a question of saying it." He smiled then and she saw the madness lurking in his eyes. "I planned it, Melissande. I did it for us. I wed Marie so that you and I might have more together. That was what kept me away so long."

She regarded him with horror, but Arnaud was so delighted with himself that he could not keep from sharing the tale.

"Did you not always love to administer estates? Well, now you have two to run and I have more lands to hunt."

Melissande took a wary step backward, but Arnaud did not notice.

"You see, Marie is a glutton of the worst kind. She has wine with her midday meal and if there are no guests compelling her to show some manners, she does not share the bottle, even with me." He grinned.

"There are no guests at Perricault this day, so I poured a certain herbal concoction that I had obtained earlier into the wine bottle. It is always left to stand in precisely the same place in the kitchens. Perricault is nothing if not superbly run." He spread his hands. "I, of course, have been off hunting today. It was easy."

"But surely a physician will treat her?"

"Ah." Arnaud made a mock sad face. "Tragically, the physician has gone to Lyons to acquire supplies and will not return for a fortnight. No one will remember that I suggested it would be a good time for him to go."

"But surely, someone will suspect foul play?"

Arnaud shrugged. "Marie always has a sour stomach. Likely a result of her continuous overindulgence. No one will suspect a thing until it is too late."

Melissande stumbled backward in the cold water. "What do you want from me?"

"What you promised me once before. After a sufficient mourning period for my dearly departed Marie, I should like to wed."

"But I am wed already."

Arnaud's smile did not waver. "I did not say what I hunted this night."

Melissande's heart stopped before it took off at a gallop. Arnaud was mad. Raving mad. And he intended to kill Quinn.

But the only way she could possibly save her child was to cooperate with whatever scheme Arnaud had in mind. Otherwise Melissande would likely suffer a fate not dissimilar to Marie de Perricault's.

Melissande summoned a frown that she hoped masked her horror. "But, Arnaud, why would you do such a thing? Why did you not simply return to wed me years past?"

His eyes gleamed in the darkness and he stepped forward. Melissande schooled herself not to step backward. "I did it for us, Melissande. Imagine. Perricault shares borders with Annossy. The estates could be merged. And Marie wanted me from the very start. It was almost impossible to resist all that wealth.

"I must confess, though," he said as he leaned forward. "All along, you, Melissande, loomed large in my memories. I recalled your independence and your beauty each time I listened to that shrew."

Melissande swallowed at the coldness in Arnaud's eyes, but when he offered her his hand, this time she took it. For the sake of her child. She stepped onto the shore by his side, hoping that somehow she would be able to save Quinn, too.

Even after his accusations, Melissande loved Quinn and she could not stand back to watch the father of her child killed before his time.

"I have a proposition for you, Melissande, and as the clever woman that you are, I know that you will see its merit."

Melissande cleared her throat and tried to smile encouragingly. "I am most interested, Arnaud. Please tell me more."

Quinn dismounted when he heard the voices and crept slowly forward through the woods. He had seen someone give chase to Melissande and followed the trail of broken bracken through the woods, his heart in his mouth. He had heard the splash and feared the worst, until Melissande's voice carried to his ears.

She was alive.

Quinn's eyes narrowed as the silhouettes of the pair ahead came into view. He saw immediately that Melissande favored her hip as she climbed to the riverbank. His gaze flicked to her steed and he noted the beast's odd stance. Quinn's lips thinned with the hope that the horse could be saved.

It was only then that his gaze lit on the slight man beside Melissande. Quinn's blood ran cold, for he would have recognized that one anywhere.

It was Arnaud de Privas.

Quinn recalled how Melissande had fled before Arnaud, which made no sense if she was plotting with the man. And Melissande would not have seen a horse injured for nothing. She had insisted to Quinn earlier that she had not seen Arnaud for years.

The lady deserved a chance, at least. If she had told Quinn the truth, she was in no small danger. Quinn paused and listened.

"I am most interested in your proposition, Arnaud. Please tell me more."

Her voice was strained. Encouraged, Quinn abandoned his horse and crept forward stealthily. He caught a glimpse of Melissande through the trees and his heart contracted at her pallor. It was not his imagination that her smile was stretched thin.

Quinn did not know her game, but he would grant her the benefit of the doubt.

"This is an idea of which I am proud," Arnaud declared. "And one of which you will surely see the merit. You see, should Sayerne, Perricault and Annossy be united into one estate, it would be huge beyond belief. And I would be its lord."

"But the estates are not united." Melissande's voice was calm and inviting. Quinn imagined she was deliberately coaxing Arnaud to explain.

The woman was wise. Quinn smiled with pride in the darkness. It was always better to understand the intent of one's opponent.

"Not yet, not yet. But with Marie's untimely demise today, I am the unattached Lord of Perricault. And you hold Annossy already. And your spouse holds Sayerne. Should he die in a similarly untimely fashion, Sayerne would pass to your hands. Then, once we are wed, all three estates will be mine."

Melissande cleared her throat delicately. "Clearly you do not know the situation. Tulley has not yet invested Quinn with Sayerne's seal and has no intent of granting me with the seal of Annossy."

"What? This cannot be." Arnaud was incredulous, then he chuckled in the darkness. "Melissande! Clearly you lie! The man told my own man that he held Sayerne."

"Your man?" Melissande asked in evident confusion.

"Yes, yes. The man taken prisoner on the walls of Annossy. If I had known it was this Quinn de Sayerne who battled me, I would have done more than nick his thigh. I would have finished him, then and there, and would not have fled Annossy in such an untimely manner."

Quinn watched Melissande's mouth drop open in shock. This was news to her and he felt guilty that he had doubted her word. "It was *you* who led the attacks on Annossy!"

"Of course. An Annossy weakened by 'marauders' would be easier to attack without Tulley becoming involved. I am afraid that you might not have fared well in that circumstance, Melissande, but that is all behind us now. My ambition has spread beyond merely uniting Perricault and Annossy. Everything has changed."

"You had no intention of keeping your pledge!"

"Why would I? Perricault has much richer properties than Annossy, if a less attractive mistress." He shuddered, then his gaze fixed on Melissande again. "When Jerome's mercenaries came through Perricault last fall after my nuptials, I had the idea of how to annex Annossy. I led that attack over the walls of Annossy last month and discovered what had happened to you.

"When I learned that you were wedded to Quinn, I realized the Fates had played directly into my hands. Here was my opportunity for three estates instead of one." He leered at Melissande.

"And a wife who enjoyed the administration that bores me so, not to mention one that is independent and more lovely." He winked at Melissande. "It was good fortune that you and Marie never saw eye to eye."

"I only knew that she had married, but not to whom."

Arnaud's smile broadened. "I wonder who was behind that?"

Melissande was clearly outraged and Quinn could easily share her feelings. His grip tightened on the hilt of his blade as his blood boiled.

"You meant to see me killed!" Melissande accused. Quinn looked to the other man, not really expecting a denial.

And there was none. Arnaud shrugged. "It was a possibility for a time," he admitted. "Although it has all worked out for the best in the end."

Quinn watched Melissande's features work but she lost the battle for control. "How can you imagine that I will wed a monster such as you?"

"A monster?" Arnaud regarded her with shock and disgust. "You call me a *monster?*"

"Yes! Yes, I do. What kind of man would coldly dismiss the demise of his own betrothed? Not to mention the murder of his wife?" Melissande spat on the grass before Arnaud's feet. "You are not worthy to sleep with the dogs."

Arnaud's face contorted with rage and Quinn silently pulled his blade from its scabbard. It was a pity that he had only his knife, but still it would be adequate to cut out this villain's black heart.

The man deserved to die swiftly and painfully at Quinn's own hand. Should Melissande be injured, he vowed, Arnaud's demise would be markedly less swift.

"I grant to you a choice, Melissande, and it is a finer one than you evidently deserve," Arnaud offered. "Your first option is to aid me in setting a trap for your husband, wed me and rule our estates jointly with me."

Melissande folded her arms across her chest, loathing evident in her gaze. "What is the other choice?"

Arnaud's lips thinned. "The other is less attractive, I must admit. Should you be unwilling to participate, rest assured that I will still claim Annossy. An unwilling bride is not beyond note and neither is a captive wife. Still your spouse will die, still we will be wed, and still Annossy will be mine before Tulley can raise a hand against me. The difference lies only in your own freedom."

Melissande looked unconvinced by the appeal of either option, Quinn noted with some satisfaction. "And what guarantee do I have that Marie and I will not share the same fate?''

"None, I suppose." Arnaud shrugged his indifference. "Once we are wed, I will not need you. It will depend on how well you please me as a wife."

"Bastard!" she hissed.

Arnaud's gaze darted over Melissande and Quinn saw the flicker of revulsion inadvertently cross her features. She schooled her expression, but it was too late.

Arnaud evidently had seen it, as well, for his gaze narrowed and he suddenly grasped her wrist. Melissande cried out, but he did not release her. "Maybe we should test your ability to please this very moment," he threatened.

Melissande screamed. She struggled and Arnaud's face darkened. "Shut up, you fool woman!"

"I would have Quinn hear all of your foul plan!"

"Do not test me, Melissande. No one will hear you here, for we are far from all listening ears." Arnaud unsheathed his blade with lightning speed and the blade glinted evilly in the moonlight. "It is no coincidence we negotiate in such a quiet locale."

Melissande's eyes widened in fear as Arnaud raised the blade high.

"You cannot do this," she whispered.

"I can and I will. I will have Annossy, with or without your cooperation. Now, which option will you choose?" Arnaud barely had time to ask his question before Quinn sprang from the woods with a roar.

Melissande gasped, the knife flashed as Arnaud pulled it downward. Melissande managed to twist out of Arnaud's grip in the nick of time. The knife missed her by the breadth of a hair.

"Out of the way!" Quinn roared. Melissande danced backward. Quinn drove his knife toward the other man's belly, but Arnaud evaded its bite.

Quinn heard the splash and Melissande's gasp as she lost her footing. He turned to find her wet but on her feet. She smiled, then her eyes widened in shock. Quinn pivoted back to face his opponent, just as the knife blade grazed his cheek.

Arnaud smiled as their eyes met. "We meet again, Quinn de Sayerne," he said. "And only one of us shall leave this place to claim the prize."

"There is no prize," Quinn said through gritted teeth.

"Ah but there is. We battle for the fair Melissande and her even fairer holding of Annossy."

"The lady has made her choice."

"The lady's choice has nothing to do with it."

"I say it has."

"And I say that you are a fool." With that, Arnaud lunged forward. Quinn twisted out of the way and brought his blade down hard. He caught Arnaud across the back of the calf, but the man danced out of range.

Arnaud spared a glance to the blood running down his leg and his eyes narrowed. *"En garde,"* he whispered.

Arnaud lunged forward and, though Quinn turned, he felt the nick of a blade across his shoulder. He pivoted and stabbed, striking Arnaud again in the same leg. The man limped away, his gaze burning as he looked up.

With a roar, Arnaud dove toward Quinn. He fought like a mad thing, tearing at Quinn's legs. Quinn lost his balance and fell, only to have Arnaud slash at his wrist. Quinn grimaced in pain, and his grip loosened on the hilt of his blade just long enough for Arnaud to kick it away.

Quinn took a deep breath and stared into the mad eyes of the man who held a blade over his heart.

Arnaud smiled. He lifted the blade high.

Quinn saw the sudden flash of a blade. Melissande drove Quinn's blade deep into the man's side. Quinn rolled out of the way as Arnaud stabbed downward. The other man yelled and lost his balance at Melissande's blow. It was not a killing blow, but the wound bled mightily.

Arnaud landed heavily on his knees beside Quinn, his blade buried deep in the earth. Arnaud struggled to release the knife from the dirt as Quinn rose. Arnaud abandoned the imprisoned blade and carefully backed away, fear in his eyes.

"You would not kill an unarmed man, would you?" he asked.

Quinn pulled the knife from the ground with a sharp gesture. "Would you not kill me under similar circumstance?" Quinn stalked Arnaud until he backed into a tree. Slowly Arnaud managed to stand with the aid of the tree and he faced Quinn with a boldness that seemed unnatural.

Suddenly Arnaud pulled Quinn's blade from his own side with a grunt. He dove at Quinn, murderous intent in his eye and the bloody blade in his hand. Quinn crouched suddenly and stabbed upward with all his might.

Arnaud's blade was buried deep in his own belly. He gasped and dropped Quinn's blade, then clutched the hilt with both hands as he fell to the ground and writhed in pain.

Arnaud glared at Quinn through half-closed eyes.

"Curse you," he whispered, and the blood trickled from the corner of his mouth. "Without you, all three estates would have been mine."

Quinn grimaced. "Without your own greed, you would have had the finest bride in Christendom."

Arnaud closed his eyes at that and his breathing stilled. Quinn turned and held out his hand to Melissande. She clung to his fingers and Quinn felt her shiver. He swept off his cloak and wrapped it securely about her shoulders, noting only now that her kirtle was soaked.

"Are you hurt?"

Melissande winced and clutched his sleeve as she tried to walk. "My hip. I fell upon it when the horse tripped." She flicked a glance to him. "Do not worry. I believe the child is fine."

Guilt writhed within Quinn that she thought she mattered no more to him than that. The lady deserved the truth, but first, he would see her safe and warm.

Quinn shuddered and swept Melissande into his arms to carry her to his horse. She huddled before him like a small child but remained silent. Quinn feared the worst. Had she not said she loved him? Was there no hope that assertion had been true? Or that it was still true?

Quinn retrieved the wounded horse from the stream and tied its reins to a tree. He did the same with Arnaud's fine black steed. He glanced down but Arnaud had passed from this world.

Quinn turned away, relieved to have this matter, at least, behind them. His gaze fell on his wife and he marveled at her strength. He would never have expected a woman to have such fortitude as to strike a blow that would save his own life. Did he dare hope that was a promise of the future?

"I shall send Bayard for the horses," he murmured.

"Mine is injured." Her voice was stiffly formal and Quinn did not know what to make of that.

"Yes, the ostler will see to it. They can bring a cart if he feels the ankle can be mended. It does not hang like a break, so do not trouble yourself overmuch."

She cast a fearful glance over her shoulder. "And Arnaud?"

"He is dead."

Melissande released a shuddering breath and Quinn was encouraged by the way she huddled closer to him.

"He meant to kill you."

That she showed concern could be no small thing. "Do not think about it now," Quinn urged. They could talk later, before the fire. "We must get you home," he murmured, hoping against hope that all would come aright in the end.

Melissande managed to smile weakly. She reached up and touched Quinn's face with her chilled fingertips. "Yes, husband. Take me home to Sayerne."

Her words encouraged Quinn as nothing else could have.

* * *

When they were safely within the walls of Sayerne again, Quinn bade Melissande wait in the bailey.

"I will be just a moment," he said with a smile that melted her heart.

She could not refuse him something so simple. Quinn disappeared into the hall and she was left alone. As Melissande waited, she wondered what Quinn was thinking. What had he thought of her confession of love? He had said nothing then and as she stood alone, she feared his response.

Did he mean to cast her out? Was he being courteous only because of the ugly encounter with Arnaud? Melissande had deliberately called Sayerne "home" in the hopes of encouraging him, but Quinn had apparently not noticed her choice of words.

The rich smell of the earth rose to her nostrils and Melissande slipped off her shoes to wriggle her toes in the sleekly green new grass. She tipped her head back and watched the stars appear one by one as the sky deepened from indigo to black. The fingers of the warm spring wind stirred her hair. The silver crescent of the moon rode high in the sky and she sighed.

If she just knew that Quinn cared for her, all would be perfect.

She heard his footfalls and turned, uncertain what to think, when she noticed the small package he carried. A smile played about Quinn's firm lips as he halted beside her. Melissande tipped back her head to hold his gaze and was lost in the warm amber glow of his eyes.

By the saints above, she loved this man with every fiber of her being. He said nothing though, and Melissande feared yet again that she had foolishly been the only one to grant her heart.

Then Quinn offered her the box.

"It is from the East," he said, his voice sounding curiously uncertain. "And the only thing I brought back from there besides my own hide."

Melissande took the small dark box, because she did not know what else to do. The moonlight picked out the inlay on its lid and she ran one fingertip across the wood in silent appreciation of the fine craftsmanship.

A vine of flowers was made of ivory on the lid, the leaves delicately traced and petals lovingly drawn. Melissande looked questioningly to Quinn.

He cleared his throat, though still his voice was gruff when he spoke. "I bought this from a woodworker in Ascalon when I heard the news of Sayerne. It seemed fitting to bring some trinket back to grace my home."

"It is lovely," Melissande said, and made to hand it back to him.

Quinn shook his head. "No. I would have you keep it." He took a deep, shuddering breath and impaled her with his regard. "The maker told me that it was a gift that I should grant to the lady who captured my heart."

Melissande opened her mouth and closed it again in surprise. She looked to her feet and was afraid he teased her only with a false promise of her true desire.

"Oh, Quinn." Melissande shook her head once as she sought the words and she pushed the small box toward him. "You do not need to confess such a thing simply because I bear your child."

"No, let me have my say," Quinn said hastily. "I did a disservice to you, for I did not confess the love dawning in my heart when I first knew of it." He took Melissande's hand within her own and she marveled at the sincerity in his intent gaze.

"I love you, my lady. I have need of a partner and a lover, a spouse and a friend with all the wisdom and understanding, all the gentleness and fire that you alone possess. I only hope that my harsh words have not changed what you said earlier."

Quinn swallowed but did not avert his gaze as he dropped to one knee. "Melissande d'Annossy, will you be my bride in every way?"

Melissande could not hold back her tears any longer. "Quinn," she whispered unevenly. "Nothing you could say could change what is within my heart. I love you as I never imagined I could love anyone. My only fear is that you will despise me for bringing Arnaud and his hate so close to your door."

"Hush, my lady." Quinn laid his fingertip across her lips. "Do not even utter his name. It was you indeed who saved me from him and that is no small thing. I am in your debt and I would take the remainder of our days to show you what that means."

His mention of the future made Melissande suddenly uncertain. "Are you pleased about the child?"

Quinn grinned outright. "How could I not be pleased to know that we have conceived a child in love? It will be a blessed babe, with so fine a mother as you."

Melissande sniffled at that and her vision blurred. Quinn stifled a chuckle that seemed most inopportune. "My lady, would you not accept me so I might stand and ease your tears?"

"Oh, Quinn! How could you doubt that I would accept you? I can think of nothing I desire more than to be your wife." Quinn's warm fingers smoothed away the remnants of her tears and Melissande smiled up at him. "Unless, of course, you would prefer to not still be my champion?"

Quinn snorted. "You shall not have another while I draw breath, my lady."

"I should hope not," Melissande murmured with satisfaction.

Quinn's lips purposefully closed over hers and she leaned against him. The inlay box pressed between them and Quinn stepped away with evident reluctance. He lifted her other hand to the lid of the box and met her gaze with mischief dancing in his own.

"Open it," he urged.

It had not occurred to Melissande that there might be something inside and she gave the box a shake now. A faint rustle greeted her ears and she looked to Quinn in confusion. He said nothing, merely lifting a brow at her curiosity.

Melissande knew he would not tell her. Carefully she lifted the lid of the box.

She caught only a glimpse of the contents before the wind danced between them and swept the pearly seeds from their sanctuary. Melissande gasped as the seeds cavorted around them in a gray cloud, then they were carried away by the wind and scattered across the bailey.

"What are they?" she asked with delight.

Quinn shrugged. "The merchant in the East said they would remind my lady of the constancy of my love."

Melissande laughed then and threw her arms around Quinn's neck. "I shall never doubt it," she whispered, and Quinn grinned.

He scooped Melissande up in his arms and he kissed her before he carried her into the hall of Sayerne. That night they sealed their vows yet again as they loved in the solar of Sayerne for the first time.

And the next spring, when Tulley came to invest Quinn with the seal of Sayerne, the bailey was covered with small, fragrant periwinkle blooms. Melissande stood in the solar window to watch the lord's arrival. She smiled as she ran her fingers across the inlay box, the image of the same flower in its lid.

She spied Quinn carrying their son to meet Tulley and her heart swelled with pride. Her smile broadened with the certainty that many more springs would arrive, only to find her secure in the love of her champion.

*   *   *   *   *

Author Note

Duke Godfroi de Bouillon was one of the nobles who answered Pope Urban II's call for the First Crusade at the end of the eleventh century. Godfroi left his estates in what is now Belgium to fight in the Holy Land. Later he was elected ruler of the conquered city of Jerusalem and chose the title Defender of the Holy Sepulchre.

Godfroi died of a fever a year later, but there is an old story that on his deathbed, he gave a box to one of his knights. He bade the knight take the box home to Château Bouillon for him and open it there. The knight did so, only to find that the box was full of seeds, which were blown into the courtyard of the castle.

Every spring, wild pinks still bloom there and the story maintains that these are the descendants of the seeds Godfroi sent home from Jerusalem almost a millennium ago.

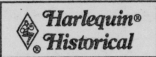

Harlequin® Historical

From the author of HEAVEN CAN WAIT
& LAND OF DREAMS comes another,
heartwarming Western love story

BADLANDS BRIDE

by CHERYL ST. JOHN

Keep an eye out for this delightful tale of an eastern
beauty who poses as a mail-order bride and winds up
stranded in the Dakota Badlands!

Coming this August
from Harlequin Historicals!

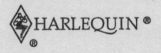

HARLEQUIN®

BIGB96-6

UNLOCK THE DOOR TO GREAT ROMANCE AT BRIDE'S BAY RESORT

Join Harlequin's new across-the-lines series, set in an exclusive hotel on an island off the coast of South Carolina.

Seven of your favorite authors will bring you exciting stories about fascinating heroes and heroines discovering love at Bride's Bay Resort.

Look for these fabulous stories coming to a store near you beginning in January 1996.

Harlequin American Romance #613 in January
Matchmaking Baby by Cathy Gillen Thacker

Harlequin Presents #1794 in February
Indiscretions by Robyn Donald

Harlequin Intrigue #362 in March
Love and Lies by Dawn Stewardson

Harlequin Romance #3404 in April
Make Believe Engagement by Day Leclaire

Harlequin Temptation #588 in May
Stranger in the Night by Roseanne Williams

Harlequin Superromance #695 in June
Married to a Stranger by Connie Bennett

Harlequin Historicals #324 in July
Dulcie's Gift by Ruth Langan

Visit Bride's Bay Resort each month wherever Harlequin books are sold.

BBAYG

You are cordially invited to a

HOMETOWN REUNION

September 1996—August 1997

Where can you find romance and adventure,
bad boys, cowboys, feuding families, and babies,
arson, mistaken identity, a mom on the run...?
Tyler, Wisconsin, that's where!

So join us in this not-so-sleepy little town and
experience the love, the laughter and the
tears of those who call it home.

WELCOME TO A
HOMETOWN REUNION

Twelve unforgettable stories, written for you by
some of Harlequin's finest authors. This fall,
begin a yearlong affair with America's favorite
hometown as **Marisa Carroll** brings you
Unexpected Son.

Available at your favorite retail store.

HARLEQUIN ®
®

Look us up on-line at: http://www.romance.net

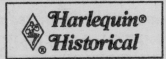

Harlequin® Historical

Bestselling author **RUTH LANGAN** brings you nonstop
adventure and romance with her new Western series
from Harlequin Historicals

The Jewels of Texas

DIAMOND	February 1996
PEARL	August 1996
JADE	February 1997
RUBY	June 1997

Don't miss these exciting stories of four sisters as wild
and vibrant as the untamed land they're fighting to protect!

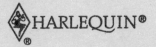

HARLEQUIN®

Look us up on-line at: http://www.romance.net